# *Resisting*

## H. L. Wegley

### Romantic Suspense

# OTHER BOOKS BY H. L. WEGLEY

**Against All Enemies Series**
1 Voice in the Wilderness
2 Voice of Freedom
3 Chasing Freedom

**Pure Genius Series**
1 Hide and Seek
2 On the Pineapple Express
3 Moon over Maalaea Bay
4 Triple Threat

**Witness Protection Series**
1 No Safe Place
2 No True Justice
3 No Turning Back

**Stand-Alone Books**
Virtuality
The Janus Journals
Slanted

**Riven Republic Series**
1 Riven
2 Resisting

# DEDICATION

Rev. George M. Docherty gave a sermon on February 7, 1954 for the Lincoln Day Observance at the New York Presbyterian Church in Washington, D.C. My president, "Ike" Eisenhower, attended. In the sermon, Reverend Docherty said, "To omit the words 'under God' in the Pledge of Allegiance is to omit the definitive character of the American way of life." Furthermore, Reverend Docherty implied that only under God—that is, under a higher rule of law—are Americans indivisible.

Four months later, on Flag Day, June 14, 1954, President Eisenhower signed into law a resolution adding those two words to the Pledge of Allegiance.

Sadly, less than a decade later—Abington School District versus Schempp on June 17, 1963—the Supreme Court declared school-sponsored prayer and Bible readings unconstitutional. That began the onslaught on "under God" in America.

As Americans have become divided on the "under God" issue, we are no longer indivisible. Nowhere is that more evident than in the halls of government.

This book is dedicated to the teachers in schools, local and federal officials, law enforcement personnel, and military members who have committed to remain "under God" come what may. *Fiat justitia et pereat mundus.* May God strengthen, guide, and protect you as you do so, and may He revive us so that we come together on this issue and, once again, become one nation under God, indivisible, with liberty and justice for all.

# CONTENTS

# ACKNOWLEDGMENTS

Thanks to my wife, Babe, for listening to me read a couple of drafts of the manuscript for *Resisting* and for catching some errors. The first draft put her to sleep once or twice. Hopefully, the rewrites have taken care of that.

Thanks again, Gail Ostheller, for proofing this novel and catching my mistakes. It definitely takes more than one pair of eyes to prepare a book for publication.

Many thanks to Daniel Greenfield and David Kupelian for their investigative reporting that allowed me to extract ideas for my story from similar events in the real world.

Thanks to our Lord for leading me through a serious illness and still leaving me with the ability to create and write stories, though I do it a bit more slowly these days.

# CAST OF CHARACTERS

**Colonel David Craig** – a recently retired Ranger commander and a national hero, age 45. He starred in *Voice in the Wilderness* and *Voice of Freedom*.

**Susan O'Connell** – the initial owner of Crooked River Espresso in Terrebonne. She's 37, a patriotic American, a team builder, and an admirer of David Craig.

**Zach Tanner** – hero of *Riven*, a radio show host and a DJ.

**Kate Alexander** – heroine of *Riven*, a new Christian, niece of the leftist Oregon governor, Sandra Harper, who Kate wants to lead from her Marxist roots to Bible-based conservatism.

**Jeff and Allie Jacobs** – hero and heroine from *Chasing Freedom*. Jeff was a world class decathlete and Allie an international scholarship student from Mexico. They have a seven-year-old daughter, **Lori**.

**Lex and Gemma James** – hero and heroine of *No True Justice*. Both are investigative journalists. They have high-IQ, nine-year-old twins, **Josh and Caleb**.

**KC and Brock Daniels** – hero and heroine of *Voice in the Wilderness*. KC knows computers, and has gained a reputation as a hacker, and Brock is an athlete and a Christian apologist with a huge blog following. Their son **Benjamin** is ten and very bright like his mom and dad.

**Drew and Beth West** – hero and heroine of *No Turning Back*. They own a horse ranch. Drew knows weapons and martial arts. **Beth**, who claimed asylum after a drug cartel killed her family in Mexico, has an MBA. Their son **Peter** is four.

**Steve and Julia Bancroft** – hero and heroine of *Voice of Freedom*. Steve is an ex-Army Ranger, Craig's weapons sergeant. Julia inherited her grandparents' mansion on Crooked River Ranch, which she uses to host meetings and provide a temporary home for those in transition. **Itzy** (Itzell), their adopted daughter from Guatemala, is 19. She is Mayan.

**Hunter and AJ Jones** – hero and heroine from *Slanted*. Hunter is a big data analyst. AJ is a barista. Their adopted daughter **Sam** (Samantha) is 13 going on 18 and is a handful.

**Oregon Governor Sandra Harper** – an antagonist in

*Riven*, heads the leftist politicians in Oregon. She loves her niece, Kate, and wants to bring her back home to her roots in the most powerful political family in the state.

**President Wendell Walker** – the main antagonist of *Riven*, a far left radical who wants to unify the nation by force.

**Secretary of Defense William Richards** – a cabinet member and confidant of President Walker who gives the president sound advice that is not always accepted.

**Radley Baker** – a vet, a half Modoc, and a pilot now serving in the Eastern Oregon militia. Radley is a short, muscular man who bench-presses well over 400 pounds.

**Shauna Jackson** – Kate's roommate and best friend since college is a beautiful, African American woman who has her eye on Radley Baker, but her sharp tongue gets in the way.

**Ned Pascal** – a trucker who lives near Terrebonne.

**Merv Bader** – owns a local construction company.

**Sherman Bender, former Adjutant General (TAG)**– a man fired for disloyalty and lack of qualifications to command the Oregon National Guard.

**Colonel Towry** - a Ranger commander from Joint Base Lewis McChord (JBLM) who is loyal to President Walker but who also tries to comply with the constitution.

**Laura Alexander** – Kate's mother and the little sister of Governor Sandra Harper. Laura is a member of the left-wing political society in Oregon.

**Major Nicholas Deke** – Former military special ops officer, now a spy planted in Oregon by President Walker. He is the brother of Captain Albert Deke who was shot and killed nine years earlier by Julia Bancroft (Weiss).

*I believe our nation is at a point where there are enough irreconcilable differences between those Americans who want to control other Americans and those Americans who want to be left alone that separation is the only peaceable alternative. Just as in a marriage where vows are broken, our rights guaranteed by the U.S. Constitution have been grossly violated by a government instituted to protect them.*
Walter Williams
Our Irreconcilable Differences
The Times News
Jan 2, 2014


*"Liberty lies in the hearts of men and women; when it dies there, no constitution, no law, no court can save it; no constitution, no law, no court can even do much to help it."*
*Judge Learned Hand*

# Prologue

*A recap of Riven*

The United States is fragmenting along geopolitical lines, blue against red, left against right. The nation's production threatens to grind down to a halt as *de facto* secession informally splits the union, threatening the fragile systems that form the nation's lifelines.

Nearly a month ago, conservative radio talk show host, Zach Tanner, advised his audience to leave Western Oregon and congregate in Eastern Oregon to avoid martial law which was declared by leftist governor Sandra Harper to quell the violence in Salem and the Portland area.

Sandra Harper's niece, Kate Alexander, is a new Christian who finds herself at odds with the atheistic aunt who used to be closer to her than Kate's own mother. Kate manages to escape both the martial law and the BOLO her aunt put out for her, and she hitches a ride to Terrebonne, Oregon, where she buys, from Susan O'Connell, Crooked River Espresso, a coffee drive-through along Highway 97.

There Kate meets the DJ she's been listening to, Zach Tanner, and they join forces with an incredible group of people living on and around Crooked River Ranch. Kate and Zach find a strong bond forming between them and there is a budding romance.

In a meeting at the Ranch Chapel, the group from Crooked River Ranch organizes a militia. David Craig, retired Army Ranger commander, heads that effort. Zach Tanner builds a radio station to broadcast to the other red states and red areas across the nation. They hope to organize and help each other defend themselves against the neo-Marxist president while they formulate a plan to unify the nation.

President Wendell Walker, a leftist, wants to unify the fragmenting nation by force—martial law, threats, intimidation of governors, and by using the military to wipe out any insurgents. However, the military is also fragmenting, and Walker cannot depend on all of the officers to carry out his commands. And if he pushes too hard, the infrastructure of the nation will fracture, leaving Walker the president of a failed state.

The Central Oregon Militia is a thorn in the president's side, and he wants to make them an example to all the other potential insurgents. When the militia leader, Craig, confronts Sandra Harper, who has kidnapped Kate to take her home and "fix her," Walker thinks he has a chance to kill them all at the same time and take over Oregon himself by using succession to place a strong Walker supporter in the governor's office. But Kate, the militia members, and an injured Governor Harper survive Walker's brutal attack.

Injured and nearly killed, Harper has an epiphany. She cannot trust the president. The other blue state governors will now not trust her nor will the red state governors. She's isolated, alone, and President Walker wants her killed before she can tell the world about his attempted murder of a governor.

Kate accompanies her injured aunt back to Salem, where Governor Harper, with Kate's influence, decides to flip Oregon from blue to red, though she knows this will create a lot of enemies in the state government, and it will take work to get the conservatives, especially the Oregon Guard, to trust her.

Since both the state of Oregon and Sandra Harper are Walker's targets, she asks militia commander, David Craig, to meet with her to work out a joint defense plan for Oregon. Craig agrees but has not yet met with Harper.

Zach Tanner has spent every spare moment with Kate, and though these are tumultuous times, he proposes to her. She accepts on the condition that Zach courts her until there is a lull in the fighting so they can marry.

The United States is now *Riven*. The story continues as red areas and red states are actively *Resisting* the increasingly tyrannical federal government of President Wendell Walker.

# Chapter 1

*Terrebonne, Oregon, July 20, day 10 of Kate's courtship*

"As soon as we climb into that chopper, we're headed into enemy territory." Drew West's voice came from directly behind David Craig who sat at the wheel of his Jeep SUV.

The huge Conestoga Wagon facade of Crooked River Espresso came into view on his right. Craig signaled to turn off Highway 97 and pushed gently on the brake pedal. "Drew, this whole world is enemy-occupied territory."

"I guess a retired special ops commander might see things that way." Steve Bancroft grinned as he looked Craig's way.

"Not my words, guys. They belong to C. S. Lewis, spiritually speaking."

"Let's focus on something more pleasant, like Crooked River Espresso and coffee." Kate Alexander's voice came low but forceful, with the intensity she displayed about ninety-five percent of the time.

Zach had his hands full courting a girl like Kate, brilliant, beautiful, and ready for action, whether it came as a political argument or a firefight.

But courting ... that was a problem Craig had never experienced. Maybe it wasn't in the cards for a middle-aged, retired Army Ranger.

Craig saw a flash of red hair in the service window as he stopped beside it.

Susan O'Connell.

He looked up into her light blue eyes made even brighter by the early morning sun.

"Does everybody want the usual?" Susan scanned the faces in Craig's jeep.

"An extra shot for me this morning," Kate said and then yawned.

Susan grinned. "You and Zach stayed out too late last night, didn't you?"

"Something like that. Zach found a big motor home he wants to buy."

AJ snapped lids on two paper cups and handed them to Susan. "For Steve and Drew. Kate's and Craig's coming right up."

Susan passed the cups to Craig and her grin faded. "Is this a good idea?"

"Coffee is always a good idea, Susan."

She poked him in the shoulder. "You know what I meant."

AJ tapped Susan's shoulder and then handed her the other two cups.

Susan gave Craig Kate's cup and he passed it to her in the back seat. When he turned and took his cup, Susan leaned out of the window, nearly falling out.

She curled an arm around his neck, steadied herself, and gave him a warm hug. "You be careful over there in lefty land, David." She withdrew her arm slowly, tentatively.

What was she—"

A jab in the shoulder jolted Craig.

It was Steve's jab. "Dude, you missed your chance."

Craig's face grew hot, almost as hot as his right hand still holding the cup of steaming hot coffee. But no way was he going to let his weapons expert know that the razzing had accomplished its intended purpose.

He gave Steve the best glare he could muster, dropped the coffee cup into the holder, then turned his attention back to the tall, slender redhead with concern creasing her forehead.

"Don't worry, Susan. We've got a full-coverage insurance policy." He stuck out a thumb, pointing at Kate, the governor's niece. "Besides, Governor Harper's had a real change of heart since President Walker tried to assassinate her."

"Knowing your political allies want you dead will do that," Kate said.

Susan dipped her head slowly. "But Salem's still packed with Walker supporters who haven't had a change of heart, Oregon's deep state. It's a dangerous place, David."

Drew craned his neck toward the window to make eye contact with Susan. "Don't worry. I've got his back, and we'll bring him safely home after we sign that peace treaty with the hostiles."

Kate leaned toward the window from her position in the back seat. "Chuck Norris has his back, and I'll keep Aunt Sandy in line, Susan. She needs this agreement as much as we do."

Craig pulled away from the service window, ending the awkward discussion and comments. "Time to drink your coffee. We board Baker's bird in twenty minutes."

When they arrived at the Madras airport, it appeared that militia member, Army vet, and now their pilot, Radley Baker, had just finished refueling the Bell 407 which was on loan from a grateful Governor Harper.

Baker had saved Harper's life by confiscating her helicopter and flying her to a trauma center in Bend.

Craig noticed Kate fiddling with the gun tucked in the holster against her back. "Remember, if you bring your weapons, they stay in the bird when we get out at the conference center. We go in unarmed as a sign we're negotiating in good faith."

He parked the Jeep.

In another five minutes, they had all buckled in onboard the Bell 407 as Baker fiddled with the controls.

Craig pulled his headset on and positioned it comfortably over his ears.

The engine whined its start-up complaint and revved until the helicopter lifted and tilted forward.

"Next stop, Silver Falls Conference Center," Baker's voice came through the audio system as the ground receded rapidly.

Baker turned to the right and they sped westward with the snowcapped peak of Mount Jefferson looming in front of them.

In a few minutes, the peak towered above them on the left as Baker cut across the north shoulder of the volcanic peak.

The nervous chatter had ended, and Craig used the time to review the main points of his offer to aid the Oregon Guard while the militia defended Eastern Oregon from federal attacks.

President Walker's previous attempts were utter failures. The next time, the militia and the Governor's Guard should expect the worst, an all-out attempt to wipe out Oregon's military defenses and to place the state under federal control via martial law.

* * *

Though she had tried to kill him a few days ago, Governor Sandra Harper knew that Colonel Craig was a man of honor, a man of his word. She could trust him with her life. She already had but was unconscious much of that time, so it hadn't been her decision to allow him to fly her to a trauma center after President Walker's assassination attempt failed ... barely.

She tapped the shoulder of her security team leader sitting in the front seat of the big sedan. "How much longer until we get there, Mike?"

"It's about ten miles, so maybe fifteen minutes, governor."

7

She settled back in her seat, but her nerves would not settle. This day should be a day that would bring a measure of relief as she signed an agreement with a powerful ally, Craig's militia. Sandra Harper would no longer be going it alone against the most powerful man in the world, President Wendell Walker.

She jumped when her official phone rang its annoying tone. "Governor Harper."

"Governor, this is Airman Gore in the Western Air Defense Sector Headquarters."

It was the voice of a young woman. And why would— reality slapped hard and her heart revved as she iterated through the possible reasons for the call. None of them were good.

"Go ahead, Airman Gore."

"I may get in trouble for making this call, but I thought you should know. I just alerted the command post of the 142nd Fighter Wing in Portland about a suspicious military plane headed your general direction."

"What military plane? Where was it coming from?"

"Ma'am, it is a Growler out of Whidbey Naval Air Station. We tried to contact it, but it wouldn't acknowledge, and it just kept flying south. I've got a bad feeling about this plane."

Her phone alarm signaled another call coming in. "Thank you, Airman Gore. I have another call that I need to answer."

"It's probably the fighter wing. They can fill you in with the details. Goodbye, Governor, and good luck."

She answered the incoming call. "Governor Harper."

"Governor, this is Colonel Adam Staten, 142nd Fighter Wing, in Portland. We were just notified about an unidentified, suspicious, and potentially dangerous aircraft headed your way. I scrambled one of our F-15 Eagles and he has it on his radar."

Was she in danger?

*Kate!*

Sandra's heart hit its red line. Kate, Craig, and the others were probably crossing the mountains in that helicopter right now.

"Colonel Staten, my niece and a militia commander are flying to meet me at a location near Salem. They are in a Bell 407 helicopter. Is it possible that—"

"Madam Governor, that appears to be the target of the Growler. That aircraft carries AIM-120D missiles. It can fire from over thirty miles away."

"We've got to stop it."

"Keep in mind we would be taking down a U.S. military aircraft, governor."

"I understand. Can you patch me through to that pilot?"

"If you're sure that—"

"I'm sure, colonel. Put me through."

"Putting you through now, governor. Wishing you good luck."

Static came through her phone, then it stopped.

"Governor, Captain Musselmann in Eagle 4, at your service, ma'am."

"Captain, a Bell 407 is crossing the Cascades about now with my niece on board and some important people coming to attend a defense planning meeting on the west side. After the president's attempt on my life, I—I believe they are in danger."

"And I believe you are right, governor. I have the Growler on radar, and it looks like it's flying a route to intercept the 407. The Growler can fire it's missiles from more than thirty miles away, so we've only got a couple of minutes, governor."

"As commander of the Oregon Air Guard, I'm giving you permission, captain, to take down that Growler if it threatens the helicopter."

"Running down the growler now. Changing frequency to contact Growler. Will be back shortly, governor."

Kate's life was on the line and the lives of other good people too. Was she a fool for asking them to fly to Western Oregon?

Thirty seconds passed. It seemed more like an hour.

The captain returned. "I caught the Growler and tried to make radio contact, governor, but he's not responding. I told him he shouldn't be this far south and suggested he turn back to Whidbey. He's proceeding southward toward that Bell 407 and he refuses to reply. That's not a good sign."

Unless she took the extreme action of destroying the Growler, Sandra would never see her niece, Kate, again. She could not let that happen.

"What do you think the Growler will do?"

"Governor, Growlers carry AIM-120D air-to-air missiles. They are fire and forget. He can fire any time now, so there's no guarantee he won't fire even if I attempted to shoot him down. And if he fires, we can forget about the Bell 407."

This couldn't be really happening. But President Walker was real enough. And the reality was he wanted them all dead. He'd already proved that. "Isn't there anything you can do to stop the Growler?"

"Blue on blue loss."

"And what does that mean, captain?"

"I can shoot down one of our own planes, governor. Are you ready to give me that order? If you do, who's going to back me up when they try to court-martial me for it?"

"What other options do we have?"

"Who's the pilot on the helicopter?"

"A militia pilot named Baker."

"Fire and forget was developed so missiles would live up to that name. But I can warn Baker and then use my radar system to try to help him avoid the attack. It's a longshot, and I need to hurry. Changing frequency now to contact Baker."

*Please, keep Kate safe.*

\* \* \*

Craig woke from his musings and sat up in his seat when a strange voice came through the sound system.

"Eagle 4 to Bell 407. Baker, do you read me?"

"Bell 407, Baker here. Who is *me*, Eagle 4?"

"*Me* is Captain Musselmann. I'm an Oregon Air Guard in an F-15, scrambled on orders from Governor Harper. Baker, you've got a Navy Growler about to intercept you. It's armed and dangerous. I'm on its tail, but its pilot will not acknowledge me."

"What should I do, Eagle 4?"

"Consider evasive action. At this range, the missile will bleed off a little speed—"

"Missile? Say again, Eagle 4."

"As I said, if the Growler fires its missile, at this distance it will slow down some before impact giving you a better chance. But, Baker, the kill rate for a jet at thirty-five miles is sixty-three percent. For a helicopter it's—"

"I get your message, captain."

"Look for something you can circle behind."

"All that's near are mountain peaks. I just passed Mount Jefferson."

"Baker, a mountain is too big. You need something like—"

"Like a rock spire?"

"Yes. A thick rock spire. You and the spire need to appear as one at the moment of impact, preferably with the rock between you and the missile. I can direct you using my radar systems, but the air-to-air missile will be incoming at over two thousand miles-per-hour. This is very dicey, Baker, but I'll do my best."

"Me too, Eagle 4."

"I'm fifty-five miles out at 340 degrees, and I'm on the Growler's tail. Holy crud! He just fired an AIM-120! Now he's turning toward home. We're at forty miles, you have roughly sixty seconds before impact. I've got both you and the missile on my doppler radar. I can keep you there. Ground clutter is not an issue. They fired the AIM a little beyond max range. Use terrain features to avoid it. That's your only chance."

"Copy, Eagle 4. Looking for someplace to hide. Wait. Maybe there is a place, Spire Rock, straight ahead. Hang on, everyone."

The wop, wop turned into a roar as the chopper sped ahead.

"What's Spire Rock?" Craig asked.

"I climbed it when I was a teenager. I think it's only a couple of miles ahead. We just have to beat the missile there and then hope we can time it so we cut around the rock when the missile arrives."

"You need to be 160 degrees from the rock. Baker," Musselmann said. "That should shield you from the AIM. You've got thirty seconds."

"Understand, Eagle 4. Trying for the rock spire. Would appreciate it if you could help us time our cut around the rock."

"We're praying for you, Baker." Kate's voice.

"I will give you what I believe are your final ten seconds. You need to go lower than the top of the spire. If the missile hits the rock, you don't want pieces of rock taking you down."

"Yes, sir. I mean, no, sir, I don't. There's the spire. Hang on, everybody, we're gonna be brushing the treetops."

"Get ready, Baker. Ten ... nine ... eight ... seven ... six ... five ... four ... three ..."

Craig's stomach flipped and flopped when Baker dropped at least a hundred feet then banked hard to the right.

"Two ... one ... may God be with you, Baker."

A thump sounded above the roar of the chopper. They had brushed a tree.

An explosion of light blinded Craig.

Like a giant hammer, the force of the detonated missile hit the helicopter, pounding it away from the rock and spinning it around in the air.

Craig slammed against the door.

Debris splatted against the chopper's fuselage, but the bird was still on its rotating wing.

Craig surveyed the front of the Bell 407. No holes in front of him. He looked back and saw blue sky through a six-inch hole in the fuselage ... a foot behind Kate's head.

But focusing on anything had become difficult as the 407 whipped back and forth.

Baker fought the controls and his eyes darted between the windshield and the instrument panel.

The tail swung to the left, then back to the right.

Baker hit the throttle and the chopper surged ahead and straightened. "Is everybody okay?"

"Yeah," Drew said. "But Kate might not be if she turns around."

"What do you mean?" Kate twisted in her seat to look behind her. "Good grief. A rock came through and it's lying behind my seat."

Static came through the speaker followed by Musselmann's voice. "Baker, I still have you on my radar. You must have made it. How's the bird?"

"Captain, thanks to your timing and your radar, we drew the missile right into that big rock spire. Looks like it blew the top off a good climbing rock. Climbers won't be happy, but we are."

"Any damage?"

"One hole in the fuselage that I know of. Maybe some smaller ones we can't see. Missed everything that mattered. Are we safe now?"

"You're safe from the Growler. It headed north toward Whidbey. The federal forces, maybe their commander-in-chief, sent it. But you can thank a young air guardsman from Tacoma. She knew immediately that the Growler was up to no good and alerted us, otherwise ..."

"Yeah, otherwise," Baker said. "We're heading on to our destination. I'll check this bird out once we're on the ground. Thanks again, Captain Musselmann. You saved our lives and probably a lot more that I'm not at liberty to disclose."

"Just doing my job, Baker. You take care. This eagle's heading back to the aerie. Eagle 4 out."

"Like Susan told Craig, lefty land is a dangerous place," Kate said.

"Somebody knew we were going to be flying today," Baker said.

"Yeah." Craig pinched his chin for a moment then nodded. "I think the governor has a mole at Mahonia Hall. And we need to have a serious talk about that as soon as we land."

"It's already on her agenda," Kate said.

Drew turned toward Kate. "And how would you know?"

"Like Aunt Sandy said, I'm more like her than I am my own mother."

Craig twisted in his seat to look at Drew. "One of these days, Drew, you'll learn not to argue with my intelligence analyst."

"So you're really going to pull her off coffee duty to analyze our meager data?"

"Our meager data now includes everything we get from Salem. But what we get from Salem can't be trusted until we find and eliminate that mole."

"Or moles," Kate added.

"That's another topic for our agenda," Craig said. "Is it feasible for Governor Harper to continue flipping the state to red when the biggest players in her staff are elected, not appointed, so they can't be replaced by the governor? Leftists." Craig snorted his derision. "All their heads are green and their hands are blue."

"Green and blue, but we aren't talking Seahawks fans." Steve chuckled. "Too bad they didn't go to sea in a sieve."

"A sieve. Do you mean like the USS Colander?" Drew laughed.

"It may take a little coercion, but maybe we and the governor can figure out how to christen the USS Colander and put Oregon's deep state onboard," Craig said.

"Green heads, blue hands, sieves—that's a lot of mumbo jumbo and nonsense, if you ask me," Baker said.

"Not mumbo jumbo. It's the jumblies, Baker. Nonsense political poetry about radical left jumblies," Kate said. "And one or more of them almost got us killed today."

"If that's what they did today, then I can hardly wait for tomorrow," Baker said.

Craig shot Baker a sharp glance. "After what just happened, let's pray we get a chance at tomorrow."

# Chapter 2

*Silver Falls Lodge and Conference Center, Oregon*

For the first time in nine years, Craig struggled to shove danger, near disaster, and death from his mind so he could concentrate on the subject at hand, securing the state of Oregon.

Kate, seated behind him, was planning her wedding. Zach had almost lost her a few minutes ago. That led to the thoughts of Susan. But she wouldn't have lost much, would she?

*She can't lose what she doesn't have, dude.*

Craig tried to ignore the annoying voice inside his head.

Who was he kidding? Though they had just met a short time ago, they were a matched pair. Only a fool would bet against the odds of them forming a relationship.

"Craig, sir."

"What's up, Baker?"

"Uh, more like what's down. There's the Conference Center." Baker pointed down and to their right.

That's what he needed to bring his wandering mind back where it belonged, something visual. "Do you mean that green postage stamp surrounded by forest?"

Baker grinned. "That's an illusion. It disappears after a few years of flying. Don't worry. It'll open up to a nice sized lawn, our landing pad, once we get down to about five hundred feet."

"If you say so." Craig twisted in his seat to look back at Kate.

She held a notepad in her lap and wrote furiously in it. Kate stopped and looked up at him. "Craig, I'm concerned about Aunt Sandy's ... uh, I mean the governor's opposition. She has enemies embedded in the administration that have to be voted out of office and others that can't be fired because they are state employees."

"We need to ensure your aunt's safety, Kate. Otherwise, anything we plan today is an exercise in futility. We won't leave here today until we have a solid, joint defense plan that neutralizes as many threats from her opposition as possible." He shook his head. "Who would have thought the governor of Oregon would have a serious deep-state problem?"

"She wouldn't have if I hadn't ..." Kate's gaze dropped to the notepad and her pen fell to the floor.

Craig's neck muscles cramped in a complaint for being twisted so long. He turned back toward the front of the cabin. "No. It's not your fault, Kate. And it's much better that she's pointed toward the truth instead of remaining an atheistic leftist with a Marxist bent."

"Yeah," Kate said. "You're right."

"Well, I'm sure not left. Are you doing okay after that runt of a pilot nearly got us killed?"

"Craig, sir, this runt saved your bacon."

"After you sizzled it in a frying pan," Craig said.

"I stopped shaking after I saw that hole behind my head." Kate grinned. "It was a reminder that we had been protected by a runt and a loving God."

"Hang on, everybody. The runt is gonna set you down on a nice patch of grass." Baker worked the controls and the Bell 407 slowed, hovered, and dropped onto a lawn nearly fifty yards wide.

Craig climbed out as the rotor spun down.

Drew and Steve hopped out of the door behind him.

"I'm going to stay out here and check out this bird for any other damage from that misguided missile," Baker said. "See you in a bit."

The lodge and conference center lay to their left, surrounded on three sides by large fir trees.

Three Oregon state vehicles had parked near it. They appeared to have a comfortable capacity of about twelve people.

The state officials likely outnumbered the militia representatives three to one. But with Kate as his wild card, it didn't matter.

Kate moved ahead of Craig and scurried through the main entrance.

By the time Craig entered the lodge, Sandra Harper had Kate wrapped in a warm embrace.

The governor's security guards had moved to the back of the entryway, present, but obviously trying to remain inconspicuous.

The depth of the aunt-niece relationship had allowed it to survive two worldview changes, harsh words and deeds, and had saved Craig and his men's lives at least twice.

He almost laughed thinking about his initial distrust of Kate because of her aunt. That gave Craig another reminder that God's wisdom and His ways were beyond understanding.

As Craig approached, Kate released her aunt, and Kate's gaze darted back and forth between him and Governor Harper. "So today we're forgetting the ideology to accomplish the necessary?" Kate said.

"Kate, in hindsight, the ideology only seems good for justifying what we want even if it is immoral, unethical, or illegal. President Walker drove that point home with an assassination attempt on all of us with that Hellfire Missile. Wouldn't you say so, Colonel Craig?" She stepped toward him and shook his hand.

"I would agree, governor ... one quick question." He lowered his voice. "Are you comfortable with the people you brought? I mean—"

"I know what you mean, Craig. Yes, I've pruned my staff brutally over the past several days. You may speak freely here."

"Good. That leaves one other issue before we get into the more laborious details of our joint security agreement. What can you tell us about Deke?"

Harper pursed her lips and nodded. "Major Nicholas Deke. I found his rank, but his records aren't in order. They appear to have been partly purged."

"Aunt Sandy, Deke's the one who kidnapped me and mysteriously got away when the missile hit the house."

"And he's the only one who could have directed that attack helicopter to the house. That attack could only have been authorized by the president. So Deke must have been planted by Walker. But I don't have positive proof at this time," Harper said.

"Deke's a concern but so is your safety, governor," Craig said. "The best way to assure that is for me to meet face-to-face with the commanders of—"

"Colonel Craig, that's partly why we're having a meeting to coordinate security of the state. Waiting outside of this room, I have the Director of Joint Staff, who has also assumed the administrative duties of TAG. I also have commanders of the 162nd Infantry Regiment, the Headquarters Detachment in Salem, and the 142nd Fighter Wing in Portland. These four, along with the commander of the 173rd Fighter Wing in Klamath Falls, who couldn't make it today, represent the most important Guard organizations you will need to coordinate with. I believe you already talked with the 142nd Fighter Wing today."

"We did indeed, governor."

Kate looked up at Craig and smirked.

"You can wipe that silly grin off your face, Ms. Alexander," Craig said. "I agree. You two *are* a lot alike."

"Then I take it you approve, Colonel Craig?" Governor Harper raised her eyebrows.

"Yes, but I'm *actually* retired Colonel Craig."

"Let's not sound so superannuated. With your time in service, you would be the ranking officer here today, and you were a special operations commander. That will command their respect a lot more than calling you the leader of a rag tag militia from backwoods Oregon."

"Ouch." Steve Bancroft flashed a grin at both the governor and Craig.

Craig shot him a cease and desist look. "I believe you've already met Sergeant Bancroft, though you might not have been awake enough to remember."

"Glad to meet you again, Sergeant Bancroft. And you have my deepest gratitude for saving my life with your shot that crippled the Apache helicopter."

Bancroft nodded. "But I'm just a lowly, rag tag weapons sergeant, Madam Governor."

"Nonsense. The people Colonel Craig has surrounded himself with stand head and shoulders above any under my command. Of course, the Guard are only part-time soldiers."

"And last but not least, meet Drew West, alias Chuck Norris," Kate said.

"Army Rangers and Texas Rangers," Sandra Harper said. "Good to meet you, Mr. West."

A door opened at the far end of the room. Four men in dress uniform entered.

Craig's faded fatigues and scuffed chukka boots would probably paint him with Bancroft's color, a rag tag militia commander. He needed to say something to gain these men's respect.

When Harper finished the introductions, Craig found the words he needed to put commanders on the defensive without insulting them.

"I'm anxious to hear your plans for gaining dominant superiority in all four contested operating domains—air, land, sea, and cyberspace. Also, I'm curious about your plans for counterespionage, especially since we have evidence of ongoing espionage activity."

Four faces with pleading eyes turned toward Governor Harper.

"We would like to hear your ideas first, Colonel Craig. Considering time in service, I believe you are the ranking officer here."

Harper had let them off the hook and given Craig a chance to point them in the direction he wanted this agreement to go.

While Kate took notes, Craig iterated quickly through items on a list comprising a high-level strategy that had the militia guarding the land from the southeast corner of the state north to The Dalles. The Guard would take the other borders. Kingsley Field, home of the 173rd Fighter Wing, would guard the air on Oregon's southwestern, southern, and eastern borders. The 142nd Fighter Wing in Portland would take the rest.

"There are still communications issues to resolve since the militia isn't on any of the defense networks," Craig said.

"Shall I give the Guard an action item, Aunt Sandy?"

"Yes. It should go to the Director of Joint Staff."

"What about the coast?" Harper asked.

Craig continued. "For the Oregon Coast, we have to use our ground troops, because the Coast Guard, District 13 for the Oregon Coast, reports to Department of Homeland Security, not to the state governors. They still need to carry out their federal mission regardless of what is happening within the states they are protecting. Here's what I suggest,

Governor Harper. You draft a letter to the District 13 commander in Seattle and tell them what we expect from them, what our intent is for defense of the state, and that you see no reason we can't cooperate and fill our responsibilities without stepping on each other's toes. I believe they will play ball with us because it demands nothing of them that they're not already doing, except to leave us alone."

"Excellent, Colonel Craig," Harper said.

Her commanders looked at one another and nodded their approval.

"Now for counterespionage and cyber activity. The militia will take care of Eastern Oregon and I assume you will use your police to handle Western Oregon, governor."

"Yes."

"But the wild card is the FBI residing within the state," Craig said. "They report to their headquarters in Washington, DC. And who knows where each agent's true allegiance lies. Unfortunately, they have most of the cybersecurity skills."

"Then I will rely on my state police," Harper said. "We have some cybersecurity experts."

"That's fine. We have one of the best in the nation, KC Daniels. But remember, you may have to consider the FBI as hostile intelligence agents. And they do have SWAT teams."

"Yes. They have one in Portland. But I also have one, Colonel Craig, in Salem."

"Well, that brings us to the most dreaded topic of the day," Craig said.

"You mean the next move by President Walker to try to take the state of Oregon. He won't wait long."

Harper had thoroughly taken over as a military commander. That was impressive for a politician who had only served as an administrator. Like her niece, she was a quick study.

"I believe you're right, governor. He definitely wants Zach Tanner. He's already tried to kill you, and he still wants the militia neutralized."

"Let me try to summarize what we've agreed upon," Harper said.

Kate flipped a few pages back in her notebook.

"For responsibilities for the geographical areas, we'll go with your defined areas of responsibility, Colonel Craig. For any attack from the air we alert the Air Guard. Whoever detects it must immediately report it to me and to you, as commander of the militia, so we can both respond as necessary. On the ground, the Guard will have to be vigilant, looking for any movement of federal troops. And they can't rely on the FBI for help. In fact, we will consider the FBI as enemy intelligence agents. Finally, we must step up surveillance and intelligence-gathering efforts to detect any planned attack as early as possible."

"Have you got all that, Kate?" Craig said.

"Got it, Craig."

"If I were Walker, I would launch an attack as soon as I could plan and prepare for it," Harper said. "He's losing face and confidence each day that he lets Oregon stand in opposition to him. And, when he attacks, he will concentrate his forces to assure a victory."

"I believe you're right, governor. He will attack the militia first, because that gives him the mountains as a barrier to help hold the ground he's taken, allowing him to set up a staging area to amass troops before launching an attack on Western Oregon."

Craig paused. "Governor, we may need your help if we're attacked. Can you have a force of say a hundred well equipped guardsmen who can deploy on a moment's notice?"

"I can."

"Good, Craig said. "Before this is all over, we will both have to rely on each other. Even if the nation is fragmented, the U.S. military is the most potent fighting force in the world, and POTUS is the most powerful leader in the world. The only question is, how many soldiers believe they can fight for this president without violating their oaths of office?"

"None should believe that," Steve said.

"I hope you're right, Steve. I *pray* you are right."

# Chapter 3

*Washington DC, President's Private Study*

President Walker ended his phone call with Major Deke and swore, assaulting his two enemies using the dregs of his vocabulary. Governor Harper and Craig, leader of the Oregon militia shouldn't even be alive, let alone be having a meeting.

Secretary of Defense Richards' anapestic knock sounded on the study door.

Maybe he could find out what was going on behind the scenes in Oregon. Surely Will Richards had some choice bits of intel to share.

"Come in, Will. The door's unlocked."

"Mr. President, Oregon's declaration of war on the USA is about to end in failure for that rogue state. I'm happy to report that the Growler from Whidbey fired its missile and David Craig is history."

"Are you saying the missile took down the chopper with Craig in it?"

"That's exactly what I'm saying. We have confirmation of the missile firing at the Bell 407 helicopter with Craig and other members of the militia onboard. This is an AIM-120D, a fire-and-forget missile. Once locked on its target, it runs it down at two thousand miles-per-hour and takes it down. There were reports of a loud explosion on the western slopes of the Cascades."

"Then would you like to explain to me why Major Deke just reported that, as we speak, Craig is in a meeting with

Governor Harper at some out-of-the-way lodge near Salem?"

"I—I don't see how that's possible, Mr. President. And I don't have an explanation. Are you sure Deke isn't mistaken?"

"Will, Deke had binoculars on the building and watched Harper and her entourage enter, and a while later, Craig, Harper's niece, and some of Craig's militia entered. Now if, as you say, the Growler pilot had his sights on the chopper, would you like to explain to me how he missed his target?"

"A Bell 407 helicopter evading an AIM-120 missile ... the only thing I can think of, sir, is that at the far range of the AIM-120 there's a little wiggle room because the missile slows a bit and that might—"

"Do you hear what you're saying? If the chopper could evade a missile coming in at Mach 3, they must have known it was coming."

"But we kept this mission off the books at Whidbey. How could they have possibly known they would be fired upon? We must have a traitor, either at Whidbey, at JBLM, or at the Western Air Defense Sector."

"That's what I want you to find out. Find the traitors in our camp and eliminate them."

"But I—"

"Just do it, Richards. And the next missile we fire at the enemy will hit its target. Do you understand?"

"Yes, Mr. President."

"You are dismissed. I need some time to think."

*And I need something for this headache.*

# Chapter 4

*Julia and Steve Bancroft's home, Crooked River Ranch*

Craig pulled out the notes Kate had prepared from their meeting with Governor Harper. He laid them on the coffee table and scanned the room.

This group had rapidly become family and, as such, he should let them visit a while before covering the items of business he had placed on the agenda.

He scanned the group seated in a large circle in the great room. Susan sat beside Craig, Kate and Zach sat by Steve, Julia, and Itzy. Hunter and AJ sat on the large couch beside Brock and KC. Drew and Beth sat in folding chairs beside Jeff and Allie. Next were Lex and Gemma followed by all of the kids from thirteen-year-old Sam down to four-year-old Peter, Drew and Beth's son.

Shauna and Baker had brought in chairs from the kitchen and they sat behind the couch beside Allie and Jeff.

Steve and Julia stood.

All eyes in the room seemed to have focused on them.

Julia smiled and hooked her arm around her husband. "Steve and I want to make an announcement."

"I knew it. They're gonna start charging us rent," Shauna said. "Kate, I'll need more hours at Crooked River Espresso."

"Hold it. Hold it." Steve's voice boomed out the commands. "Julia, you tell them."

"A few weeks after Christmas, there's going to be someone else living in this house."

"Kate and I will be out by then, Julia," Zach said. "That will free up two bedrooms."

"We're going to have a baby."

Craig let them have fifteen minutes to congratulate and talk about the good news. Then it was time to get down to the business at hand.

He raised his voice, "KC how's it going getting Zach's radio station online and hidden?"

The room quieted at the sound of Craig's voice.

"I've already set Zach up for live streaming on the Internet. It was the best alternative to rebuilding towers every time somebody decides to blow them up along with Zach and the radio station."

"So we've eliminated the need for towers and a powerful transmitter?"

"Yes. For now," Zach said. "If things ever return to normal, I would still like to have the flexibility a traditional station provides. But for now, I can hide on the Internet, broadcast, and my network stations can take the feed that I stream to them. They can rebroadcast it however they choose. Now, we can go worldwide. I can still answer call-in questions live, as long as KC can keep me hidden. That's a way to get useful info about the status of the break-up of states, and we can assess how the people are faring across the country."

Zach paused. "I'm looking for someone who can back me up for, you know, a short honeymoon after the wedding."

"Got any takers?" Craig asked.

"Got one possibility. A DJ at the news station in Redmond."

"A more important question," Craig said. "Do you have a wedding date yet?"

Kate took Zach's hand. "We're hoping the treaty with my aunt will lead to a reduction of hostilities, at least for a

while. That's when we'll finalize our wedding plans. So …
it's all on your shoulders, Colonel Craig. You wouldn't
deprive a girl of realizing her biggest dream, would you?"

"Pressuring me. Kate, you ought to know that doesn't
work with me." He grinned. "I'm hoping for a time of peace
too. But, knowing Walker, I think he'll try to take out the
militia at least one more time before he settles down and
licks his wounds."

"Zach did find a motorhome."

"Yep. Craig, you're about to have a new neighbor down
at the Ranch RV Park. The park owner cut me a good deal
on monthly rent because of my work with the resistance.
Back to the radio broadcasts. I have broadcast capability
set up in Julia's study. We had a high-speed business line
installed for broadcasting high-quality audio. We also set
up Internet broadcast capability in two local radio stations."

"Does broadcasting from this house endanger Steve,
Julia, and Itzy? And what about the days we babysit the
kids here?" Allie asked.

"You have to consider Zach, Kate, and Shauna. They
live here too."

Craig glanced at KC. "Is this safe? I mean can he be
traced?"

"For now, it's safe." KC brushed a stray red curl from
her face. "It's safe because no one can find Zach's physical
location. If I detect any danger, Zach can move to one of the
other locations that he's prepared."

"Aunt KC," Josh said. "How will you know if the NSA or
the FBI have found Zach's router?"

"Josh, I'm running a daemon on the computer we
stream from. It monitors the router and sends me an alarm
if router probes come from any suspicious IP addresses, like
from Maryland or anywhere in the DC area."

"But they can't probe unless they figure out what you're
doing with the domain name servers, right?" Caleb said.

KC reached across and mussed Caleb's hair. "Caleb, would you like to take over for me? I can find other things to do."

"Caleb would never do that, Aunt KC. He's afraid he might get somebody killed if he makes a mistake. But he never seems to worry about that happening to us."

"I do worry about us too. Josh, remember that time when—" Caleb stopped, then made eye contact with Josh. "Ipo wona si,"

Sam stood, hands on hips. "It's not polite to talk in your language around other people, Caleb. They might think you're saying nasty things about them behind their back."

"Thank you, Sam," Gemma said. "But that was supposed to be my line."

"I'm sorry. But there are stories Josh shouldn't tell in front of other people," Caleb said. "They wouldn't understand, and they might think we're juvenile debutantes."

"Juvenile delinquents," Sam said. "I oughta know. I helped them once when—"

"Don't, Sam." Caleb's eyes pleaded with Sam.

"But you saved that old duffer from falling in the canyon," Sam said.

KC studied Sam for a moment. "This wouldn't have happened near the green on hole number five, would it?"

"Brings back memories," Brock said. "You know, Kace. Twenty years ago."

"Oh, all right." Josh blew out a blast of air and shook his head. "We had this little flipper we took out of an old electronic game. We got an infrared sensor to actuate it. If somebody tried to hit their ball across the canyon from the tee to the green, to turn that par four hole into a par three, while they were walking around the dogleg on the fairway, behind all the trees, we'd move the golf ball to the hill on the back of the green. When the golfer got close to the flipper, hidden in the grass, it would flip the ball and start it rolling. The golf ball would roll down the slope onto the steeper slope by the canyon then it would really take off until it—"

"Yeah," Brock said. "Until it fell six hundred feet to the bottom of the canyon."

Caleb nodded. "Except this guy wouldn't stop chasing it, and he slid, headfirst, until he was hanging over the edge. He couldn't move or he would slide over the cliff."

Sam laid a hand on Caleb's shoulder. "That's when the three of us ran out from our hiding place and grabbed his ankles."

"We held on while he screamed and yelled," Josh said.

"Yeah. Until the other golfers got there and pulled him out." Caleb said. "And the ball wasn't even a Titleist. He almost cracked his noodle for a cheap old Noodle."

"And that's why Caleb won't help KC," Josh said. "He's afraid he might endanger everybody if he messes up."

Brock chuckled. "All's well that ends well. Unless they called the course marshal on you three."

"They didn't," Sam said. "They just wondered what we were doing there. The wild goat herd wasn't far away, so we just said we were following the goats and didn't realize we were alongside the golf course. They thought we were heroes, and we thought being heroes with everybody shaking our hands was better than riding to the clubhouse with the marshal so he could turn us over to our parents."

Craig blew out a long sigh. "Now that we've established that the sins of the fathers and mothers are visited on the next generation, is anyone interested in learning what our defense agreement with Governor Harper looks like?"

"Wait a minute," Lex said. "The parents with sins are Brock and KC, not Gemma and I."

Craig smirked. "I could tear up this agreement and let Walker shoot missiles at us."

"Tell us about the agreement," Lex said.

The room grew silent.

Craig explained the border defense responsibilities for the Guard and the militia and their responsibilities to defend each other. "But what really expands our capabilities is that we get support from both the Air Guard wing in Portland and the wing at Kingsley in Klamath Falls. The only thing I forgot to clarify is whether this would include CAS, close air support, if we get into a battle with federal troops. But I know the F-15 Eagle pilots are trained for that and they got a lot of experience in Afghanistan. So I'm assuming they will come to defend us if we get pinned down."

"Yes," Baker said. "And the good thing about that is the federal troops have no fighter interceptors in the Northwest. For the past several years, they've all been assigned to the Air Guard."

"What about that Growler from Whidbey?" Drew said.

"It's no match for an F-15," Baker said. "It wasn't designed for the same purposes. F-15s would blow those Growlers out of the air in a few seconds."

"I'm feeling a little better about this defense agreement," Zach said. "I was getting a little paranoid at first with the big bullseye painted on the back of all my shirts."

"Well don't get too comfortable, folks," Craig said. "Walker has egg on his face and a burr under his saddle ... us, the militia. We're making it look like he can't handle red areas let alone red states. That will provoke more rebellion and stronger resistance. So I think we need to prepare for an all-out assault by the strongest force President Walker can muster. He needs to make an example of us or risk losing his ability to govern."

"Would he fly over in bombers?" Benjamin asked. "That would be the easiest way to get rid of us."

"Let's pray the man isn't that evil, Benjamin," Craig said. "Or that he can't find any bomber crews willing to drop bombs on American citizens."

"Yeah," Caleb said. "Because that would be unprostitutional."

Gemma's eyes rolled and she shook her head.

The rest of the adults burst into laughter.

Craig chuckled. But Caleb's mistake might not be far from the truth ... if unprostitutional were a real word.

# Chapter 5

*Washington DC, Oval Office*

After two hours of intense tightrope walking, President Walker dismissed the Saudi ambassador. The bump in the road of the two nations' relationship had been smoothed ... for now.

Many ambassadors had left the country when the United States began to seriously fracture. But, evidently, the Saudis thought this was a good time to win concessions from the Americans. Walker hadn't given them any, had he?

It was difficult to think about anything but the domestic problems he faced. Problem number one was shutting down the militia in Oregon and their propaganda campaign headed by Zach Tanner, a campaign that now had reached coast-to-coast.

Deke was supposed to be ferreting out Tanner's location so they could eliminate him. But Walker's most trusted operative hadn't reported in two days. Was this another failed mission? It seemed that every time he made an aggressive move against—

Walker's secure phone rang. He looked at the caller ID. Deke.

"President Walker here."

"Mr. President, I'm sorry for the delayed report, but this is the first opportunity I've had to call you in forty-eight hours."

"Major Deke, have you had your sat phone with you for the past forty-eight hours?"

"Yes, sir. But—"

"But you couldn't remember my number? Failure to report in such critical times is unacceptable."

"Mr. President, I've been operating concealed, in close proximity to the militia. I couldn't use my phone."

"Why were you playing hide and seek with the militia?"

"Don't you want to eliminate Tanner and his radio network that the insurgents are using against us?"

"Just tell me what you found, Deke."

"I found that the GPS tracker on Tanner's truck, placed by Governor Harper's spies two weeks ago, is still on the truck and is sending its signal."

"Can you track Tanner's movements?"

"Yes. I was studying the pattern of the truck's location when Tanner broadcasts. But I really don't need to solve that mystery. I just need to verify that Zach has just driven his truck. If he is still driving or if he stops, either way, you can take him out. That will degrade their little propaganda network, leaving only Lex and Gemma James and Brock Daniels as mouthpieces for the rebels."

"Aren't you forgetting Governor Harper?"

"Mr. President, taking out the governor is a much more delicate matter. I thought you might like to handle that in a less violent manner."

"You mean arrest her and try her for treason?"

"Yes, sir. Something like that."

"Deke, how do we avoid the four thousand guardsmen who will protect her? She also has a state police security unit?"

"After Harper flipped the state, many Oregonians in high places don't like her. They are a vindictive lot. We just need to find a Judas among them. Which do you prefer that I focus on first, finding a Judas or Zach Tanner?"

"I want Tanner as soon as we can get him, and I don't give a rip about collateral damage."

"Tanner drives a blue Dodge, late-model pickup. I'll text you his GPS tracker's frequency and let you know when he's available. But you'll have to be ready to go on a moment's notice."

"Give me twenty-four hours and I'll be ready. If I can identify his tracker signal, Zach Tanner's charmed life is over. And for what I have in mind, all I need is a moment's notice."

# Chapter 6

*Crooked River Ranch RV Park, Craig's motor home*

Craig's secure cell rang. He set his razor on the bathroom counter, swiped some shaving cream from the side of his face, and planted the phone against his ear.

The caller ID said Jeff Jacobs, the former Olympic champion. Craig had put Jeff in charge of the militia team charged with gleaning intelligence from what the militia had confiscated after the Apache attack on the house where Governor Harper took Kate. Maybe Jeff had found something in the rubble.

"Craig here."

"Craig, sir, this is Jeff Jacobs. There's been an interesting development from something we found after the Hellfire Missile killed Harper's men at that house near Sisters."

"Shoot, Jeff."

"One cell phone had a lot of pictures on it, almost like someone was documenting the Oregon State Police security squad's mission that day. Well, one of the pictures had a man in the background. We don't think he was a state trooper. We sent the picture to Kate. She said the guy was Deke, the same dude who had kidnapped her."

Bingo. The snake may have coiled and struck for the last time. "That's good news, Jeff."

"There's more, sir. You probably knew that one of our men, Burright, used to be a PI. We turned him loose with that picture and he found out some very interesting things."

"Hopefully, like where the man lives?" Craig said.

"Not quite, but almost," Jeff said. "We found several people who had seen Mr. Deke, and we verified that he eats dinner several times a week at the Black Bear Restaurant in Redmond."

"That dude is spying on us and feeding his info to Walker's people."

"You're probably right, sir. Thought you'd want to know about it."

"Thanks, Jeff. For the next day or two, I've got Deke. I'll call Burright and tell him where to pick up Deke's trail."

Craig ended the call. But someone other than the mysterious Deke kept intruding into his thoughts. And Craig had an idea that would allow him to spend some time with her.

He glanced at the wall clock. 8:10 a.m.

Susan had been working the early shift at Crooked River Espresso, so she would be there until 2:00 p.m..

If he stopped by and asked her to dinner, Susan would come. He knew that. He also knew how to talk to a group of warfighters in almost any situation, even if it was a mixed group, men and women. But talking to one woman in an intimate setting ... it had been so long since he'd done that.

Thinking about it seemed to shake his confidence. Maybe it was a bad idea. It would be better to have a good friend like Susan than to lose her because he'd bungled the romantic approach and lost hope of any kind of a relationship with this incredible woman.

*Dude, you sound like a teenager with a crush on the girl next door but afraid to tell her.*

He needed to go now, or his courage would evaporate as he systematically talked himself out of this opportunity.

Craig slipped on a camouflage t-shirt, tucked it into his jeans and headed out the door.

Ten minutes later he pulled up to the service window at Crooked River Espresso.

Shauna rose a couple of inches—probably on her tip toes—looked down into his big Jeep SUV, and stared at his face. Slowly a crooked smile twisted her lips. "Craig, are you here for coffee or for Susan?"

Was he that obvious? "Is that the kind of question you ask customers these days? Who broke you in here? Was it Kate?"

"It's the kind of question I ask men who pull in here so anxious to see that special girl that they forget to wash all the shaving cream off their face."

Craig winced, then stuck his head out the window to look in the big side mirror. It was worse than leaving a little shaving cream on his face. He'd only shaved one side of his face. On the other side, two days' growth of salt and pepper beard covered his cheek and half of his chin—at least that's what it looked like through the shaving cream he hadn't wiped off his face.

He ripped a tissue from the box sitting on the console, wiped his face, and looked again into the mirror.

Shauna frowned down at him. "Dude, if that's the latest beard style, I don't think the ladies are going to care for it."

"Shauna, just tell me where Susan is." The words had come out a little harsher than intended.

"And you're supposed to be an officer and a gentleman?" She stuck out a palm at him and shook her head. "That's okay. I've been called munchkin and midget and a few other things. I can take a little rudeness."

He opened his mouth to ask again.

"Susan just drove into the parking lot. She ran over to the store on her morning break. Now, I don't know what you came to ask her. But, Colonel Craig, I'm going to give you some advice. Keep the right side of your face turned away from her if you want her to say yes." Shauna smirked again.

"I'm beginning to see why Baker calls you motor mouth. Do you give him the same verbal abuse?"

"I don't know. Never thought about it. But that runt still comes around almost every evening."

Susan approached from where she'd parked her car. "Whatever she gives Baker, he must like, because he sure hangs around this place a lot when Shauna's working. Our coffee is good, but ..."

"Susan, I need to talk to you about something important that has come up."

Susan looked up at Shauna watching them through the service window. "I'll only be a few minutes, then I'll cover you for your break."

Shauna nodded and gave them another twisted smile.

Susan hurried around Craig's jeep to climb in the passenger side. She would be sitting on his right so—

"Dude, you blew it. The answer is no." Shauna laughed.

Susan climbed into the Jeep. "What is Shauna talking about?" She studied his face for a moment. "Did you, uh..." She covered her mouth and looked down at the floorboard.

Maybe it was best not to try explaining. He drove out of the service line and parked at the edge of the lot. Craig felt his gut tighten as he formulated his question. "I got a call this morning from Jeff. It seems there's a short undercover assignment that I could use your help with. Would you like to go with me?"

She had quickly regained her composure when he asked for her help. "I'd like to, but how long is this assignment?"

"It's just dinner tonight in Redmond."

The corners of Susan's mouth curved upward ever so slightly. "David, are you asking me out on a date?"

"Sort of a date. But it's more than that."

* * *

*More than a date? What did that mean.*

Susan sensed she was frowning and forced a smile onto her lips. "Of course, I'd like to go. What kind of place are we going to? How should I dress?"

"It's casual. Just dress so you don't look conspicuous. We don't want to draw attention." David's eyes roved over her long red hair and stopped on her face.

His thoughts were obvious. He didn't think she could avoid drawing attention.

This was entirely new coming from David Craig, a man who seldom said anything about people's appearances. It was flattering that he liked hers, but she wasn't sure how she felt about that.

"I see you're having some second thoughts. I needed somebody to go with me, so we appear to be a couple. The man who infiltrated the Oregon State Police to spy on Governor Harper, then kidnapped Kate, and escaped from the Apache attack is named Deke. We think he was planted here by Walker to provide intel about the militia. We need to find out where he's staying. He will probably be having dinner at the Black Bear Diner in Redmond. That's where you and I will be dining."

Having dinner in the same room with the president's secret agent. This could be a bit dangerous. "Are we going to track him to his house?"

"No. After we leave, I'll call our man, Burright, an ex-PI. He'll tail Deke after we've followed him for a few blocks."

"Sure, I'm up for dinner and a little intrigue."

But how much of this would be pretense and how much would be a real dinner date with David? She would have to wait to find out.

"I get off at two o'clock. When do I need to be ready?"

"About six-thirty. I know you have to get up early tomorrow to open up the shop, so I'll have you home by eight-thirty."

"Do you know where I live?"

"It's my business to know where our people live. Your house is on NW 19th, right?"

"Yes. But you won't get to meet my mother tonight. This is her evening for ladies' Bible study at her church."

"That's okay. It's a bit early for family introductions."

Family introductions? Why had he said that? He was thinking ahead in an enticing direction, but it was too early for anything enticing.

"In this topsy-turvy world, it's seldom too early for anything." She opened the passenger door to get out. "See you at six-thirty and, David ... maybe you should change that blade in your razor."

* * *

Susan stood from her seat near the living room window when David Craig's Jeep SUV pulled in on her graveled driveway.

Her mom's grandfather clock bonged half of the Westminster Chime.

He was punctual. But what else should one expect from a retired special forces commander?

By the time she locked the front door and turned toward the driveway, David was crunching through the gravel in his newly shined chukka boots and wearing a no-tuck western shirt over what appeared to be a brand new pair of jeans. And he had shaved.

She chuckled. They were a matched pair, though her jeans had encountered laundry detergent several times.

He stopped when he saw her. His eyes went straight to her red hair which contrasted with the navy-blue denim shirt. Though David didn't voice them, his eyes and the expression on his face spoke the words, "I thought I said inconspicuous."

She had endured years of torture about her carrot top while growing up and had vowed she wouldn't take any more abuse about her hair. "I'm sorry. I didn't have time to dye my hair."

"No, I'm sorry … for staring. Your hair is perfect. Besides, I'm the only one of us he might recognize but, if Deke's a red-blooded male, he won't be looking at me."

The easy-going yet confident smile on his face—the one she had seen him give to the men he worked with—sucked all of the awkwardness out of the moment.

She grinned at him. "Just don't call me carrot top and we'll have a great evening."

"Consider it done, CT."

"CT? You keep that up and I'll sentence you to two hours of tongue lashing by Shauna Jackson."

"According to Baker, she can deliver it. That's why he calls her motor mouth. Who would expect that from a cute little thing like Shauna?"

"You should have heard her yesterday. A teenage guy drove through to order coffee, and when he made a vulgar proposition to her, Shauna cut loose with every non-profane insult known to man … or woman. She started with, 'If you were standing here looking at the trash I'm looking at, you'd puke.' It went rapidly downhill from there. The poor young kid's face looked like he had a third-degree sunburn when he peeled out onto the highway."

"Speaking of peeling out onto the highway. We need to head for Redmond if we want enough time to finish our meal before Deke decides to duck out of the place."

Fifteen minutes later, David escorted her through the double doors and into the Black Bear Diner.

The waitress led them to the dining area and asked where they would like to sit.

David quickly scanned the room, then drew Susan's gaze and nodded toward a booth along the wall.

A medium-height man sat alone. He had short cropped hair, and a lean but muscular build. The hungry look on the man's face, his hawkish nose, and wide eyes, looked to Susan like a cross between a vulture and a demon.

Then he looked at Susan and studied her until the feeling that he was undressing her with his eyes forced her to avert her gaze. Demon had overshadowed vulture.

David had chosen a small table out in the open area. It gave them a clear view of Deke's booth. And it gave Deke a clear view of Susan.

After they were seated and given menus, David studied her for a moment. "Sorry, Susan. Maybe this wasn't a good idea." He lowered his voice. "This guy gives off bad vibes."

"I think they're evil vibes," She whispered. "But I guess a man must be evil if he plots the assassination of a governor and all of her security troops ... and he meant to kill you too, David."

"Susan, we don't have to stay. If you want to leave, I can call Burright as we're headed out and he can take over for us."

"No. Let's stay. I can take anything this guy dishes out. I was just telling you what I think of him."

"I had to get up so early that I missed breakfast. So that's what I'll order." David had quickly changed the subject.

"Sounds good to me too, especially Bruce's Meat Lover's Omelette."

"You keep eating like that and you'll have a heart attack before you're fifty."

He smiled briefly. "That still leaves me a few more years to ... well, for other things."

"I'm having the California Omelette."

After the waitress brought them water and took their orders, a thought struck her. How would David handle it if Deke left suddenly?

The next few minutes were filled with casual banter about nothing of significance. David's concentration was clearly on Deke. Maybe he was worried that the man would leave suddenly, and they would lose him.

"Here come our meals," David said. "Ma'am I'm expecting an important call sometime this evening and I'll need to leave immediately. Could you please bring our tab now, I'll leave cash, and a nice tip, if you could take care of it for us."

The waitress smiled. "Sure. We serve a few doctors who have that situation all the time."

Susan was taking the last few bites of her omelet when Deke asked for his bill. She nodded toward Deke.

"I noticed," David said. He pulled out his wallet, pulled out two twenties, slipped them under the bill, and set his unused spoon on top. "As soon as he exits the door, we get up and head for it. Try to get his license plate number. I have a text for Burright ready to go. We'll just need to add some details."

After Deke passed them on his way to checkout, Susan picked up her purse and set it in her lap.

David sent a message to the man called Burright and started composing another. He stopped and looked up at her. "Let's go, Susan."

After they exited through the main entry door and rounded the corner to the side parking lot, a black van pulled out of a parking spot and headed toward the east entrance.

"David, hurry. He's turning onto 4th Street."

"Watch him, Susan. Tell me if he goes north or south."

"He turned south."

"Which way is he going at the intersection."

"Don't pull out. He's turning onto Cedar and will come by right in front of us."

"Great. Get his license plate while I contact Burright."

"It's 672JXW."

"Got it, and now so does Burright. I'm calling him, so keep your eyes on that van."

"He turned right onto 6th Street."

"Burright, Craig here. We're following Deke. He's driving a black van. I just sent you the license plate number. He's headed south on NW 6th Street just passing West Antler Avenue. He's in the right lane ... So you're at the corner Southwest Cascade and 6th? ... Great. You've got him in two more blocks. Good luck."

He turned to Susan. "Good job. Now if we can find where he's staying, we might be able to listen in on him and figure out what Walker has him up to before they can spring anything on us."

For the ride home, Craig seemed to retreat into some inner world, probably where he played his war games and laid out strategies.

At the moment, it seemed to be a world she wasn't allowed to enter with him. Would that ever change, or was this what it would be like to be the wife of a dedicated warfighter, a commander of warfighters?

Should she even be asking herself such hypothetical questions at this point? She glanced at the intense look on the face of a man born to lead, one who risked his life for others to keep them safe and free. A man of his word. How could she not ask?

Craig pulled into her driveway and stopped. His gaze met hers. "It's been a really long time since I had dinner with a woman. It was very nice, even if we had to deal with Deke. I enjoyed it, Susan."

She opened her door to get out.

He remained in the driver's seat.

It was nice. He enjoyed it. Was this how the evening would end?

It seemed that Craig wanted to say something, but he didn't. Until ...

"Good night, Susan."

"Good night, David."

He backed out and drove away.

It wasn't what she had pictured for the end of their evening. Maybe it was the undercover part that had restrained the relational aspects.

Or was it her. Susan hadn't been enough for Jerry, her fiancé. She had almost married him, until he left suddenly and the vile truth about him was exposed.

But David Craig was a warfighter, a patriot, a man of honor, too good a person to ever let her down. But did he view her as a person of value? Jerry hadn't. He had left her, nearly at the altar. And what he had left Susan for made her sick to think about.

# Chapter 7

*The next morning, Washington, DC*

President Walker stood behind the lectern in the James S. Brady Press Briefing Room. He had been answering the media's obnoxious, harassing questions about the state of the union for forty-five minutes.

"One more question."

"Mr. President."

"Mr. President."

He pointed to the dark-haired woman seated on the left side of the room. "Yes?"

"Mr. President, I'm sure you are monitoring the critical systems that keep our nation functioning and provide the necessities for families and businesses. What plans do you have to keep our nation together and functioning, and does that require changing our form of government in the future?"

"In the future, our government must take into account that the world has been shrinking at an incredible rate. The only future that makes sense is a global future. We're all members of the human race, and we will live or die together as such. Anyone who believes otherwise—"

"But, Mr. President, not all human beings want to live under a global government. They want—"

"It's survival of the fittest. Perhaps those you are referring to are not fit to live. No more questions."

The noise in the room rose to an ear-splitting volume.

Walker hurried off the platform and headed toward his private study. When he turned the corner by the Cabinet

Room, Will Richards caught Walker with both hands on his shoulders to prevent a nasty collision.

"Will, I need to see you in my study as soon as possible."

"How about right now, sir?"

The president nodded and Will followed him down the hallway to the study.

"Have a seat, Will. I'm concerned about the press. Even the friendly media outlets seemed hostile today. I need you to tell me how Oregon's declaration of war on the United States is playing in the news." Walker rolled his office chair up to his desk. "Are we seeing any outrage?"

"Outrage? I don't think so. A lot of people are laughing, but even more are cheering them on."

A flash of heat burned under his collar. Walker swore. "Then this attack needs to prove that Oregon made a bad— no, a deadly decision. The militia must pay, and Governor Harper must be removed from office and convicted of treason. Are we ready to finalize the attack?"

"Mr. President, there are some loose ends and some troubling constraints."

"Constraints? We have almost the entire military at our disposal."

Will's bushy eyebrows pinched until they nearly touched. "What about air support, especially close air support? Oregon has all the fighter interceptors in the Northwest on their side. How can we counter that?"

"Couldn't we use the 211th Aviation Regiment?"

Will shook his head slowly. "Sir, the 211th is all choppers. They do have Apaches, but they could easily be shot down by F-15s that can fly at nearly five times their speed. Besides, they fly out of West Jordan, Utah. That's 600 miles. They would have to refuel. But that's also a Guard Unit activated and under the governor's command. Governor Udall would never let you have the 211th. If they flew at all, it would be to defend the rebels."

"So you're telling me we're stuck using JBLM in Tacoma?"

"It's only three hundred miles to the target area."

"We had some problems the last time we flew through the Western Air Defense Sector, can we still find a loyal crew and get them safely to Eastern Oregon?"

"I believe we can find somebody from the 16th Combat Aviation Brigade, 1st Battalion. If you want Apaches, their 229th Aviation Regiment has them."

"Didn't we get one of their choppers damaged last time?"

"And that's why, Mr. President, that might have been the last time—"

"I am the president, the Commander-In-Chief."

"But you've got to find someone who will still obey your orders or you're the commander who's not a chief. So far, the gutless governor of Washington has towed the line, despite some opposition in the ranks."

"What about Colonel Towry. Can we use him again?

"Probably, sir. But remember what happened last time? He got himself into that standoff situation and put his men in danger."

"I'm willing to overlook that. It wasn't Towry's fault."

"No, it wasn't, Mr. President. No one could have predicted that little hate triangle that formed or that it would turn violent in the way that it did."

Walker swore again. "Or that Harper would kidnap her own niece and leave us to kill each other rather than taking out Tanner's radio station."

"Do you want me to set up a telecon with Colonel Towry for tomorrow?"

"Yes. Check my schedule and then set it up, Will."

"Yes, sir."

"How are we doing with consolidating blue states on the East Coast?"

"Mr. President, I told you how to reign in the East Coast. Just ask each governor if they want federal protection from the militant rebels who will try to take over their states. If they ask for protection, you tell them that in these uncertain times, you need to know whom you can trust, so protection can only be bought with demonstrated loyalty. They'll get the message."

"I can hear Smarty Pants Pandolfi asking me what I mean by 'demonstrated loyalty'."

"You can tell Pandolfi, and any others, that you mean their media outlets must stop supporting dissenting voices and start supporting their president. That might help break Tanner's Resistance Network, or whatever he's calling it now."

"You mean tell the governors to censor the media?"

"Behind closed doors, of course, but have you got any better ideas?"

Walker didn't reply.

The Oregon situation still troubled Walker. They needed to ensure victory in this next attempt. "I'm having second thoughts about an immediate attack on Oregon."

"Do you want me to hold off contacting Colonel Towry?"

"No. We need to talk to him. But with all the uncertainty about loyalties in the military, I have a smaller army than I expected. Consequently, I prefer not to be fighting simultaneously on two fronts, which is almost certain to happen in Oregon."

"Eastern and western Oregon are allied against you, Mr. President. How can you avoid a conflict with two fronts?"

"Maybe we should let Oregon take care of the Oregon problem."

"What do you mean, sir?"

"I mean Ms. Sandra Harper has made a lot of enemies by flipping her state politically."

"Yes, she has a deep state problem that cannot quickly be resolved."

"And so perhaps we deal the militia a crippling blow while the Oregon deep state, with a little incentive I provide, buries Harper about six feet deep."

# Chapter 8

*Crooked River Ranch Espresso, Terrebonne, Oregon*

Susan dodged Shauna's arms as they reached in to grab a grande-sized coffee cup.

"You never did tell me how that dinner date with Craig went. He doesn't seem the romantic type, but he's sure easy on a girl's eyes." Shauna batted her long eyelashes and waited.

"You want the truth?"

"Lie if you want to, but I'll know it if you do."

"I wouldn't lie, Shauna. But there's not much to tell. We were there to locate and tail one of Walker's spies, that guy named Deke."

"Did you?" Shauna filled the cup with milk and started the hissing steam treatment.

"We did, then we handed him off to another militia person, Burright. He was supposed to follow Deke to where he lives, but I haven't heard how that turned out."

"How did the date turn out?"

"Did anybody ever tell you you're nosey?"

"Lots of people. I can't repeat what some of them said, but it sure wasn't nosey. Here comes another customer." Shauna moved toward the service window. "I've got this one. Hmmm. I don't recognize this guy. He shaved his head bald and he's not that tan. He's gonna fry his noggin in the desert sun."

The car stopped at the window.

"Welcome to Crooked River Espresso. What can I get for you?"

"Is Susan here?"

"Yes, she is, but I can—"

"I'd rather have Susan, please."

Shauna nodded then walked across the narrow shop and nearly bumped into Susan. "He wants *you* to wait on him."

A bald head. "Do you think he's a skinhead?"

"I don't think so. Maybe he just likes redheads. Or maybe he doesn't like, you know … me."

"That's why I asked if he's a skinhead. I'll wait on the guy and send him on his way." Susan walked to the service window. "I'm Susan. May I help you?"

"How about a tall, iced latte and maybe you can tell me how to get in touch with the local militia."

*Not on your life, buddy.* "If you give me your contact information, I can have someone call you."

"Perhaps you can put me in touch with David Craig."

"Why are you asking?"

"Well I heard he's been talking to Governor Harper and I have some info he should know about her."

"Craig and Harper? I'm afraid I wouldn't know anything about that." *And if I did, I wouldn't tell you, skinhead.*

"That's funny. I thought you were dating him."

"I don't know who would have told you that." *Except maybe Deke.*

After three or four red flags, it was time to get rid of this guy. He was probably a spy.

Susan poured the contents of his drink in a tall-sized cup of ice.

"Hey, Susan. I've got the camera ready and the light's just right to take that picture you wanted of our menu sign." Shauna shot the picture with her cell before anybody could react.

Both Susan and the man would be in that picture.

When she set the coffee cup on the counter, the man snatched it. Threw a five at her and roared away to the highway.

"That was some quick thinking, Shauna. I think we just saw a spy blow his cover. Send me that picture. Craig needs to know about this guy."

She hit Craig's number on her speed dial. "Craig, this is Susan. A very suspicious guy just left here in a hurry after asking questions about you and Harper. And he wanted a contact for the militia. Shauna took his picture and he took off."

"Sounds fishy. Send me the picture and I'll see if anybody recognizes him."

She sent the picture to his cell and waited for him to receive it.

"I don't recognize him. But Drew is tapping my shoulder. Just a sec."

"Drew says this guy contacted him about joining the militia. He gave him a form to fill out, but the man didn't return it. He just asked questions. One was about our relationship with Governor Harper."

"Did you ever find Deke's place?"

"No, we didn't. But I think this guy might be Deke's replacement, at least for the spying part of the mission. Assassination on the other hand..."

"He thought you and I were dating. The only way he would have thought that is if Deke told him. That means we didn't fool Deke at the Black Bear."

"It also verifies that he's a Walker plant. And it means Walker is still gathering information for some kind of attack."

"What do we need to do?" Susan asked.

"We need to go on high alert, DEFCON 2. I'll broadcast the message to everyone in a few minutes. And we need to have a conference tonight at Julia's house. You need to be there Susan, along with Drew and some others. It's a good thing Julia and Steve are so accommodating."

Susan nodded, but was still trying to absorb the impact of David's decision to go on high alert.

David obviously read the angst in her voice. "Susan, if we detect any signs of an impending attack, we'll move the families to the designated shelters. I'll invoke the joint defense plan to move guard troops in by helicopter and have Harper put her two fighter wings on alert. Don't worry, we have a plan for this."

"Do you really think Walker is going to launch an assault on the state of Oregon? "

"At some point he has to. If he can't get Oregon to surrender, he's going to lose all the red states and maybe turn some blue states red. That could cost him the entire nation. It's a loss he can't afford, so Walker will come soon in an attack planned to wipe us out. And when he comes, a depraved man like him won't give a rip about our families."

# Chapter 9

Craig pressed send and his message announcing DEFCON 2 was broadcast to every member and supporter of the Central Oregon Militia. "We are now one defense readiness condition from officially going to war."

Kate looked over at Craig from her desk in Julia's study where she was working on intelligence reports. "Does that mean we—"

Craig's cell rang, playing *Oregon, My Oregon.* It's your aunt, Kate. I'd better see what she wants."

"Craig here."

"Craig, this is Sandra. Something very disconcerting happened today."

"Are you okay and is Western Oregon still secure?"

"I think so."

"Governor Harper, you don't sound convinced. What happened?"

"There was an attempt on my life. A sniper shot through a window and—well, it was a close call."

"A window? Your office doesn't have windows a sniper could use. Where were you?"

"I had to meet with Layla Thomas, Secretary of State, to decide how she was going to keep public records for the businesses in Eastern Oregon, many of which have stopped corresponding with Salem. When I entered her office on the first floor and walked to her desk, I passed a window on the back wall. The window looks out to a parking lot along Court Street. Someone shot at me from the parking lot. The shot went through the window. Evidently the glass deflected it slightly, so the bullet only grazed my head."

*Grazed her head?*

Craig stifled an old habit and cut some choice words before they flew off his tongue. "Whose idea was it for you to go to the Secretary of State's office? Was it Ms. Thomas's?"

"It was. She called to ask me about meeting with her. My security people are investigating the incident. And I saw that woman sweat for the first time when she tried to answer some of their questions. I'm convinced she was part of the conspiracy, but there had to be others."

"Are you sure you're okay?"

Kate stood by her desk. "Craig, what happened to Aunt Sandy?"

"Just a minute. Kate is asking about you." He turned to Kate. "Someone tried to shoot your aunt, but they missed. She's fine. We're just trying to decide what we need to do."

Kate clenched and opened her fists several times. She looked as if she might bolt and run... straight to Salem.

"Kate, let me finish talking with the governor and then you can help me get the word out. We have a meeting scheduled for this evening. Now we have another agenda item."

Kate nodded but the crease on her forehead deepened as she sat on her chair watching Craig talk with her aunt.

"Do you have any other suspects?"

"Besides Layla Thomas, we suspect Sherman Bender was involved. There may have been others and we haven't identified the shooter yet."

"Do you have people around you that you can trust—I mean absolutely trust?"

"I believe I can trust every member of my security guard, but I suppose there's always the possibility of a traitor hiding among a group that size."

"Keep your most trusted people around you at all times. Remember, you are surrounded by Oregon's deep state and those people consider you a traitor. Now you know how far they will go to get rid of you."

"Yes. They made that clear. If your leaders are meeting tonight, let me know what comes out of that meeting. We may have to modify our plans based on the failure of this heinous assassination attempt. President Walker may feel compelled to move against the state immediately after he hears about the failed attempt on my life."

"You mean the failed coup?"

"It was that too." She sighed sharply into the phone. "And I'm starting to get really angry about that."

"I understand. Stay safe, governor. I'll get back to you after our meeting. As you said, we may have to make some new plans, because Walker is probably starting to panic as each attempt to stop the resistance in Oregon fails. I think we are the guinea pig for his plan to force the nation back together. He has to make an example of Oregon or he loses power and influence. And with things so volatile, that could cost Walker the presidency, his freedom, and maybe his life."

Craig ended the call and turned to Kate.

"About the meeting here tonight. We'll start at five o'clock, but I'll let Steve and Julia know it might be a long meeting. I'll contact Drew and Beth, Lex and Gemma, Brock and KC. Kate, will you call Baker and Susan?"

"Why Susan?"

"I think she needs to be here. She's starting to take on a larger role. And she is the networker that brought us all together."

"I see," Kate said.

Steve walked into the study, stopped, and scanned Craig's and Kate's faces. "What happened and how bad is it?"

Craig blew out a blast of frustration. "There has been an attempt to assassinate Governor Harper. We think the Secretary of State, Layla Thomas, Sherman Bender, and several others were involved. Harper, after getting over the shock of a bullet grazing her head, got angry, really angry. She thinks she can trust her security guard. I've already told Kate because this impacts her personally. But I'm going to let the whole group know there was an attempt to assassinate Governor Harper."

"So we can expect a long meeting tonight," Steve said.

Craig nodded. "I'm just praying we can come up with a plan to hold Walker at bay until all of the resistance sees his guilt and his weakness and we can remove that would-be tyrant from office."

\* \* \*

At 5:05 p.m., Craig opened the meeting. "We have moved to DEFCON 2. There was an attempt on Governor Harper's life. I mentioned that when I contacted you earlier. But it was only by God's mercy that she wasn't killed. The bullet grazed her head."

Murmuring spread throughout the great room.

"Is the governor okay?" Gemma asked.

"Yes. Thanks to her security detail. But she has some bruises from being pushed out of the way and a slice on her scalp where the bullet grazed her," Craig said.

"Do we know who the conspirators are?" Drew asked.

"About half the people in the Willamette Valley." Shauna gave a derisive snort.

"We've only heard two names, so far," Craig said. "Layla Thomas and Sherman Bender."

"Aunt Sandy needs me over there," Kate said. "Her security detail is all men. That won't cut it when the Oregon deep state is as deep as Crater Lake. I need to act as her personal bodyguard until we have a handle on this. It might even involve someone on her security team."

"Kate, leave that to the professionals. I don't want you in that kind of danger," Zach said.

"Kate is right," Craig said. "Our intelligence says we're beginning to see that the majority of Oregonians will follow their governor into red statehood. Evidently, the governor's opponents feared losing control, completely, so they tried to stop the trend by killing the leader, Sandra Harper."

"I still think it's a bad idea," Zach said.

"Kate is smart and perceptive," Craig said. "She knows how to use her gun and she loves her aunt. What better qualifications are there for a personal bodyguard?"

Zach opened his mouth to speak.

"Zach, if she's determined to go, it would be ill-advised for you to try to stop her, especially since you're trying to set a wedding date … if you get my drift."

Zach nodded but didn't say anything.

"Kate can handle the job of protecting the governor, but what about keeping operations going at Crooked River Espresso?" Craig said. "It's been a good source of information for us."

Baker gave Shauna, sitting beside him, a twisted smile. "Munchkin makes a mean mocha and has been filling in there off and on. She and AJ can handle the coffee and the info."

"Yes, they can," Susan said. "I've watched them work together. They're a good team."

Zach took Kate's hand. "So what about our wedding?"

She leaned against his shoulder. "Zach, as soon as things settle down, I still want to become Mrs. Tanner."

"Until then, I need you to be careful, Kate. Really careful."

"Like you were when you charged that house under heavy gunfire and dove through the window to rescue me?"

Zach opened his mouth then closed it again.

"I have my Sig Sauer, and I know how to use it. And you're broadcasting from the Internet now, so you're safe." Kate glanced at KC. "Right, KC?"

"Kate, I won't let Walker know where Zach is broadcasting from. He's as safe as he can be. And if anyone figures out what I'm doing with domain name servers, we'll disguise his location another way. But what about your intelligence analysis?"

"Susan can do that," Kate said. "In fact, she's already been compiling info on our mysterious spy."

"I agree," Craig said. "As much as Kate and Susan talk, she's almost up to speed already."

"And how would you know that?" Kate said.

"I have my sources." Craig shot Susan a glance.

"I see," Kate said.

"About that wedding ..." Susan said. "... as soon as we see a wedding window, I'll coordinate with Pastor Bousman about using the Ranch Chapel. But you two might not have much opportunity for a honeymoon. There's no safe place to go."

"They have a perfect place to go," Beth said. "Zach and Kate can use our cabin in the hills above the Deschutes River. It's a beautiful place and it's isolated. Nobody will bother you."

"Now that that's settled, let's move on to the *main* agenda item," Craig said.

Susan gave him a piercing glance.

"I mean move to the *next* agenda item."

Susan's piercing glare softened to a warm smile. "That's what I love about you, David. You're so perceptive."

"Perceptive? I do know a dagger when I see one, especially if it's pointed at me."

The men in the room chuckled.

But the ladies just stared at the men.

Maybe Craig should, for future reference, file the reactions he had just seen. With women, relationships trumped war ... every time.

But what was going on between Shauna and Baker—staring at each other? And Baker had, there was no other way to describe it, gaga eyes. If this trend continued, Craig would have a whole army of men and women married to one another. That could turn out to be tactical torment when it came time to fight.

Maybe the news he was about to announce could return them to being an army on alert at DEFCON 2.

"Here's our situation," Craig said. "It has changed a bit after the Portland and Pendleton Guard gave Kate some radio intercepts from Washington state. They picked up both voice and data over the defense networks—messages from federal troops at JBLM. Something is being planned that involves transporting troops from Washington using Chinook helicopters."

KC laughed. "It's difficult to maintain security when your military communications networks weren't designed to handle secession."

"Yes," Craig said. "Part of the military is suddenly the enemy, and nobody remembered to prune the communications network to remove the 1st Battalion, 168th Aviation Regiment. That's how Pendleton heard about it."

"Communications networks don't handle blue states flipping to red, either." Steve said.

"So ..." Susan said, "... we have a failed coup and a deep state opposing the governor in Western Oregon, a spy in Central Oregon assessing our capabilities, and intercepted communications indicating that our president wants to attack us."

"That's about the size of it," Craig said. "Has anyone got a prognosis?"

"Give me a few hours and I might have one," Susan said.

"I told you she could handle this." Kate looked at Susan and smirked. "I can also tell you *why* she *wants* to handle it."

Craig caught Allie's gaze which alternated between him and Susan.

Allie nodded her approval of Kate's remark, but the room went silent.

"Sounds like I need to fly the 407 over the Cascades again." Baker had broken the awkward moment. "When are we going to do this?"

"Early this evening, Kate said. "So Baker can get back before dark."

"Do you want me to go along like the last time?" Drew asked.

"I'll go," Craig said. "The governor, Kate, and I need to have a private conversation."

Shauna's gaze started on Baker and wound up on Craig "Do you think I could—"

Baker hooked Shauna's arm and refused to let go when she tried to pull it free. "I think Munchkin needs to stay home this time. Not that she isn't good company. But this could be a volatile situation on the West side. And as we saw in our last trip, the Witch of the North isn't good like she was in the Land of Oz. She casts her spell with Hellfire Missiles and AIM-120s."

Craig nodded and grinned. "Volatile situation? If motormouth Munchkin came along, I guarantee the conversation would be volatile."

"You white folk need to watch your words, 'cause, from the neighborhood where I grew up, I got some choice ones I could use on you."

Julia looked at Itzy sitting in a chair along the far wall beside Sam. "Let's see ... white, black, and we've got brown covered with Allie and Itzy."

"Red too," Baker said. "I'm half Modoc. That's why I got shorted on height. But I've got some other things that make up for it." He flexed his huge biceps.

"Modoc? A red man?" Shauna said. "I thought you were just a runt that tanned really fast." She gave Baker a crooked smile.

"John Ito, one of our recruits, immigrated from Korea," Drew said.

"Okay, people," Craig raised his voice. "Before we start singing *Jesus Loves the Little Children*, we have a trip to Salem to plan, and we don't want a Growler for company this time."

# Chapter 10

Craig glanced at his cell as Baker revved the engine of the Bell 407 for takeoff.

*7:20 p.m.*

They had rushed the meeting at the Bancroft's to squeeze in this flight to Salem and back before dark.

When Craig slipped his headset on, Kate, seated behind him, had already started a conversation with Baker.

"We need to make sure the plan in place will keep my aunt safe," Kate said. "If anything were to happen to her, there would be chaos across the entire state. Layla Thomas is a suspect in an attempted assassination, but she's also next in the line of succession to be governor. At least half of Salem would probably welcome her."

"Yep. A real mess," Baker said.

"We won't leave Salem until we're sure Governor Harper is safe from everything but a nuclear attack," Craig said.

"I hope that was hyperbole for effect," Kate said.

"It was. There are some extreme orders President Walker might give, but they would never be carried out by the military. We can safely say that an order to bomb any target in the USA is on the do-not-obey list. But I've got a question for you, Kate."

"What's that?"

"Why did you pick that seat when there's a big patch in the fuselage right behind your head?"

"This is my good luck seat, Craig. I bet you don't have one."

"No, I don't have a hole right behind my head. Don't want one."

"A thousand may fall at your side, ten thousand at your right hand, but it will not come near you—"

"I'd say six inches is pretty near you."

"You didn't let me finish ... no harm will befall you."

"Psalm 91. I've prayed that a few times before going into battle. Where you're going, Kate, I suggest you lean pretty hard on that tenth verse, the 'no harm' one."

Kate didn't respond.

Her faith, courage, and loyalty continued to impress Craig. Zach certainly knew how to pick a good woman. But Kate's non-stop intensity would wear Craig down. A woman like Susan O'Connell, on the other hand ...

It remained quiet as they crossed the Cascade Mountains.

"No Growlers and we made it in record time," Baker said. "We'll be landing in five minutes. They kept the governor at the hospital after they examined her. Her security team said it was safer there than back at the capitol building."

The familiar helipad came into view and Baker eased the bird down onto the cross painted on the landing pad.

Before the rotor could spin down, a uniformed man emerged through the door by the elevators.

As Craig and Kate climbed out, the man walked their way.

"Colonel Craig, I presume. I'm State Police Special Operations Commander, Major James Sellers."

Sellers stuck out a hand and Craig took it. "I recognize Kate. She's been on the front page of the paper a few times recently. Let me take you down to the conference room where we're keeping Governor Harper until we can make other arrangements for her safety."

"Lead the way. Major Sellers."

\* \* \*

"A conference room in Building A—I know the way," Kate said. "It's the same conference room in this building where some rude State Police captain interrogated me. We almost got into a fight."

"That would probably have been Captain Robbins," Sellers said. "He can be a bit overzealous at times. But you can relax, Ms. Alexander. Robbins won't be in the conference room this evening."

When they entered the conference room, Aunt Sandy stood.

Kate hurried to her and wrapped her up in a firm hug.

"My goodness," Aunt Sandy said. "You are strong for a such a slender girl."

"How are you doing? Does your head hurt, Aunt Sandy?"

"Head? I can hardly feel it. I didn't know I'd been hit until the blood trickled down my neck. Now I'm getting angry. Thomas and some others wanted to hand Oregon to Walker, a gift with a blue bow tied around it."

"Well I've come to be your bodyguard for as long as you need me," Kate said.

"I have an entire team to guard me, Kate."

"But I can shadow you all the time, everywhere you go."

She studied Kate's face for a moment. "I have a woman on the security team who can escort me to the lady's room and such. I don't want to put you in any more danger. I've done enough of that already."

Craig came alongside Kate. "You look pretty good for someone who's just survived an assassination attempt." He gave her his confident, winning smile. "What's the status on Layla Thomas and the shooter?"

Aunt Sandy sighed. "Let's sit down around the table. This may take a while."

Major Sellers pulled a chair out for the governor. "Would you like me to brief them, Madam Governor?"

"Jim, you can stick around to correct me if I get something wrong, but we have a binding agreement between the governor and Colonel Craig, and I want to live up to my side of it."

Kate and Craig sat at the table beside the governor.

She folded her hands on the table. "The assassin hasn't been identified yet. We're looking at video for the parking area along Court Street. He's on the loose somewhere in the city."

"He?" Craig said. "Are you sure of that?"

"No. The shooter could have been a woman. We should find out soon."

"What about Layla Thomas?" Kate said.

"That cursed little traitor is under surveillance and the phone messages of her talking with Bender should be enough to try both of them for attempted murder."

Craig turned toward Aunt Sandy. "You've got a deep state problem and Thomas is part of that. But isn't she an elected official? And won't there be other elected officials? You can't simply remove them from office because they are a danger to you."

"During a state of emergency, I am granted powers that allow me to deal with such people for the duration of the extreme circumstances. I've practically memorized the paragraph in that section of Oregon law. It says that during a state of emergency, the governor has complete authority over all executive agencies of the state government, and I have the right to exercise, within the areas that I designate in my emergency proclamation, all police powers vested in the state by the Oregon Constitution in order to effectuate the purposes of the emergency proclamation."

Craig grinned. "So you can temporarily remove any person who's a perceived threat. They might kick and scream about it and even challenge your action, but their challenge won't be ruled on until you have the state back firmly in your control and have rounded up all the guilty parties in the conspiracy."

"Yes, Craig. That's true as long as I play my cards right."

He chuckled. "And when you start arresting people and charging them with things that can put them away for life, I'll bet the rest of your opponents will back off and simply wait, hoping to get their way after the next gubernatorial election."

"That's what I'm hoping for, Craig. But the wildcard is President Walker. What's he planning? Who will he attack first?"

"He wouldn't start wars on two fronts at the same time, would he?" Kate asked.

"No," Craig said. "And he's got a logistics problem. He has no fighter-interceptors, and it's pushing the limits of his helicopters' ranges to try to attack from JBLM or from Utah. Besides all that, he hates Zach Tanner and wants him off the air."

Kate drew Craig's gaze. "So you think he'll try to take out Zach and the militia leaders first."

"I do," Craig said. "If he can neutralize the militia by taking out their leadership, he can use all of Eastern Oregon as a staging area to attack the west side. But that still leaves him with one problem."

"Don't you mean two problems?" Kate said. "The fighter wings at Kingsley and Portland."

"Yes. He will have to strike the militia with a blow to essentially cut off its head then quickly bring in fighters to maintain some degree of air superiority, or he's finished." Craig turned to the governor. "So that gets you off the hook for a while with regard to Walker. You take care of your security issues and we'll deal with Walker."

"Kate?" Her aunt drew Kate's attention. "Surely you can see that I will be okay here and will soon have things under control. You're needed more in Eastern Oregon."

It wasn't what Kate had planned, but she could see that her aunt was in much less danger than Zach and the militia.

She blew out a sharp sigh. "Okay, I'll go back to the east side."

"But dealing with Walker may still require some assistance from your Guard, governor," Craig said.

"I'll select a company of the Guard and keep them equipped and ready to go if you need them. I'll move some Chinooks down from Pendleton to provide transportation."

"That would be perfect, governor."

Soon, Kate and Craig headed toward the elevators to take them back to the roof where Baker had remained with the helicopter.

At 8:25 p.m., Baker lifted off the helipad and quickly climbed up to altitude. "You know, the Department of Fish and Wildlife put a nice entertainment package on this bird. I'll bet we can pick up Zach's radio broadcast from the Redmond station if you'd like to hear it."

"Good idea," Kate said. "I'm still worried about my aunt. She has a lot of enemies seeking ways to attack her. Maybe Zach can help this day end on a more positive note."

"Zach should come on in another minute or so."

Music played through the sound system for a couple of minutes, then the fanfare for Zach's show sounded.

"This is Zach Tanner with Thoughts for Today coming to you via the Restore America Network.

"Today, we clearly have a president with tyranny on his mind. The Tenth Amendment states that 'all powers not delegated to the United States (i.e. the federal government), by the Constitution, nor prohibited by it to the states, are reserved to the states or to the people'. Related to that,

Thomas Jefferson said, 'To take a single step beyond the boundaries thus specifically drawn around the powers of Congress is to take possession of a boundless field of power, no longer susceptible of any definition'. And that, my fellow Americans is tyranny, and it's what President Walker did when he trampled on Oregon's sovereignty by trying to murder its governor to put his own person, a Walker supporter, in the governor's office.

"You see, tyrants kill for their own purposes. To blazes with the justice system. Their thirst, their life's blood, is power. And they take it any way they can get it.

"Noah Webster once said, 'The supreme power in America cannot enforce unjust laws by the sword; because the whole body of the people are armed, and constitute a force superior to any band of regular troops that can be, on any pretense, raised in the United States'. And he was right. That army now is over a hundred million with an average of five guns each. It's the largest army in the world, many times over the next largest, the Chinese army.

"And, as Samuel Adams told us, 'If ever a time should come, when vain and aspiring men shall possess the highest seats in Government, our country will stand in need of its experienced patriots to prevent its ruin.' We have such patriots rising across this land to stop a vain and aspiring man in the highest seat of government, President Wendell Walker.

"On the radical left, where Wendell Walker stands, the fighting never stops. Drop your guard, fellow Americans, and you will be sucker-punched every time.

"This is a long, dirty, no-holds-barred war that has warmed on a burner for decades but now has become a fiery furnace. The war has divided our government and our people along a line in the sand dividing two diametrically opposed worldviews, one based upon truth from the Author of truth, the other upon lies from the father of lies, Satan.

"One worldview is a path to hell and destruction, the other to life and freedom.

"July the 4th, which we recently celebrated, represents the signing, 250 years ago, of a document that was a masterpiece of political, philosophical, economic, and spiritual thought, conceived in liberty and dedicated to the proposition of equality. The world will never see this again, yet it is ours. We have it. We own it. And as Americans we must fight for it and the freedom it bestows or we will lose them forever. And now we are engaged in a great civil war testing whether our nation, so conceived and so dedicated, can endure.

"We fight lies with truth. We fight immorality and debauchery with God's absolute morality. We fight attempts to place us in bondage by exercising our freedom. And if our evil opponents in this war come to harm us, remember the words of Nehemiah:

"Don't be afraid of them. Remember the Lord, who is great and awesome, and fight for your families, your sons and your daughters, your wives and your homes. We, the people of Oregon, are doing just that. Will you join us by fighting for your homes and families in your state?

"We are instructed to, 'If possible, as much as depends on you, live peaceably with all men.' But if that is not possible and we must fight, fight to win! Otherwise there is no use in fighting at all. If you want to learn how to do that, contact us via our web site, RestoringAmerica.org. We can help you.

"One last thought—freedom only lives in the hearts of people, and if it dies there, the legal system, the justice system, the Constitution—nothing can bring it back to life. So we the people have got to keep it alive.

"May God bless you. May He bless Oregon, our beautiful state. And may God bless America.

"This is Zach Tanner signing off from the Restore America Network."

"Freedom lives in our hearts," Kate said. "And people like Wendell Walker want to kill it."

# Chapter 11

*Washington DC, 3:00 p.m. EDT*

Will's knock sounded on Walker's private study door.

"Come in, Will. It's unlocked."

Will entered then closed and locked the door behind him. "Remember when you said maybe we should let Oregon take care of the Oregon problem."

Walker motioned toward the chair by his desk. "Yes. What's up?"

"An assassin just shot Governor Harper."

Walker swore. "So I was right. Oregon is taking care of itself. Who's taking her place, Layla Thomas?"

"No, Mr. President. Thomas and Bender are about to be arrested as accomplices. The assassin is still at large, and Governor Harper escaped with only a bullet crease ... on her head."

Walker swore again. "Is anyone competent in that blasted state? No one in Oregon ever gets their job done."

"Aren't you overlooking Colonel Craig and his militia? They're getting the job done. And what about Zach Tanner?"

"Don't mock me, Will. I'm not in the mood for it. But speaking of Zach Tanner—the GPS tracker is still on his truck and working, isn't it?"

"It was as of yesterday when we talked to Deke."

"Colonel Towry said he needed twenty-four hours advance notice to deploy troops, but only two or three hours to send an Apache."

"But we suspect that Growler from Whidbey was picked up by air defense radar and then someone at WADS tipped off the Air Guard in Oregon."

"So what are you suggesting?"

"The Apache should not fly a direct route. Coming in from the north sends it right over the Western Air Defense Sector's headquarters near JBLM and gives away the direction to the target."

"We can't send it out to sea and then come in from the west. Coming in from international waters would be sure to draw attention."

"Sir, we should send it to Eastern Washington, let it hide behind the Blues or the Wallowa Mountains as it makes its way southward, then come in from the east, the least likely direction for an attack."

"How far is that route?"

"Mr. President, I already checked that out. It's about 650 air miles. The Apache can't make it back to base without refueling, which we don't want them to do after hitting the target. That means they stop at Madras Municipal and quickly top off their tanks, then proceed to the target, near Redmond."

"The last time we used Madras, the mission failed."

"Partially failed, sir. And that was due to a lucky shot by some ex-Rangers. There won't be any Rangers guarding Tanner's truck, trying in desperation to shoot down an Apache with an RPG. As I said, last time they were lucky to have damaged the chopper before it completed its mission."

"When should we launch the attack?"

"Now!" Will said.

"Let me call Deke first." Walker hit Deke's secure cell number.

"Deke here."

"This is President Walker. Are you still tracking Tanner's pickup?"

"The tracker's still working. I check up on it once or twice a day to verify that."

"When was the last time you checked?"

"This morning, about 7:00 a.m., Tanner drove his truck in to Redmond. He stopped in town, then he went to the radio station site that we hit on the edge of town."

"If the truck moves, track it, Deke."

"Will do, Mr. President."

"I am most interested in where that pickup is in about three hours."

"Yes, sir. That's around 3:00 p.m. Pacific time."

"Let me know if the location changes." Walker ended the call. "Time to call Towry."

"Do we still plan to follow up Tanner's elimination with an assault on the Central Oregon Militia?"

"Of course, Will. That's how we planned it."

"But we wanted the leaders of the militia to be together in one place so we could behead the seditious snake with one blow."

"If we kill Tanner, they will gather to decide how to replace him. The most likely spot they will meet—according to Deke the only spot they meet anymore—is the Bancroft's house. So we eliminate Tanner. Our spy watches for them to congregate at the Bancroft house, and then we send in the ground troops."

Will nodded but didn't say anything.

"I'm going to call Towry now." Walker dialed Colonel Towry's number.

"Mr. President, I was wondering when you would call."

"Have you made all the arrangements for a large troop movement?"

"I have. What about the attack on Tanner?"

"Launch it now."

"I will, sir, as soon as we finish this call. When do we send the troops?"

"Give the Apache time to reach the target, then send the Chinooks carrying the Humvees and the troops to the staging area."

"Any other instructions, Mr. President?"

"No, Colonel Towry. Just carry out your orders."

Walker ended the call.

*Now let's see how Tanner fares with no Rangers around to interfere.*

# Chapter 12

Susan watched Kate drive away in Zach's blue pickup. "Where's Kate going?"

AJ looked up from the milk she was steaming. "Her car's in the shop today. She's driving Zach over to the old radio station site where he's trying to salvage that NETX400 transmitter that Walker nearly destroyed. Then she's taking Zach's truck over to Julia's to help watch the kids. Julia's got them all today."

All meant Lori, who was seven, Josh and Caleb, Benjamin, Peter, who was four, and two toddlers from other militia men. Kate must have realized Julia would need help, especially since her morning sickness had recently started. Sam and Itzy were there also, but teenagers weren't always a lot of help.

"How busy has it been so far?" Susan asked.

"It's been slow. Shauna and I can take care of the shop if you want to help Julia."

"Thanks. I think Julia could use the help."

Fifteen minutes later, Susan parked behind Zach's truck in the big circle drive. She walked through Julia's house to the kitchen and looked through the kitchen window to the backyard.

The little kids were on the playground equipment.

Sam and Itzy stood beside the smallest kids, keeping things under control.

Julia sat with Kate at the table in the shade of its big umbrella.

When Susan opened the back door and stepped into the yard, she nearly bumped into the big object in Benjamin's hands.

He swung the four-foot-wide flying machine away from her. "Sorry, Aunt Susan."

"It's okay, Benjamin."

These kids had a lot of aunts and uncles who weren't relatives, just part of a big family that formed and bonded when Oregon began to fall apart.

Josh and Caleb studied what looked like a large drone.

"Are you going to race it next month, Benj?"

"I can only control it up to one-hundred miles-per-hour, then I start losing control on the turns. This is an X class drone, but to race with those world-class pilots, I've got to get up to two hundred and be able to pass other drones without crashing it."

"It goes two hundred miles-per-hour?" Caleb asked.

"Yeah," Benjamin said. "I got it up to two hundred once out in the desert, away from everything. But that was just flying it straight."

"When we helped you build it, I didn't think it could actually go that fast," Josh said.

Those three cousins were amazing. Even brighter than their brilliant parents. But a ten-year-old had no business flying anything at two hundred miles-per-hour.

Susan walked over to the umbrella table where Julia sat holding her stomach and looking rather pale. She laid a hand on Julia's shoulder. "Looks like a rough morning."

"It's not that bad. If you've ever experienced projectile vomiting from Ebola, like I did, this is child's play. No pun intended." Julia gave her a weak smile.

"Sorry I asked." Susan sat down beside Julia. "Don't think I want to hear about projectile vomiting."

"At least the kids are all under control, for the moment," Kate said.

Susan laughed. "If 'under control' includes three middle-grade boys trying to figure out how to control a big racing drone at two hundred miles-per-hour."

"Benjamin just brought it over to show Josh and Caleb. The boys all helped build it, but Benjamin's the only one who's seen it fly. KC and Brock only let him fly it out in the desert, away from anything they don't want to be damaged."

"At least it's a quiet day. I don't know what I'd do if I had to chase kids around the yard while my stomach was churning."

Susan studied Julia's small frame. The stories she'd heard about Julia's exploits nine years ago—was it possible that a woman who probably didn't weigh much over a hundred pounds could survive Ebola and then run as far and as fast as Julia had only weeks after she recovered?

Today Julia could just rest. This would be a quiet, relaxing day for her. She had certainly earned it.

* * *

Craig turned onto a paved road that climbed the steep hill leading to the potential home site on top of La Follette Butte. The owner had given Craig permission to put a honey bucket at the site, because it was eight miles to the nearest services in Terrebonne and even farther to Sisters.

The new sentry, John Peterson, who had joined the militia a few days ago, lived up Whychus Creek, so Craig had stationed him on La Follette Butte, about two miles west of the Deschutes River and about ten miles east of Sisters. The top of the butte was accessible via the road the real estate speculator had made in hopes of selling the land to a developer.

From the butte one could see ten of the volcanic peaks in the Cascades. It was perfect for detecting any military force approaching from the west by land or by air.

Craig stopped his Jeep at the end of the pavement and got out.

Peterson sat on a folding chair underneath a large umbrella stuck in a pipe that had been driven into the ground. He stood as Craig approached.

"Good morning, Peterson. Have you seen anything of interest today?"

"No. It's been really quiet. I'm not superstitious, but it's so quiet that it makes the hair stick up on the back of my neck. Have you heard anything I should be concerned about, Colonel Craig?"

"Not a thing. How far is your place from here?"

"It's about three miles as the crow flies. But about twelve miles as the car drives. The Whychus Creek canyon and an escarpment are in the way. No real need to carve out a road that cuts through to Whychus Creek, so people just drive down near Sisters and get on Highway 126."

"I'd hoped you wouldn't have much of a drive to get here when we assigned you to this lookout while things were still touchy between us and the governor."

"Speaking of the governor—her niece rode with us to Terrebonne the night we left Salem. Her name was Kate Allen or—"

"Kate Alexander?"

"Yeah, that's her. Seemed like a really nice girl. Smart. Do you know her? She was going to buy a coffee shop."

"She bought it. But she only helps run it part time. She's been working for me analyzing intelligence info. She's also planning a wedding. Her and Zach Tanner are getting hitched."

"Tanner. Well I'll be. He's the reason we decided to leave Salem when we did. Our family's been safe over here, and we're thinking about staying, permanently. Tell Kate hello from the Petersons. The kids still talk about the stinky girl who climbed in our car in the middle of the night."

"Stinky? That doesn't sound like Kate."

"She had to hide out in a doghouse when her aunt sicced the Salem police on her. Smelled like a dog when we—"

Craig's cell rang its sentry alarm. Something was happening somewhere.

"Craig here."

"Sir, this is Bob Daggett at Madras Municipal. Got bad news to report. A doggone Apache helicopter is refueling as we speak. It came in fast like and headed straight for the fuel. They're pumping it like the chopper's about to die of thirst."

*A lone Apache? The target is probably Zach Tanner.*

"The pilot is putting away the fuel line. Copilot is in his seat. The pilot is getting in. I think they're gonna leave now."

He needed to guess the target and alert the people there. "Keep watching them, Daggett, and give me a vector from the airport as soon as they head out."

"Engine is revved up. They're lifting off. They lit out like pheasant on the wing. Heading, about two hundred degrees."

Craig already had his area map up on the screen and centered it over Madras Municipal Airport. A heading of two hundred was straight toward the Bancroft's house. Was Zach still there? Regardless, whoever was there needed to be told to take cover.

Steve was in Bend getting supplies.

Craig hit Julia's cell number in his contacts.

"Hello."

"Julia, this is Craig. There's an Apache headed toward your house. It could be there in six minutes. Who all is there?"

"Me, Kate, Susan ..."

Craig winced when he heard Susan's name.

"... and all the kids are in the backyard, including the two new toddlers we just acquired."

The reality came like a punch in the gut. They could all be dead in another six minutes. He had to think. What could save them from a Hellfire Missile and the M230 chain gun that could shoot through an armored tank?

"Is Zach there?"

"No. But Kate drove his truck over today, because her Toyota was in the shop."

That had to be it. Zach's truck was the target. If it was sitting in the driveway, the Apache pilot would make sure he got Zach by destroying the vehicles, the house, and anyone in the yard. That bird would shoot as many missiles as it needed to accomplish that.

# Chapter 13

The speakerphone was on and Susan had heard Craig's taught voice tell them their situation.

In five minutes, the whole area could be one big fireball.

Sam had trotted over and stood beside the three boys. All of them were listening.

"Should we cram into my SUV and drive away?"

"No, Julia," Craig said. "If that Apache spotted you, and I think he would, you wouldn't stand a chance."

"Not even if I drove as fast as I can?"

"The Apache would pursue you at over two hundred miles per hour. You can't get away and it would leave you no place to hide."

Susan watched the change come over Kate. Eyes darting. Ready to bolt. Then her eyes focused on the corner of the house nearest where Zach's pickup was parked.

Zach's truck. He's the target and she drove his truck over. She thinks she made them all a target. Kate was going to drive the truck away and try to draw the Apache's fire.

Kate's about to be married, yet she was willing to sacrifice herself, lose her life with Zach, to save the kids. Susan couldn't allow that to happen. But before anyone made themselves a sacrifice, they needed to hear Craig's advice.

"You've got about five minutes, Julia. Here's what I want you to do. Round up all the kids, everyone there, but do not go into the house."

"Okay. But where—"

"Take them to the big boulder by the garage. Stack your bodies against that boulder like sardines in a can. Do that on the opposite side of the rock from the garage."

"I'm giving the phone to Susan and rounding up the kids."

Josh and Caleb were engaged in a rapid conversation. Not all of it was in English.

"They must know where Zach's truck is," Josh yelled.

"Yeah," Caleb said. "Because he's not here, only his truck."

"But how would they know?" Benjamin said.

Susan took the phone, but the boys' conversation was loud and distracting. And the horror of what was about to take place scrambled her thoughts.

"It probably has a GPS tracker," Josh said.

"Then we gotta find it. Now!" Caleb yelled.

"Who just mentioned a GPS tracker?" Craig's voice startled Susan.

"It was Josh or Caleb. Either. Both. I mean—I can't tell them apart."

"Is that you, Susan?"

"Yes."

"The kids might be onto something, but I have no clue what they can do about it even if they find a tracker."

Across the yard, Julia and Itzy herded the kids toward the boulder that was around the corner of the garage. Seven-year-old Lori fell down and scraped her knee. Frightened and hurting, she started wailing.

Itzy snatched her up with her free hand while holding one of the toddlers in the other.

Four-year-old Peter tried to go back to the swings.

Julia held the other toddler but freed up a hand to grab Peter. She pulled him toward the garage on the south side of the house.

"David, I'm following the boys to Zach's truck in the front yard. I need to see what they're doing."

"Listen, Susan. Those twins, even as bright as they are, can't do anything to stop an attack helicopter. You've got three, maybe four minutes then you need to be behind that boulder with the kids. And have the adults lie over the kids. They may cry. It may hurt. But—"

"I understand, David."

Sam and Kate also followed the boys into the front yard.

Josh and Caleb sprinted to the truck with Benjamin in pursuit.

"We gotta hurry, guys," Caleb said.

Caleb opened the cab door and looked inside.

"I'll check out the bed of the pickup," Benjamin said.

"I'll look underneath." Josh laid on his back and scooted under the truck. "I found it."

Julia rounded the corner of the garage and ran toward them. "Itzy has the little ones behind the big rock. Come on. We all need to hide there. It's our only chance to survive what's coming."

Josh slid out with the tracker in his hand. "Benjamin, get your X-Class, now!"

Benjamin's expression looked pitiful. "We're gonna get my X-Class blown up, aren't we?" Benjamin stared at Josh, but when he didn't get a reply, he turned and ran into the house.

"David, you said no one was to go into the house."

"Who went inside, Susan?"

"Benjamin. He was running and he's coming back out."

"But we're running out of time. Do you hear a helicopter?"

"There's too much chaos. I can't hear anything."

"Just listen carefully for that staccato noise," Craig said.

"Aunt Julia!" Josh yelled. "Get me a roll of duct tape. Hurry! Please hurry."

Julia stepped in front of Josh. "You're going to get more than Benjamin's drone blown up if you don't stop this nonsense and get behind that boulder." Julia had become ferocious.

Josh didn't back down. "Just get the tape or we're all dead." Josh's eyes seemed to cut like a laser as he stared at Julia.

Susan shivered as she saw Josh's intensity. He would not be deterred in whatever he was trying to do.

"What's going on, Susan?" Craig's voice had a hard edge to it she had never heard before.

"I don't know, David."

"Heaven help us if they're trying to do what I think they are."

# Chapter 14

"Susan! Susan! What the heck is going on?" Craig's voice blared from the cellphone's speaker.

"Julia just ran into the garage to get something," Susan said.

Wide-eyed, Sam approached Susan. "If Craig's worried, this is really bad, isn't it? Are we all going to die?"

"Susan, listen for a helicopter. Do you hear one?"

"No, David. I don't but there's such a commotion here that I might not hear it until—"

"The second you hear anything like a helicopter, run behind that rock. Please, promise me you will."

"I will, but Josh, Caleb, and Benjamin have some scheme they think will save us."

"You're not all going to die," Kate said. "There's only one thing that's going to get blown up and it's this truck. I'm going to drive it down the highway."

Susan sucked in a breath so hard she choked on it when she realized what Kate was doing.

"Does Kate intend to drive off in Zach's truck? That sounds like something that girl would do." Craig's voice blasted from the phone.

"She might intend to, but she's about to have a wedding, and I'm not going to let her—gotta go, Craig. Here, Sam." Susan shoved the phone at Sam. "It's Craig. Just answer his questions."

"But I—"

"Do it, Sam!"

"Don't go, Kate," Josh said. We just need to get rid of the tracker."

Benjamin shot out of the front door and scurried across the front lawn carrying his big X-Class drone.

"And we know just how to get rid of the tracker, we think," Caleb said.

Kate stopped at the edge of the front lawn. "What do you mean by 'we think'?"

"Caleb and I read about the new missile guidance system the Army bought for Hellfire Missiles. It tracks a GPS or other signals to a location, and in the final hundred yards, it uses the GPS signal from the tracker to hit the target. Maybe that's how they plan to blow up Zach's truck."

"Yeah," Caleb said. "They used to use image recognition to follow the target until they hit it."

"What if Zach's truck is an image target? And what if Zach is in the house, not the truck?" Kate said.

"That's why they're probably gonna blow up the house before they go away," Josh took the drone from Benjamin.

"But what if they're just marking the truck and firing the missile?" Benjamin said.

"That's why I need to drive the truck away." Kate said.

"Does anybody hear an Apache?" Craig's voice blasted from the cell phone. "I think I hear one through the phone."

"I can't hear anything with everybody yelling," Sam said.

Julia ran out of the garage with a big roll of tape in her hand.

"We've got to try to save Kate and the truck," Caleb said.

"And take down the Apache at the same time," Josh said.

"You mean take it down with my X-Class racer?" Benjamin said.

"We don't have any time to waste," Josh said. "Aunt Julia, give me the tape!"

Josh grabbed the tape.

Benjamin held the drone. "Put the tracker on the center, Josh. No, not on top or I can't control it. Put it in the center but underneath."

Caleb steadied the fuselage as Josh wrapped the tape around it.

"Guys," Benjamin said. "The batteries are low. I didn't think we would fly it 'til next week, so I didn't charge them. I don't know if there's enough charge left in my batteries to fly for more than a minute."

"We have to try anyway," Caleb said.

"If we do this right, we shouldn't need more than a minute," Josh said.

"I think I hear a helicopter," Sam said.

It *was* a helicopter. In the distance but growing louder.

Susan pushed Sam toward the rock near the corner of the garage.

"Sam," Craig's voice. "Tell them to get behind the rock."

Kate whirled and sprinted toward the truck.

Susan's pulse redlined.

Kate was going to drive the truck away from the house. The Apache pilot would never let that truck escape. Kate would die in a few moments unless ...

Susan blew out a blast of frustration. Then came resolution.

She ran full speed after Kate.

# Chapter 15

Kate sprinted toward Zach's truck at an incredible speed.

Susan could never catch her in time.

"Kate, you gotta wait 'til the last second, so they see you," Josh yelled.

Kate slowed. She nearly stopped as she processed Josh's message.

Maybe this was Susan's chance.

An adrenaline surge gave Susan more speed than she'd ever had.

As Kate turned back to look at Josh, Susan crashed into her.

The impact sent Kate sprawling on her face in the grass.

The truck keys flew out of her hand and landed on the gravel drive by the driver's door of the pickup.

Susan scooped them up, jumped into the truck, and locked the doors.

Kate jumped up and pounded on the window. "Don't, Susan!"

The engine started on the first try.

Susan mashed the accelerator to the floor and prayed Kate's feet were not under the edge of the truck as it lurched forward. But broken toes were better than a broken body.

Kate appeared in the rearview mirror. She was on her feet using her sprinter's speed to catch the truck before Susan could navigate the circle drive and reach the road where she could accelerate to highway speed.

Kate caught the truck as it turned onto Rim Road. She grabbed the top of the tailgate with both hands.

The truck pulled Kate down the highway at over thirty miles per hour.

Kate kept pace with huge bounding strides as the truck accelerated.

Now she was trying to get into the bed of the truck.

Susan couldn't let her do that.

She stomped on the brake pedal, sending Kate smashing into the tailgate.

Susan gunned the engine.

Kate fell to the pavement.

In the side mirror, Susan saw Kate's spent body struggling to get up.

After she stood, Kate put her hands on her hips and stared at the truck speeding down Rim Road.

But at the top of the side mirror, the reflection of a menacing-looking silhouette appeared against the deep blue sky.

The Apache.

* * *

Craig had just listened for the last sixty seconds as Sam gave him the play-by-play of the events unfolding in front of the Bancroft's house. But the Apache had to be bearing down on them.

"Sam, you need to run to the rock and get behind it," Craig said.

"No, sir. You need to know what's happening."

"But I can't help you whether I can hear you or not. Go, Sam."

"I'm staying here. If you'll be quiet, you can hear what's going on. They launched the drone. Benjamin is flying it, but Josh looks like he wishes that he were. That thing is fast. I could hardly follow it with my eyes as it flew toward the canyon. I'm going to get closer so you can hear the boys on the speakerphone."

"Fly it just over the rim," Josh's voice. "And keep it below the top, headed north toward where the Apache will appear."

"Some of the kids ran out from the corner of the garage," Sam said. "But Julia is dragging them back to that big boulder. Kate's back now. She's helping. But it looks like her knee's bleeding and she's crying."

"That's it, Benj." One of the twins' voices. "Drop it just over the edge of the cliff so the Apache can't see it."

"There's the Apache." It sounded like Benjamin's voice.

Sam came on the phone again. "Josh is telling Benjamin to wait until it gets closer for whatever they're going to do."

"Sam, you need protection, now."

"Benj and the twins are my protection. I trust them."

Craig bit his tongue to keep from lashing out at Sam. The events would play out quickly now and either Sam was right to rely on two nine-year-old boys and their ten-year-old cousin or she was a fool.

What the boys were trying to do was becoming clear. But if the boys had done their homework, they knew they had at best a fifty percent chance of this working. Either the missile would lock onto the image of the target, Zach's truck, or it would track the GPS signal.

The boys wanted the missile to track the GPS signal coming from the tracker they had taped onto the drone. And they clearly planned to send that drone up into the Apache.

If the boys were wrong, Susan was about to die. And that cataclysmic event would end a dream that had been revived in Craig's heart for the first time in nine years.

"My batteries are really low," Benjamin's voice. "I don't know if they'll last long enough."

"They've got to last until it makes a one hundred-fifty-mile-per-hour climb up to the Apache."

"I know, I know," Benjamin's frustrated voice rose in volume.

"Did you hear that, Mr. Craig?" Sam said.

"I heard. Now, Sam, please run to that boulder."

"I can't We're all going to live or die together. But this is beginning to look impossible. Here comes the helicopter. You'd better pray, sir. This looks really bad."

"I have been praying ever since we knew an Apache was headed toward the ranch," Craig said. "Can you see Susan in the truck?"

"Yes. She slowed way down and is just creeping down the road. Why would she do that?"

"So the pilot can see his target," Craig said. "She doesn't want it to be you, Sam, or any of the others."

"I know." Sam's voice broke. "Susan wanted it to be her, because Kate and Zach are getting married." Sam was sobbing now.

'Watch that chopper." Josh's voice. "If he hovers really still, it means he's aiming. That's when you have to—"

"He's aiming!" Sam said.

"Now!" Josh's voice.

"Benjamin's drone just came up from the cliff," Sam said. "It's zooming up right underneath the Apache. Fire and smoke came out of the Apache. It's a rocket."

"But the line of smoke turned and—" An explosion drowned out Benjamin's voice.

"Sam, what happened? Is Susan all right?"

Craig's cell sounded the alert for an ended call.

Had Sam ended the call, or had the missile ended Sam? And what about Susan?

# Chapter 16

Craig raced down Terrebonne-Lower Bridge road hitting a hundred miles-per-hour on some of the straight stretches. The junipers lining the road were only a blur of dark green. But was that his speed or his welling eyes?

The turn-off to the ranch lay only a quarter of a mile ahead. Craig hit the brakes.

He could not erase the picture in his mind of Susan driving a blue pickup down Rim Road and then disappearing in a ball of flames.

Losing the cell call all but confirmed the picture.

But what about all the kids and the women who were watching them? Were they safe?

If not, it was Colonel David Craig's fault. He was the man responsible for everyone's safety in Central Oregon, just like Lieutenant Craig had been responsible for his team in Afghanistan., the team that had been ambushed and decimated.

And what had happened as Josh, Caleb, and Benjamin carried out their crazy attempt to take down an Apache with a racing drone?

He turned onto NW 43rd Street and stomped on the gas pedal.

Two minutes later he turned onto Rim Road. When he rounded the first turn, Zach's blue truck came into view. It had been parked on the left shoulder.

Susan stood beside it watching Julia's house a quarter mile away.

Craig's breath left his lungs in a single blast as the knot in his stomach unwound. She was safe. But what about the others?

He opened the driver's door and stepped out. Beyond Julia's house, a plume of multi-colored smoke rose into a powder-blue summer sky.

A group of women and children had congregated on the lawn, watching the spectacle about two hundred yards to the north of the house.

Burning remnants of the Apache lay scattered on the edge of the precipice. Other parts of the chopper had plunged down the cliff into bushes and Juniper trees where, on the edge of the golf course, a growing desert wildfire sent flames forty or fifty feet into the air.

Susan looked his way for the first time. Her eyes widened and she ran toward him.

By the time he closed the driver's door, Susan had closed the distance between them, and she ran into his arms.

She cried softly as he held her against his chest and watched the fire grow.

"Is everybody okay?"

She didn't respond.

"Are you okay?"

She looked up at him through teary eyes and nodded. "But, David, I didn't think I would ever see you again."

"Ever is a long time. But I had the same thought after I learned that you had some bad plans for yourself."

"I mean *ever* as never again in this life." Those eyes held a rich blend of expressions ranging from resignation to self-sacrifice through amazement to—

Before he could take in all the wonder and goodness of the woman looking up into his eyes, she kissed him.

Emotions and adrenaline surged through Craig and he became more than just a willing recipient. He finished properly what Susan had started.

Afterward, she beamed a smile at him and Craig brushed the tears from her cheeks. "I take it that means everyone at the house is fine and that the boys brainstorm was successful."

Sirens from the fire department two miles away began their piercing wailing.

Susan nodded then craned her neck to look toward the house. "The fire is from the helicopter, or what's left of it." She turned her head back toward his. "But there's another fire that you and I have started, David. I hope that you don't—"

He pressed a finger firmly over her lips. "Fire isn't always destructive, Susan. There have been too many cold winter days and nights in my life."

"So, you didn't mind?"

"No. I didn't. But now I need to have a talk with three boys who didn't mind."

"David, they saved the children. They saved all of us. Don't be too hard on them."

"Just hard enough so they know not to make a habit of taking life-risking chances. No matter how bright they are, they will lose if they keep playing Russian Roulette."

"All right, Colonel Cavalier, what would *you* have done in their situation?"

"I would have shot at the chopper until I emptied my M4's magazine, then I'd have either gotten chewed up by the chain gun or blown all to blazes by a Hellfire Missile."

"Blazes?" Her eyes widened. "But I thought—"

"Blazes ... I wasn't thinking. To be absent from the body is—"

"Is to be present with the Lord."

"Yes, and now I need to go act like the Lord when I speak to those boys."

Susan gave him the enigmatic smile she seemed to have mastered. "Be careful, David. They might just turn the tables on you."

# Chapter 17

When Craig pulled his Jeep into the circle drive, Zach's blue pickup, with Susan at the wheel, was on his rear bumper.

Julia held a phone to her ear.

After he climbed out, he heard Julia mention KC. If KC saw a chopper explode and crash between her and Julia's houses, and if she thought it was an Apache, she was probably frantic to find out if Benjamin was okay.

Craig interrupted Julia. "Tell KC I'll bring Benjamin home when we're done debriefing here, because I need to talk to her."

Kate stood on the edge of the front lawn watching Susan and Craig. "I saw you two, and it looked—"

"What happened to your eye, Kate?" Craig had cut her off.

She nodded toward Susan. "She gave me this black eye."

"Kate, you're an athlete. How could you have let her—"

Kate pointed an accusing finger at Susan. "Craig, she blindsided me. I still ran the truck down and was climbing in when she hit the brakes."

"Susan, you could have hurt her."

"David, she was trying to hurt herself, if you'll remember. And right now, I'm having a hard time feeling apologetic."

"It's all right," Kate said.

"All right. All right." He blew out a sigh. "This was my fault. If I had been doing my job, that Apache wouldn't have made it to the ranch.'"

Kate turned toward Julia who stood beside the three boys.

Susan gave him an accusing frown. "And how would you have stopped it?"

"That, Ms. O'Connell, is confidential information."

"And that's a convenient answer."

"Cabe and I can tell you how you can stop an Apache attack," Josh said. "You start, Cabe."

"Okay. Think about this. A call comes in to the 142nd Fighter Wing from someone in the Western Air Defense Sector up by JBLM."

"My turn," Josh said. "The fighter wing scrambles an F-15 Eagle and shoots the Apache down before it can even get to Madras."

"And how did you get that information?" Craig's gaze raked over the three boys.

"We didn't get it. We figured it out. You don't have any other auctions," Caleb said.

"Yes, I do. I can auction you three boys off."

"Huh?" Caleb shrugged.

"Well, that should tell you how this Apache got through to the ranch," Josh said.

Craig looked from Joshua to Caleb. "Our people saw it refueling at Madras Muni. But you're saying you know how it got through?"

Both boys nodded. Benjamin didn't say anything, but he was smiling.

"Okay, tell me how that Apache snuck up on us."

"It couldn't sneak in unless WADS missed it," Josh said.

"Yeah," Caleb said. "But they don't miss anything. So it had to displease WADS, right?"

"If you meant deceive, yes, that would displease them. But how did it trick the Western Air Defense Sector?"

"It couldn't fly west over the ocean, or WADS would have spotted it," Josh said.

"Yeah," Caleb said. "They watch everything from the north and the west. That means it flew to the east, probably circled around the Walla Walla Mountains, and came in low from the east."

"It's the Wallowa Mountains, Cabe. They couldn't see the Apache on radar because of the mountains," Josh said. "And you're lucky the sentry at Madras saw it or we'd all be toast."

"What made you guys think that the Hellfire Missile had the signal-tracking guidance system and not the older system?"

"Think about it," Caleb said. "If you were planning to take out an enemy that got away every time you tried to get them, you know like Zach did every time Walker tried, would you use the old technology or the new stuff to get him?"

"I see your point. I guess that old adage 'know thine enemy' is still true today."

"Told you, David." Susan ended the reminder with her enigmatic smile.

"Yeah. You told me. If I could double their ages, I would draft them into the militia and turn them loose on the president."

Susan laughed.

His words, "told me", reminded him of the Petersons. "That reminds me of something I was supposed to tell Kate."

Kate broke off her conversation with Julia. "Did I hear my name again?"

"Yes. I met someone today who said to tell you hello."

"Who would that be here in Central Oregon? Nearly everyone I know is at the house ... or will be shortly."

"Our new sentry out on the hill above Whychus Creek, John Peterson."

"Whychus Creek. The Peterson's cabin. That's the family that stopped along the Santiam Highway, picked me up, and gave me a ride to Terrebonne. Are they doing okay?"

"Doing fine. I think they are putting down roots and plan to stay."

"It looks like someone else is putting down roots too. Do they plan to stay?" Kate's gaze alternated between him and Susan.

Craig looked away across the desert. "There's a lot of work to be done before that question gets answered."

"It didn't look that way to me." Kate laughed. "Zach and I aren't waiting for anything except a lull in the action that lasts long enough for a wedding ceremony."

Susan hooked his arm with hers. "That's your and Zach's choice."

Kate focused on Susan. "Yes, it is. What's yours?"

\* \* \*

President Walker left the Oval Office and headed across the hall to his private study.

When he opened the study door, his secure cell rang.

The caller ID looked like Colonel Towry's number.

"President Walker here."

"This is Colonel Towry at JBLM. Mr. President, we have a bit of a mystery to report."

If there was one thing he didn't like it was mysteries.

"Go ahead, Towry."

"The Apache has disappeared. We confirmed that it refueled at Madras, then nothing."

"Apache helicopters attack, they don't do David Copperfield vanishing acts."

"Just reporting, sir. There's nothing on radar in that area. Of course, we can't see it near the ground because of the terrain. But even worse, no comms."

"We can't send your men in until we know what happened. Find out, Towry, and report to me the minute that you do." Walker ended the call.

His phone rang again almost immediately. He selected some choice words for Towry then glanced at the caller ID. It was Deke. Maybe he could unravel the mystery.

Walker answered.

"This is Major Deke, Mr. President."

"Deke, do you know what happened with the Apache attack?"

'That's what I was calling about, sir. I was on a ridge about a half mile away watching as the Apache closed in on the target. Tanner's truck took off with somebody on foot chasing it. Then three boys launched something that looked like a big drone."

"Get to the point, Deke. Enough of this cockamamie story. I want to know about the mission and the Apache."

"I was almost there, Mr. President. The boys' drone flew hidden by a bluff until the Apache hovered, preparing to launch the missiles. Just as the first missile launched, the drone came up from the bluff at an incredible speed and was headed for the bottom of the Apache. That's when the missile did a U-turn, came back, and hit the helicopter. There was a ball of fire and the Apache came down in pieces."

"Are you sure that's what happened?"

"I had my wide-angle binoculars on it. That's exactly what happened."

"And three boys took down our Apache?"

"No, Mr. President. You took it down by insisting on the latest, greatest technology which comes along with certain vulnerabilities that even kids can exploit."

"Don't get impertinent with me, Major." His gut was tightening. Bile rose in his throat and heat flashed on the back of his neck. Walker was losing it. He needed to calm down.

"How old are those boys, high-school-age, college-age?"

"No. I believe they were Lex James' twins, who are nine, and KC's and Brock Daniels' son, who is ten."

"And we let them take down a sixty-million-dollar attack helicopter?"

"No, Mr. President. It gives me no pleasure to say this, but *you* did."

Walker swore until his well of vile words went dry. He took a deep, calming breath. It wasn't Deke's fault, not this time. Somebody's head was going to roll, but it sounded like the person responsible for this catastrophe was the helicopter pilot, and he couldn't have survived.

"What happened to the Apache after the Hellfire Missile hit it?"

"It went down in pieces, sir. Started a wildfire at the base of the bluff and firetrucks came to put it out. This will be reported and—"

"I don't care what people in Eastern Oregon report. Deke, do we have addresses for all the known leaders of the militia and of the resistance effort?"

"I gave all the info I had to Secretary Richards."

"How complete is it?"

"We know where the important people live except for David Craig. He uses a post office box number in Terrebonne. And their pilot, a vet named Radley Baker, does too. But if you threaten any of them, Craig will show up."

"Threaten them? You idiot. I want this to be a surprise. They should all be dead before Craig knows anything. Towry should be able to take care of that."

"Mr. President?"

"What now, Deke?"

"Towry might not be the man for—"

"Are you trying to get the glory for yourself, major?"

"No, sir. Just trying—"

"Good. Keep trying, Deke. I'll call you when I need you."

Walker ended the call with Deke and immediately dialed Towry's number.

"Colonel Towry, we lost the Apache helicopter to an unfortunate accident, so I want you to go in on a night raid with a small force and take out everyone at the addresses I will give you."

"Are these addresses of houses, sir?"

"Yes."

"And we're hitting them at night?"

"Of course. The only way to get these people is to surprise them."

"Are they houses where families live?"

"Some of them."

"Mr. President, this is not the attack that Secretary Richards and I have been discussing."

"But it is the attack that I need."

"Sir, we were talking about luring the militia out into a battle, a military conflict. What we did today, trying to take out Zach Tanner because he was an enemy agent, was a stretch, but still justifiable. But Will and I never discussed going into houses and killing fathers, mothers, and their kids."

"But surely you can see, Colonel Towry—"

"Sir, what I can see is that I'm not your man for this mission. Goodbye, Mr. President."

Towry had ended the call.

And maybe he had ended his career. But what if this was typical of what he could expect from a military that operated under certain antiquated rules of warfare? This was not the time for rules, it was the time for expedience.

He needed to bring Will Richards in to get his opinion on how to strike a deadly blow to the militia, now, before

Oregon turned from a plum ripe for the picking to a mother bear defending its cubs.

Mother bear. That description might fit Sandra Harper now that her allegiance had changed. And, under her command, she had four thousand troops, two Air Guard wings, and an undefeated militia as an ally.

Could it be that trying to pick the ripe plum by attacking the militia had become plumb crazy?

Walker picked up his secure phone.

Will Richards was the best person to answer that question.

# Chapter 18

Julia and the three boys were still outside talking to the police and a fire marshal who were getting information about the helicopter crash for their reports.

But Craig sat in silence in the great room, trying to wind down from the tense action of the previous thirty minutes.

Susan sat beside him on the couch and Kate sat on the far end of the couch.

He nearly jumped to his feet when the front door flew open.

Craig relaxed when KC stepped into the entryway. She glanced through the huge doorway to the great room and headed straight for the trio seated on the couch.

"Well, Benjamin looked okay."

"He's got all his fingers and toes, but I came close to tanning the hides of three boys who—"

"David, you did not." Susan shook her head. "Any fool could see that you were proud of those boys, regardless of what you said." She looked up at KC. "They saved all of our lives, KC."

"Josh and Caleb have been in that situation before. It was the first time for Benjamin, but something tells me those three are going to impact this whole nation if they can keep from killing themselves in the process." She paused and looked down at Craig seated beside Susan. "Julia said you wanted to talk to me."

"We need to find out more information about Walker's plans to attack us. After today's debacle, he's probably foaming at the mouth while he tries to launch another attack."

"So it's hacking you're asking about?"

He nodded. "But performing cyberespionage against the president is a pretty tall order."

"Yes, it is. But that doesn't mean it's impossible." She pointed at the entry to the hallway. "Let's go into the study and get online. I've got some ideas."

He knew KC was a brilliant network analyst who could also hack with the best, but ... "Just like that? You've got ideas to hack the president?"

"Craig, the weak link in any security system, as you probably know, is the people. They are creatures of habit and some of them form bad security habits. We just need to find out what those are for Walker."

Craig stood, took Susan's hand, and pulled her to her feet. "Come on. Let's watch KC work her magic."

Kate headed for the front door. "I'm going to help Julia and the girls with those kids. Their adrenaline level was sky-high after all the excitement."

Craig and Susan followed KC down the hall to the first door on the right, the study.

KC scurried to the computer chair, slid into it, and grabbed the mouse. "There's this guy a lot of people follow who calls himself Pi, you know like the Greek letter Π. Most people believe he's someone on the president's staff and that he knows a lot about the innermost workings of this administration."

"I've heard of him," Craig said. "Doesn't he have something like a cult following?"

"Uh, *he*, might be a *she*, Craig. I've seen increasingly the—I wouldn't call it an acronym as much as it is a pseudonym—URAQTΠ. When someone tweets it to her, she responds with IMAQTΠ."

Susan laughed. "You are a cutie pie? Sounds like they're talking about Shauna. If I've ever seen a cutie pie, Shauna is it."

Craig chuckled. "Baker sure thinks so, but he won't admit it to any of the guys. We're, uh, getting off track here."

"Back to Π," KC said. "Π might be a cult leader, maybe a bit of a nutcase, but she does have access to the president, or at least his staff. She might even be a member of the National Security Council. Anyway, Π knows things that someone without a security clearance would not know. And she makes posts to a web site which keeps her anonymous but hints at all sorts of special knowledge."

"For example?" Susan motioned toward KC.

"Supposedly, Π knows about Walker's connections to the families that own the biggest banks in the world."

Susan sighed and shook her head. "But, KC, that could just be a wild conspiracy theory."

"We've heard that one before," Craig said.

"Okay. Try this one. About a month before Walker fired his White House chief of staff, Π told that it would happen." KC's eyes darted back and forth between Susan and Craig. "No thoughts? ... All right, call me gullible. But I think there's something to this person, and since I need some quick inside info about the president's behavior, I'm going to try to make contact with Π."

Craig huffed a sigh. "How long is this going to take?"

"Look. It's going to take less than five minutes, or it's not going to happen tonight. Have you got five minutes to spare?"

Susan grinned. "This I've got to see. A world-class hacker goes after the contact information for a world-class, anonymous, conspiracy theorist who may or may not exist."

KC's red eyebrows nearly touched at Susan's remark. But she began typing furiously on the laptop keyboard.

"Can you tell us what you're doing?" Craig said.

"Tell you, yes. Explain it, I don't have that kind of time, Craig."

"Ouch." Susan looked at Craig and smirked.

"Then just tell us," Craig said.

"I'm hacking a certain server on the dark web. I do not recommend that you try this, because the admins over in dark territory have painful ways of retaliating. You know, they might give control of your laptop to people who run ransomware for fun and profit."

"Doesn't that bother you," Susan said.

"No. They'll never get a chance to load ransomware on this machine. Okay, I'm on the server as superuser. This is the only way I know to maybe find a valid email address for Π. Now I just *grep* through the binary database file and pipe its output through strings and—bingo."

KC straightened in her chair. "I'd bet good money that this is Π's email address. Let's check its domain ... here it is. It's a server in the DC area owned by some person or organization I've never heard of." She paused and studied their faces. "Am I boring you?"

"No comment," Craig said.

"He's pleading the fifth, KC. Just tell us what your email message says."

"At least Susan's honest." KC gave Craig a crooked smile.

"Okay, here's what the message says. I'm using my professional pseudonym and hoping that will get Π's attention. She should be old enough to remember Brock and I being in the news."

"KC," Susan said, "You two weren't only in the news. You're now in the history books."

"Here's my message. 'From KC Banning-Daniels. Subject, desperate, need to find out about black operation Walker is planning. What computer does he use in his private study? Please provide info about the machine's configuration and about his personal use of the machine, especially any careless habits. The only way I can pay you is through my organization accomplishing its mission. How would you like to have your country back in six months or less? Your confidential friend, KC Banning-Daniels'."

"That would get my attention," Susan said.

"Send it," Craig said.

"I just did. And it hasn't bounced back. I assume it was delivered by the mail server on the other end. Now we wait. But this could take a while."

KC's eyes did that back-and-forth thing between Susan and Craig that she had been doing a lot since she arrived. "It's after five. I'm going to wait here and hope for a reply." She paused, "If you two want to go to dinner or something, I'll call you if I get a reply."

He looked at Susan trying to read her eyes.

She folded her hands in her lap, clearly waiting for him to take the lead.

"How about the Black Bear Diner minus Deke?"

Susan gave him her warm smile. "I'd like that."

*And I could get used to seeing that smile every day.*

\* \* \*

Craig and Susan followed the waitress into the dining area of the Black Bear Diner. The waitress was the same young woman who had seated them night before last.

"Would you like a table in the middle of the room again?"

So she remembered them. A woman like Susan was hard to forget. Why hadn't she found someone to marry? Rather, why hadn't someone found her? Maybe they had. She seemed to be the prize catch in Central Oregon.

"We would like a quiet place this evening," Susan said.

Craig motioned toward the booth where Deke had sat. "How about that booth?"

"You got it."

The waitress left them with menus in their hands.

Susan lowered her menu until it rested on the table. "David, how do you deal with facing death every day while you do your job? I saw you today and heard the tension in your voice."

"How did you face death today driving Zach's truck while you waited to be blown away?"

"I ..." She didn't finish. Probably couldn't.

He shouldn't have asked. It didn't really apply to her question. Craig needed to move the conversation along. "Normally, I prepare so that my men always come out on top in any battle. Know thine enemy is the key, just as it is in spiritual battles. In fact, many of our military battles only occur because of spiritual battles, good versus evil being played out on an international stage. But today I hadn't prepared and didn't know what the enemy was doing. I dropped the ball and our people could have lost their families. I could have lost ..."

"But this is what you think God has called you to do. That's obvious."

"Yes, but his calling doesn't guarantee my success at carrying out my mission." He was treading closer to that dark moment he would forget if it were possible. He hadn't talked about it with anyone since the reports were filed explaining the death of most of his men twenty-one years ago, when First Lieutenant Craig had led them into an ambush.

"When you stopped near me on the road after the attack, there was something in your eyes I had never seen before. I wanted to erase it."

"You did. You told me everyone was okay, and you ..."

Susan smiled then it faded. "Surely you don't go into battle over and over again with the kind of fear that I saw. No one could do that and keep their sanity."

He was past the point of no return on two journeys, one to reveal the cause of his fear and the other to tell Susan about it. And that was something he had never done with any woman.

"Keep my sanity? There's something that happened more than twenty years ago that almost stole it." He paused. "It was my first command of a team of Rangers. We were in the mountains of Afghanistan, near Balamorghab, when I saw a group of Taliban we believed were responsible for killing several U.S. soldiers and slaughtering Afghan civilians. They led me into an ambush, one that I should have anticipated. Most of my men were killed."

Images of bloody, lifeless bodies created an unwanted slideshow that played in his mind.

Craig's hand tightened on his menu, crumpling it until it was unusable. Unusable, like David Craig knew he had been and feared he might still be.

Susan took his free hand and his grip on the menu relaxed. "I would imagine most special forces commanders who did what you did for an entire career have such stories to tell."

"Perhaps. But, Susan, I'm not most commanders. I'm me. And I will never fail the people I'm responsible for again. But today I thought..."

"Despite what you thought, God used three young boys to save us and, in doing that, he taught them a life lesson that they will never forget. If they use their special gifts for good purposes, God will honor their sacrifice and miracles can happen."

This remarkable woman had given him a perspective on today's events that David Craig could never have gained on his own while remaining defeated by his fears.

If only he had her insight and her comforting presence to draw on every day, maybe he—maybe he shouldn't go there. Not yet.

"Susan, maybe you should teach the middle-grade boys' Sunday school class at the chapel."

"Heavens, no. Little boys with wild imaginations scare me to death, especially when their IQs are too high to measure. But tell me why you joined the military and went into special forces."

The waitress approached them with an ordering pad and a pen in hand.

"First, we'd better order," he said. "I think I'll have breakfast again."

"Me too. The breakfast menu looks fantastic."

The waitress left with their order, and Craig focused on events of his childhood. That's where his dreams had started.

"Nearly every young man has a dream. Some have it from childhood. Like many who enlist, mine was to make the world a safer place for the people I love ... for all Americans."

"Dream big. That's what my granddad used to say," Susan said.

"I thought maybe I had accomplished my dream nine years ago when we took down President Hannan and swore in Ben Tucker as president. Then I retired after my third deployment to Afghanistan, but I didn't leave the world a safer place. Look at America now. It's coming unglued and it's a powder keg. Maybe here in Central Oregon I'll finally get the chance."

"You've accomplished more than anyone here hoped or imagined. From the moment you walked into that meeting at the chapel, everyone believed we—this tiny community in Central Oregon—could change the course of this entire nation. I believe in you, David, and I see God using you."

"Excuse me." The waitress stood beside the table. "I don't mean to interrupt, but your food is ready and ..."

She set their plates in front of them then stared at the thoroughly crumpled menu.

"Sorry about your menu," David said.

"We have plenty of menus. We get toddlers in here who do almost as good a job on them as you did." She grinned at David then took the menus and left.

"Let's eat," he said. "Hopefully, I can do that better than a toddler."

She didn't reply. Probably because her mouth was filled with a large bite of jalapenos with a touch of egg, something that looked like it could cause a three-alarm fire.

Two-thirds of the way through her three-alarm omelet, Susan stopped eating, fanned her mouth, and took a big gulp of ice water. Beads of sweat glistened on her forehead, indicating she had had enough of her omelet from hell.

Maybe she was ready to talk now.

"I didn't get to hear your plans and how you came to own Crooked River Espresso."

"After hearing your aspirations, mine seem small and selfish by comparison."

"The biggest dreams that capture a human heart are never small, and with someone like you, I know they would never be selfish."

"But you haven't heard mine yet."

Her eyes took on a distant look, as if peering into a different time. "I had a father who was, let's just say, distant. He was seldom home. My mother wasn't good at showing her appreciation, even after I helped her through some health challenges. Besides my parents, I had a fiancé, Jerry Fanning, who left days before our wedding."

"Left? Don't you mean broke off the engagement?"

"No. He just drove away and never came back." Susan sighed heavily. "I found out he had a second life that I knew nothing about."

She stopped and twin frown lines deepened while her gaze grew intense. "That life was filled with vile things, prostitutes, pornography, and even some drug use. I wasn't enough for Jerry. All that left me wanting—David, I just want to really mean something to someone ... to know they value me as a person."

"Value you? I want to tell you something, Sue. I—"

"Please, David." In an instant, her face had turned from serious and intense to tormented. "Don't call me that. I'm not Susie Q, not Susie, and not Sue. Just Susan."

"Got it ... Susan."

Craig had gotten the picture and didn't need to hear more agonizing details. Time to change the subject. "Is Susan ready to order dessert?"

His cell rang.

He checked the screen. "It's KC. Maybe she has some news."

"Craig here."

"This is KC. I've got some things you need to hear, and we need to act on them quickly. Is dinner winding down?"

"We can come over now."

"Good. I'll package everything into layman's terms and be ready to explain it when you get here."

"See you in about twenty minutes." He ended the call. "First I was worse than a toddler. Now KC says I'm just a layman."

"What?"

"Nothing. I'm just a little cranky tonight. KC has some news that we need to hear. Dessert will have to wait."

Twenty minutes later, David and Susan entered the study at Julia's house.

KC sat hunched over the laptop.

She had pulled up two chairs beside her.

"Have a seat and I'll show you what I found."

"I take it that Π was helpful," Craig said.

"Yes. She gave me a couple of tips that should be enough to accomplish what we need. First, she confirmed that the network topology of the White House complex, including the West Wing, hasn't changed since I worked there nine years ago. Of course, the routers are newer, but since I know the topology, if I get through the firewall, I can locate and log on to the router Walker's laptop is connected to and can search the connected devices to locate his laptop."

Craig gave KC his well-rehearsed incredulous look. It usually persuaded people to explain their plans.

"Π told me that Secret Service agents have said President Walker often leaves the laptop on in his private study and leaves the browser open. If I find the laptop with the browser open, I should be able to hack the browser to get to the operating system. There are plenty of ways to accomplish that. Once into the operating system, I will leave a little spy, a daemon that monitors the laptop's microphone and starts recording when steady sounds, such as voices, are detected."

"Aren't sound files big if you record several minutes?" Craig said.

"They can be, but only if you're an audiophile. I'll do a low-quality sampling of the sound to keep the files small. We just need to be able to make out the words."

"How do you retrieve the files?" Susan asked.

KC smiled. "That's the easy part. The daemon will wake up the system late at night and will send any sound files to a well-hidden server on the dark web. I will run a program on my machine that looks for any files, downloads them, erases them on the server, and then gives me an alert to check the file."

"I can see how that might work, KC," Craig said. "But you have as much as a twelve-hour delay if the conversation happened in the morning, say halfway around the world. That delay could leave us without enough time to respond to an attack."

"The program residing on my computer and the daemon on the president's laptop have only been designed in my head. The code hasn't been written, Craig. I'll change the daemon to look for the first period of inactivity after the conversation stops. Unless the president talks all day, without a break, we will be notified soon after he ends a discussion. Probably within an hour."

Their time might run out before a project like this could be finished. "It sounds pretty complex. How long will it take to write all this code?"

"I'll write it tonight before I go to bed. I can test it in the morning and deploy it at the first opportunity. Probably tomorrow night."

Craig shook his head. "KC, I've worked with a few software developers and none of them worked anywhere near the speed you're talking about."

"It's not that big a deal. I don't have to write, test, and document the code to MIL-STD-498, which is probably what you're used to seeing. That takes a lot longer. But my code just needs to work. I'll code it in a high-level scripting language, maybe Perl. Something that can be compiled to a binary after it's working. Programming at that level isn't much different than sitting at the computer with a console or command-prompt window up and typing in commands."

"If you say so." Craig met KC's gaze and studied her eyes for a moment. "We had a close call today, KC. Just make sure that you don't do anything that lets Walker's people trace this back to us."

"That's not gonna happen, Craig."

"David, how about having that dessert we missed? My mom's at home probably getting out the ice cream about now."

"Sounds good, Susan."

When they all stood, Craig's phone rang.

"Craig here."

"This is Drew. I went out to spell John Peterson at La Follette Butte lookout. Craig, he's been shot."

# Chapter 19

When Craig parked his Jeep at the top of La Follette Butte, Peterson was sitting in a folding chair under a large umbrella that was unable to block the glaring rays of the sun which now hung low in the northwestern sky.

Drew stood behind Peterson with one of his hands clamped on the wounded man's left shoulder.

Craig, Susan, and Kate climbed out of the Jeep and hurried toward the two men.

Kate had insisted on coming because she wanted to thank the Peterson's for taking a risk on a lone hitchhiker in the middle of the night.

"How bad is it, Drew?" Craig asked.

"It's low in the shoulder but above his lung, and the bullet seems to have missed all the arteries and bones."

"How are you doing, Peterson?"

"Compared to what? I've never been shot before, so I don't really know. It could have been a lot worse."

"How did it happen?" Craig asked.

"I think the shooter was coming to check out what we had up here. We've got a chair, a big umbrella, and a honey bucket."

"But you weren't in the chair," Drew said. "He could have been coming to use the honey bucket."

"Maybe," Peterson said. "But he was surprised when I stepped out from behind that juniper tree." Peterson nodded to their left.

"What did the guy look like?" Craig asked.

"Medium height. Wiry but strong looking and ... he looked evil. Evil as sin."

"Deke," Susan said.

"Yeah, Deke," Kate echoed. "Peterson, how is your family doing?"

"They're all just fine. Good to see that you're doing well too, Ms. Alexander."

Craig sighed. "I need to call your wife and let her know about—"

"No." Peterson cut him off. "We should wait until they check me out at the hospital, and then I'll call her. If I tell her, she'll be much less upset than if she hears about it from someone else."

"Your cabin is along Whychus Creek about two miles from here, right?"

"Yes."

"When you call her, tell her there is the possibility of an attack, but the safest place for her and your kids is at your cabin. It's highly unlikely that any part of a battle will be fought there. Tell her if there's any change to that, we'll call her and let her know. By then, you should be back from the hospital anyway. With that wound, they'll check you out, clean it up, patch it up, and send you home."

"I hope it's that simple," Peterson said. "Here comes the ambulance."

The ambulance arrived with its lights flashing but without the siren.

Two men hopped out and trotted over to Peterson.

The shorter man pointed at Drew's hand applying pressure to the wound. "Good job. I'll take over now. We need to have a look at that gunshot wound."

Drew removed his hand from Peterson's shoulder and stepped aside.

A small amount of blood oozed from the back of the shoulder.

"Well, if you're determined to get shot in the shoulder, that's one of the best spots to pick. But it is a gunshot wound, so we'll take you to St. Charles in Bend. I don't think you'll be needing it, but they have a level two trauma center."

After the paramedics loaded Peterson and headed down the paved driveway, questions scrolled through Craig's mind. What was Deke up to? Was this part of getting intel for Walker before an attack?

"We need KC to get access to the president, so we have something firm to plan for. Unfortunately, we have no idea when or if she can find out anything definitive."

Craig focused on Susan and Kate who stood side-by-side near the large umbrella. "What do you think is happening—your gut feel?"

"Walker is planning an attack," Susan said. "We need to prepare for it."

"Yes, we need to plan for an attack," Kate said. "One that includes boots on the ground. But for the timing, we need help from KC."

"Deke being spotted by Peterson may make them feel that they've tipped their hand," Drew said. "They may strike immediately because they fear losing the element of surprise. I would prepare for an attack tonight, just to be safe."

"It's about 8:00 p.m.," Craig said. "We still have a couple of hours before it gets dark. Just in case, let's make a plan to ward off a nighttime attack. We should meet with all the militia leaders at Steve's and Julia's house."

"I can drive, David, so you can start calling people," Susan said.

"Thanks, Susan. We'll need air support if we risk getting overrun by a large ground force. So the first person I need to call is Governor Harper to get approval to put the fighter wings on alert."

"Won't air support stop a large force in their tracks?" Kate said.

"Only if we know where they are so we can direct the air support." Craig said. "Close air support, CAS, must be precise. Otherwise, it could get our militia killed."

"I see what you mean," Kate said.

"But it's not like the fighter wing doesn't have any experience. Ever since we got into it with the radical Islamic groups in the Middle East, we've been averaging over twenty thousand CAS sorties a year. But the critical part is that when CAS is needed, it's needed immediately, or someone is going to die. That's why I should call Governor Harper first."

Susan slid in behind the wheel of Craig's big Jeep SUV. Craig rode shotgun and Kate took the back seat.

Drew followed them in his pickup.

Before they reached Julia's house, Craig had gotten Harper to place both fighter wings on high alert for instant response.

Craig had also broadcast a message to the militia leaders informing them of the meeting this evening at Julia's house to discuss details of their response to Walker's attack.

"You didn't need to put Baker on the distribution for the meeting message," Kate said. "Baker's probably there already visiting with Shauna."

"Those two fight too much to ever really be a couple," Craig said.

"David, that's how some people flirt," Susan said. "You know, sparring with words that have double meanings."

"Words like runt and motor mouth do not convey affection," Craig said. "And as for double meanings, I think both are singularly hostile."

"I'll bet you they end up together," Kate said.

"All's fair in love and war," Susan added.

"That's just it," Craig said. "You can't tell if they're in love or at war."

As acquaintances became friends and other relationships grew even deeper, Craig could not let Walker hurt these people who were quickly becoming family to him. No matter how devious and calculating Walker's plans, Craig would foil them. He couldn't live with himself if he didn't.

Susan, behind the wheel, glanced his way. "Are you okay, David?"

He wasn't, but he didn't reply.

\* \* \*

Before opening the meeting in the Bancroft's great room, Craig stuck his head into the study.

KC was still glued to the laptop, typing furiously.

Rather than break her concentration, he strode back to the great room and called the meeting to order.

Craig asked Brock to open in prayer.

As Brock prayed for wisdom and strength for what lay ahead, Craig's mind became a broken record, asking repeatedly that he would not fail these people. They deserved better than that.

After Brock closed the prayer, Craig scanned the room and noted that KC was still not there.

He would lay out the problem and hope KC had something to add before much longer.

"My brothers and sisters, we go into the coming events as family and as a member of this band of brothers and sisters, I pledge to you my loyalty and everything I have to offer to bring you all safely through the battle we are facing.

"Tonight we face a bigger federal force than we have yet seen, and we must end this meeting with a plan that keeps us and our children safe from a rogue president, Wendell Walker.

"After his previous attempts failed—"

KC's bright red hair lit the entry way to the great room. She held a sheet of paper in her hand.

"Before we make any plans, we need to hear from KC. She has been working on getting information about Walker's plans to attack the militia. KC, what have you got?"

She walked to the front of the room beside Craig and waved the piece of paper.

"As some of you might know, I have been working on — let's just call it what it is—hacking Walker's laptop." She stopped as chuckling spread around the room.

"My little digital spy recorded part of a meeting between Will Richards, Secretary of Defense, and the president. They talked on the phone with a man called Major Deke. Is this the same Deke we've been concerned about?"

"That confirms it," Susan said. "Deke is Walker's spy. But has he done all his damage, or do we still need to worry about him?"

"We need to worry about him until we eliminate him," Craig said. "He can direct the attackers to target our weakest defenses. That makes him an existential threat to us."

Baker and Drew seemed to be having an intense conversation between the two of them.

"Drew, do you and Baker have an idea you'd like to share with us?"

"Sir, from what we already knew, what KC discovered, and a few details I learned from Peterson, Baker and I think we can take out this Major Deke ... if you can spare us for twenty-four hours."

"I can spare you for a day provided we aren't attacked and provided you're ready to drop what you're doing and help defend Central Oregon if we are."

Baker jumped up. "Let's go, Drew. We've got a spook to stop."

"Spook?" Shauna shrugged. "This isn't Halloween."

"It means a spy," Drew said, rising to his feet.

Shauna stood too. "Drew, keep an eye on this pint-size pilot. A runt like that needs somebody to protect him."

"Munchkin ..." Drew grinned, "... in hand-to-hand combat training, everybody in the militia is afraid to go up against this runt."

"Does that include you, Chuck Norris?" Shauna gave Drew her crooked smile.

"Shauna, this pint-size pilot can bench press four hundred pounds on a bad day," Drew said. "He could bench press four munchkins like you all stacked on top of each other. But don't worry, I'll have his back."

Shauna's gaze tracked the two until they left the room.

"I had some more to tell you before we got interrupted," KC said. "I heard more from President Walker."

"Let's hear it," Craig said.

"It sounds like Walker is coming after the militia leaders and their families."

The low buzz of voices turned to a loud cacophony.

Craig raised his voice above the noise. "This won't be the first time we've seen Walker's willingness to murder innocent civilians. Keep that in mind when we encounter his men in battle."

Steve, who had been silent for most of the conversation, gave a derisive snort. "Being a person of honor is not a prerequisite for joining the radical left. They've already murdered sixty million kids and it hasn't bothered them. Murdering a half-dozen more won't either. How about another assault on the West Wing, Craig?"

Steve had missed the assault that took down a president nine years ago. But, hopefully, they wouldn't need a repeat performance.

"Maybe, Steve. But all in due time. Right now, we need to focus on securing our families and ensuring we prevail in battle if we're attacked."

"I have more info," KC said.

Craig nodded at her. "Let's hear it."

"Some colonel from JBLM refused to lead this operation. Will Richards suggested that they create a Special Ops team for a black operation, headed by Deke. They plan to come in the night and hit all of our houses, Drew's and Beth's, Lex's and Gemma's, Brock's and mine, Steve's and Julia's, but they weren't sure where you were staying, Craig."

A rare expletive blasted from his lips before he could stifle it. "They're trying to behead the militia, then they will try to finish it off. We've got to move all the families we think might be in danger to a safe place. Then we'll lay a trap for them. But we need to move everybody tonight, under cover of darkness and, hopefully, while Drew and Baker have Deke too preoccupied to observe what we're doing."

Steve and Julia exchanged what appeared to be knowing glances. Craig watched them for a moment. "Steve, Julia, what are you two thinking? It isn't as if you haven't been in this situation before."

Julia took Steve's hand and wrapped both of hers around it. "The Skylight Cave. If we can get everyone in tonight without being seen, Walker's men will never be able to find us."

# Chapter 20

Something didn't feel right. Had Walker made a mistake when he gave Deke the reins of this mission?

The anapestic knock on his private study door meant Will stood outside. Maybe he could set Walker's mind at ease about the raid on the Oregon militia to exterminate them.

"Come in, Will."

His Secretary of Defense closed the door behind him then looked across the small room at Walker and waited.

"Yes, lock it."

Will locked the door and sat across the desk from Walker. "Mr. President, you look like the cat that just swallowed the canary. So what have you done?"

"Last night I had a long conversation with Major Deke."

"And you gave him responsibility for your raid?"

Walker nodded. "Towry was too skittish."

"What organization is Deke recruiting his men from?"

"None in particular. He's calling former military men that he knows, ex-SEALS, ex-Rangers and some from private security organizations."

The creases on Will's forehead deepened. "Sounds like he's creating a band of misfits. They will be vicious and dangerous, but you can't control a group like that. They play by their rules not by their commander's orders."

"So you don't think Deke is the man for the job?"

"Mr. President, I don't think the men he's selecting are the right people for the job, and you will have to live with all the repercussions from their attack." Will paused. "Tell me again why Towry backed out of the assignment."

"This is a night raid on militia leaders' houses to behead that rabble in Central Oregon."

"Sir, don't you mean a raid on the militia's families? Won't wives and kids be in those houses?"

"They might be but—"

"Mr. President, Major Deke has a checkered record and was nearly court-martialed on two occasions. Can you trust him?"

"What do you mean by *trust him*?"

"Sir, I mean trust him not to repeat the barbaric treatment of the enemy ... you know, like the actions in Afghanistan that nearly sent him to prison."

"I checked his records and he was exonerated of all charges."

"No, sir. Not exonerated. They just weren't able to convict him. But some of his men insisted that Deke had tortured men, assaulted women, and then killed entire families all without proof that they were supporting the enemy. As I said, he's vicious."

He should either agree with Will or object to his assertions. But truth be told, it would not trouble his conscience if Deke repeated such atrocities with the militia leaders.

For the trouble they had caused Walker, stifling his efforts to re-unify the nation, all of the Oregon militia members deserved something vicious. It would strike terror into the hearts of other resistors in the red states and red territories. It would force unity through power and fear. At a time like this, that was exactly what he needed to bring the nation back under his control.

Will sat silently for several seconds with his lips pursed. "Sir, your eyes betray your thoughts. Vengeance and intimidation might appear to be the way to end the fragmentation of the nation, but it could also blow up in your face. You might incite such a violent reaction, including a rebellion among federal troops, that you lose control of the military. If that were to happen, you might have to run for your life."

Run for his life? He would never believe that unless he saw it. It wasn't going to happen.

"Mr. President, if you really knew the troops, if you understood them, you would weigh that possibility. Please, sir, consider it now. Tomorrow might be too late."

Though he wouldn't tell Will Richards, a moment of clarity revealed the truth. Walker was more like Deke than like Towry. And that showed Walker how to proceed in this black operation.

His likeness to Deke had taken Walker all the way to the presidency, while Towry was lucky to have made colonel.

*And that's why Deke is the right man for this job.*

# Chapter 21

*10:00 a.m. the next day, the president's private study*

The press was pressuring Walker's administration mercilessly for information about his plan to unify the nation. He had given his press secretary some talking points that would partially satisfy the ravenous reporters at the morning press conference.

Beyond those talking points, the actual effort to subdue the state of Oregon and bring it back into the union must go well. If so, Walker could point to Oregon as an example of what other red states and territories should expect if they persisted in their rebellion.

However, if this operation failed, it could signal the end of Walker's presidency and either split the nation indefinitely or turn the United States of America red for the next fifty years.

Those were the stakes if Walker pursued forcefully subduing Oregon. But with their surprisingly strong militia and its treaty with Governor Harper, Walker had no other options than to send a powerful military force.

To be certain he succeeded in crippling the militia, he had to ensure that Harper's Guard troops, all four thousand of them, did not enter the fray. Maybe Towry would be more amenable to that role, defending the Cascades so Harper's Guard did not cross the mountains.

Regardless, Towry needed more time to prepare and Deke needed to strike in sync with Towry's availability.

Walker slipped out his secure cell and hit Deke's number.

"Deke here."

"Good morning, Major Deke."

"Our JLTVs still haven't arrived. When will we be ready to launch the attack, Mr. President?"

"There's been a bit of a delay."

"Sir, what kind of a delay are we talking? A few hours? And what's holding us up?"

So Deke was getting impatient. He needed to tell the man something. "I need some time to get Colonel Towry onboard."

"Permission to speak frankly, Mr. President?"

"Speak what's on your mind."

"Towry is a wuss. Pardon my derogatory remarks about a fellow soldier. But why do we need him, Mr. President? He hasn't been willing to participate in our operation to completely wipe out the militia. That makes Towry a dangerous man, one we can't rely on."

"Deke, we face the possibility of Governor Harper's Guard showing up. They could move as many as four thousand troops in from the west. And Harper commands the two Air Guard wings. I need Towry to protect your men from the Guard while you exterminate the militia."

"Sir, you said you needed time to get him onboard. Is there a possibility he will refuse again?"

"That's not likely. But he does need time to plan and get approval of the logistics for this operation, because he'll be flying his men in from JBLM. He needs Humvees for mobility."

"It sounds like he needs a whole fleet of Chinooks to deploy to Central Oregon. And my men need at least three Chinooks for our equipment. How do we ensure that all the birds get through after what happened to that Apache a few days ago?"

"There was a problem at the Western Air Defense Sector Headquarters. I was assured that it will be taken care of."

"Mr. President, most of the people manning that sector are Air Guard personnel."

"Yes, Deke, but they are Washington Air Guard. They are not under Harper's command. If there is a traitor there, or a procedural issue, I was assured that it would be thoroughly dealt with."

"That sounds good, sir. But I will feel a lot better when those JLTVs are sitting in front of me ready to drive. My gut says, sir, that every hour we delay, the more risk we have to deal with."

"Rest assured, Deke, that we won't delay one more hour than necessary. So if you and your men are ready, the attack should start in about thirty-six hours."

"If that's what it takes, I can wait thirty-six hours to exterminate these pests. We'll be ready, Mr. President."

Walker ended the call.

Now to ensure that Towry will be ready.

He placed the call.

It went directly to voice mail.

Walker left a message emphasizing the urgency of a return call.

Five minutes later, his phone rang.

He glanced at the caller ID. Towry.

"President Walker."

"Mr. President, you said you have an urgent matter to discuss with me."

"Yes, Colonel Towry. We are expecting an engagement with the Central Oregon Militia, but we fear the Oregon Guard under Governor Harper will come to the militia's aid. We want to prevent that by blocking the pass. Will you help us."

"Of course. As long as I'm not victimizing civilian men, women, or children."

"You won't be. Can you get enough men in position to defend the mountain pass in twenty-four hours?"

"Do you mean by tomorrow night?"

"Yes."

"Normally, I would need forty-eight hours."

"You have thirty hours to get your men in position."

"Considering the potential size of the Guard army, I would prefer four hundred men. But the logistical constraints will probably leave me with one hundred men, weapons, and vehicles brought in via helicopter."

"Can you be ready by tomorrow night?"

"It might raise some eyebrows at the base, but I'll make it happen."

"How will you get your troops in position given that the position could move from one pass to another?"

"You let me worry about that. Just don't start the conflict before 2300 hours tomorrow evening or you might get an unpleasant surprise."

"I understand. But I want you to let me know when you have landed and then give me periodic updates via this phone."

"Will do, Mr. President."

Walker ended the call.

If Deke and Towry both did their jobs, in forty-eight hours, Oregon would be ready to surrender to the federal government, and Walker could start the process of formally removing the rebellious governor, Sandra Harper. Then he would rattle his saber in the next governor's face.

*What could possibly go wrong?*

# Chapter 22

*8:00 p.m. PDT, Julia's house*

Craig stood at one end of the great room at Julia's and Steve's house. "Is everybody here now?"

Susan walked halfway down the right side of the room and leaned against the wall. "They're all here, David."

"Did you find a place for your mother, Susan?"

"Yes. She's with a friend from our church, but I could have stayed with her at my place."

"You and I have been seen together around Redmond. Anybody associated with me is in danger and needs to leave this area."

Susan gave him her patented Mona Lisa smile. "Is that what we are, David? An association?"

It was not the time to raise that issue. "Moving along—since all the women and children will be in the cave for the duration, did anyone *not* bring enough supplies for your family to last for a week?" Craig looked around the room.

No one responded.

"Good. The water situation has been taken care of. Steve has enough plastic water jugs for us and the spring comes out of the ground near the cave. I understand there's a glorified fifteen-foot ladder for entry into the cave. Lori and Peter are our two youngest. Will they be okay using the ladder? Before you answer, remember our latrines are outside the cave."

"Peter climbs like a monkey," Beth said.

"Lori will be fine," Allie said.

"Great. We will start leaving here at 10:00 p.m.. Vehicles will leave one to two minutes apart, and we will congregate in the parking lot at Creekside Park in Sisters." He paused. "Any questions?"

Allie waved her hand. "Craig, please remind us one more time why we're doing this and why all the secrecy is necessary."

KC stood. "Allie, I know this is a lot of trouble. But the information I intercepted from President Walker said that a black ops team of special forces have planned a night raid hitting all our houses in quick succession. They plan to kill all of us. Everyone in this room ... including the children."

Sam scooted closer to AJ and curled an arm around her.

"If the raiders split into two groups," Craig said, "they could hit KC's and Brock's house then Julia's in five minutes. If they have enough men, they could send another group to Lex's place. From there in another five minutes they could be at Drew's and Beth's ranch. If they planned carefully, they could kill all of you in a ten-minute span of time. And that seems to be their goal. This should serve as a harsh reminder of the kind of evil we are fighting when we oppose Wendell Walker and his supporters."

Beth pulled Peter onto her lap, and Drew wrapped his big arm around both.

Brock looked at Benjamin and KC sitting beside him, then across the room at Steve. "What did they plan to do about Harper's Guard?"

"They didn't mention the Guard," KC said.

"If they didn't mention the Guard," Kate said, "this must be a hit and run attack on the militia. They probably have something else planned for my aunt."

"I hate to say this, Kate," Craig said. "But they may not have to defeat the Guard if they can stage a coup beginning with capturing or assassinating the governor."

Kate jumped to her feet. "If they do that, I might do some assassinating of my own."

"No, Kate." Zach pulled her down into her chair. "This is all brainstorming. If we think something's going to happen, we'll create a plan to stop it."

"Thank you, Zach." Craig said. "I should have qualified my remark and, yes, we will have a plan for every contingency. If we plan well, and trust Almighty God, we have nothing to worry about. We're told that we should be prepared for the battle, but it is the Lord who gives the victory."

Sam stood. "No, it was the horse that was supposed to be prepared then victory is the Lord's."

"Sam," Josh said, "Colonel Craig wasn't talking about Proverbs he meant what David said in First Samuel. 'This day the Lord will deliver you into my hand, and I will strike you and take your head from you. And—"

"That's enough beheading, Josh," Gemma said. "Give the meeting back to Colonel Craig."

"But, Mom," Caleb said. "Josh was getting to the best part."

"Gemma, if you don't mind, I'd like Josh to finish that passage for us," Craig said.

She blew out her frustration loud enough for the room to hear and then nodded.

Craig grinned. "Go ahead, Josh."

"This day the Lord will deliver you into my hand, and I will strike you and take your head from you. And this day I will give the carcasses of the camp of the Philistines to the birds of the air and the wild beasts of the earth, that all the earth may know that there is a God in Israel. Then all this assembly shall know that the Lord does not save with sword and spear; for the battle is the Lord's, and He will give you into our hands."

It was a dramatic recitation from the mind of a genius and the wild heart of a young boy. With what they were facing, it was just what this group needed to hear.

"Thank you, Josh."

Drew waved his hand. "About the surprise attack tonight. They wouldn't be so bold as to try to get the governor and us in a single night, would they?"

"My guess," Craig said, "... at the risk of sounding arrogant, is that they plan to neutralize the militia first. When we're no longer a serious threat, they will invoke whatever plan they have for replacing Governor Harper. That said, I'm going to call her now and warn her. If she offers to help us near term, I'm inclined to turn her down. Her troops need to protect her just in case Walker makes a move against her."

Craig called Governor Harper's secure cell but got her voice mail. He left a message for her to call him.

Now the room was buzzing with nervous chatter.

Baker's voice rose above the murmur. "How far apart are those steps on that ladder at the mouth of the cave? If they're too far, we may have to lower Munchkin down on a rope."

Shauna pounded his knee.

Laughter spread around the room.

"If Peter can negotiate the ladder, I'm sure Munchkin can," Beth said.

Shauna's wide brown eyes feigned a shocked look. "Munchkin? Beth, I thought you were on my side."

"Back to Kansas from the Land of Oz," Craig said. "We need to firm up our plan for defending the cave. The last thing we want is to be inside the cave surrounded by two hundred Army Rangers."

"I can testify to that," Julia said. "And that Deke dude, probably wouldn't care for my singing."

"It might have worked nine years ago," Steve said. "But Deke wouldn't appreciate *God Bless America*."

"Point taken," Craig said. "Our number one defense priority—don't let them find the cave."

"That's why we're going there tonight," Susan said. "But what if they find it anyway?"

"Our second priority—have sentry's stationed ready to notify us of any indication they found, or suspect, the cave."

"We easily have enough militia to cover that," Drew said. "But what do we do if the cave becomes endangered?"

"I think I have a solution for that," Craig said. "But let me run it by you all for a sanity check." He paused. "If we are in imminent danger while in the cave, we scramble the entire fighter wing from Portland. The Air Guard's F-15s can make it here in six minutes from takeoff—seven minutes from notification time if they're on alert. And they will be. The militia would form a defensive posture near the cave, and we would use Close Air Support, CAS, to protect both us and the militia outside."

"Do we assume the black ops team has any air support?" Steve said.

"For them to use Growlers again from Whidbey NAS isn't likely. It wasn't successful the last time. They have no fighters under their command. I would instead expect Apaches from JBLM. Walker's men got approval to use them against us the last time, so we can look for them again."

"Apaches would have to leave JBLM three and a half to maybe four hours before the attack if they come in the back door, from the east, to avoid detection," Baker said. "So we need our man in—"

"You mean our *woman*, Airman Gore," KC said. "She's the person who alerted us, though she had a few other like-minded friends in the WADS headquarters."

"Right," Craig said. "But we have another option to protect both the cave and our houses once we have an ETA for the incoming Apaches."

"Scramble the F-15s early?" Baker raised his eyebrows.

"Yes. We will have them cruising, hidden by the crest of the Cascades. Once the Apaches commit to a target, either the cave or our houses to the north, we send in the Eagles."

"How far is it from the ridge to the targets?" Baker said.

"To reach firing range for the F-15s it's only ten to fifteen miles. Flying at Mach 1.2, that's less than sixty seconds until the Eagles fire. The AIM-120 air-to-air missiles travel at Mach 4, over 3,000 miles-per-hour. That's another fifteen to twenty seconds until the chopper goes down. Only seventy-five to eighty seconds from my initial command until the Apaches are out of the battle."

"But, sir," Baker said. "Apaches now have countermeasures."

"Yes. Some have that new MRFI system," Craig said.

Baker nodded. "And it's integrated into their ASE for improved survivability. The eagles may have to fly closer to engage."

"But remember, Baker, when the F-15s are first detected, they will be ID'd as friendly aircraft. Our defenses are set to detect Russians and Chinese, not a group of friendly Americans."

"Right," Steve said. "All Americans love each other these days."

"We appreciate the sarcasm, Steve. But by the time the pilot realizes the Eagle isn't coming to give him a hug, and then he decides to take evasive action, a missile will be headed his way. If the Eagles shoot two AIM-120s, about eight seconds apart, at least one will hit the target."

"And we just need to get the Apache before it can launch a missile at our houses," Baker said.

"If the target is the cave," Steve said, "we'd better make sure we have enough of a safety margin so they can't launch a Hellfire Missile at us."

"We can do that, Steve," Craig said. "The cave is twenty miles or more southwest of our houses. That gives us more time because they will be coming from the northeast. The F-15s can close rapidly to within a short distance of the Apache. The pilot will only be thinking about his own safety and his electronic countermeasures at that point. He won't be trying to aim at his target. My bigger concern is where their ground troops will be and what they will try after the Apaches are shot down."

Julia dropped Steve's hand and stood.

Craig studied her for a moment, recalling the young woman from nine years ago—about five-foot-four, no more than one-hundred-ten pounds, looking so fragile that she might break—as tough as anyone Craig had ever met. She had been an avowed pacifist until she realized that worldview could not be lived out in a fallen world.

Julia had saved the lives of nearly a third of the people who would be in the cave if you counted the children unborn at the time. The intensity in those brown eyes looked like she might be attempting a repeat performance.

"There's something we need to keep in mind about Skylight Cave." Julia paused until she had everyone's attention. "We hid there nine years ago. One of our enemies might remember that and come to find the cave once they realize we're not in our houses. But we've mentioned a man named Deke who will be leading the ground troops. I killed an army officer named Deke nine years ago, because of what he was about to do to KC. It happened in Skylight Cave. Who is this new officer named Deke, and what is his real motivation for coming after us? Two Dekes in the army, both leftists, both in special forces—that's quite a coincidence. I have no way of knowing if they are actually brothers. I'm just saying that it might not be safe to expect this Deke to act rationally."

The room grew quiet.

The danger crescendoed to a screaming alert siren inside of Craig's head. These troops would be even more dangerous if they were led by a vindictive sibling who, if he felt it necessary, would turn this into a suicide mission for revenge.

Craig took a deep calming breath then faced his audience seated in the great room. "Come on, folks. It's time to load up and go spelunking."

# Chapter 23

*1:15 a.m., The Skylight Cave near Sisters, Oregon*

At night, the Skylight Cave was only a dark hole in the ground. Craig had seen daytime pictures of this long lava tube with holes in its ceiling. The eerie shafts of sunlight created luminous columns of yellow and sometimes light blue, depending on the time of day.

Tonight the cave was lit from numerous lanterns and flashlights.

The biggest problem they'd encountered so far had been privacy. The rocky floor of the cave only left enough room to pitch two medium-sized tents. They designated one the women's dressing room and the other was for the men.

Sleeping bags occupied any area with a relatively smooth gap between rocks.

The unmarried women, Susan, Kate, Shauna, Itzy and Sam found a smooth area farther back in the cave.

The unmarried men, Zach, Craig, and Baker, put their sleeping bags near the cave opening and the ladder. But Craig and Baker had volunteered to split the night watch just outside the cave's opening. They were the last line of defense nearest the cave.

While Baker stood watch, Craig came in to talk to the group before they bedded down for the night.

He called them all up to the front of the cave, near the two large tents.

"I know these are strange surroundings, but you can all sleep easy tonight. We have three lines of defense around us. First, Baker and I will be standing watch outside the cave entrance. Other militia are deployed in a half circle about a quarter mile out from the cave. Fifty men, spaced about fifty yards apart, can see all the open areas around us that might be used by approaching troops. They are well armed and will camouflage themselves by day so they cannot be detected.

'Finally, we have one hundred eighty men, fifteen detachments, stationed at critical places along all the roads that lead into this area from the east, near Sisters, from the north, near Highway 20, and along Highway 240 to the west. We have a few along a Forest Service road to the south.

"And, if we need them, we can call on the fighter wings to defend us with CAS. The bottom line is you can all sleep sound. We've got you covered."

\* \* \*

Susan could see immediately what Craig was doing by holding this short meeting. He wanted these people who had been forced from their homes to a dark hole in the ground, to feel secure, especially the children. He was a good leader and a good man. She needed to tell him that.

When Craig adjourned the meeting, he headed up the steps to leave the cave.

Susan followed him up the steps to the outside.

When she reached the top, she looked up into the night sky. The myriad of bright lights revealed the silhouette of a man.

"David."

"I thought I heard someone sneaking up behind me. It's late. Aren't you tired after the events of this day? I've heard that trying to get yourself killed is exhausting."

"And now you're mocking me."

"I would never mock you, Susan. That sounds more like something Baker and Shauna would do to each other."

"I hope you're not comparing us to those two."

"Hardly."

"Are you on guard duty now?"

"No. I was just going to check on Baker. I'll relieve him about 4:00 a.m., but I see him down by the spring. Things look fine."

"Then we can talk for a minute." She waited.

"Sure."

Susan wished she could see his face, but the darkness turned it to a shadow without any detail. "It seems as if the conflict with the president is coming to a head. It worries me."

"If I was forced to trust David Craig for my safety, I might feel the same way." He chuckled.

"That's not what I meant."

"Which is?"

This wasn't easy and David wasn't making it any more so. "Do you know, or suspect, where God is leading you, David?"

He stood silent, studying her for a few moments. "He led me back to this community that I came to know and care about nine years ago when Brock and KC were in trouble with President Hannan."

"Does that leading include ..." She couldn't continue.

"Does it include you? Before you hear that answer, you need to understand what you'd be getting with a man like retired Colonel David Craig."

That wasn't what she expected to hear. Was he still wrestling with the ghosts from his past? His perceived failure as a young lieutenant?

"David, I believe that—"

A penetrating buzz came from a spot in the darkness a few feet ahead.

Craig circled her waist with an arm, lifted Susan, and pulled her away from the threatening noise.

He set her down again and looked toward the noise that seemed to be decreasing in volume. "A rattlesnake. We must have interrupted his nighttime foray for food. Those little demons sure terrified KC."

"I'm not fond of them either."

KC? She was the first thought on his mind after the snake announced its presence. KC was now thirty. But was David still infatuated or maybe in love with the twenty-one-year-old version of KC that he met nine years ago? She'd heard the story of Craig asking about KC's availability and Brock making it clear that KC was taken. Were the memories of KC the reason he seemed reluctant to approach the subject of a commitment to Susan O'Connell?

*Susie Q, maybe you're just not enough for a man like David Craig.*

# Chapter 24

*12:00 a.m. EDT, the next night*

The mission should have launched two hours ago. Why hadn't Walker heard anything from Deke or Towry?

In late July, at 9:00 p.m., it should be nearly dark on the West Coast. Earlier in the day, Colonel Towry had told him the mission was a go for tonight, but something must be holding—

Walker's secure cell rang.

"President Walker here."

"Mr. President, this is Colonel Towry. Just wanted to let you know, sir, that the two Apaches are on their way. The two Chinooks with Deke's JLTVs are taking off now."

"Did you have any problem loading those armored vehicles into the Chinooks?"

"No, sir. With the B-kit armor package, the JLTVs are still within the payload limit of our Chinooks. Deke should be commanding his team of twelve men with two JLTVs in about an hour and a half."

"Good job, Towry. What about your men and your vehicles? Have you had any problems?"

"The Humvee troop carriers—two in each Chinook—are about four inches too wide and two inches too long for the cargo area of a CH-47. But after we reconfigured the HICHS on the Chinooks and took the winches off the Humvees, they fit. The biggest problem came when I requested permission to fly ten Chinooks across the boundary of a state that has for all practical purposes seceded. That raised a few eyebrows on the general's staff. But we explained the situation, dropped your name a few times, Mr. President, and we got permission. In about three hours, we will deliver the men and equipment to a landing site a few miles east of the pass we'll be defending."

"Once again, good job, Towry. Do you have any concerns at this point?"

"Just one, sir. My men are supposed to be guarding the pass to protect Colonel Deke while he engages the militia."

"That's correct."

"Once the hostilities begin, we could see movement of Harper's Guard through the pass. But Deke was never clear about how soon the fighting might begin. Depending upon what the Apaches do, my men may not be in position in time."

So Colonel Towry was actually worried about what the Apaches would be doing prior to Deke's arrival—like killing civilians. Walker couldn't afford to have Towry pull out of the mission at the last minute.

"Mr. President, will my men get there in time?"

"Don't worry. You'll be there in time. Besides Deke, I've had another spy in the area for a while. He's watching the Guard tonight and will let us know when they make a move. It will take Harper's troops over an hour to reach the pass, so your men will have plenty of time to get in position to block them."

"I'll take your word on that, Mr. President. Just wanted to make sure we were keeping Major Deke and his men safe."

"Colonel Towry, I do expect updates. I especially want to know when your men are going to engage the Guard, because we may lose contact for a while during the skirmish. And I want to know the minute anything goes wrong or causes us to deviate from our plan."

"Mr. President, there's nothing that can go so terribly wrong that we can't handle it. But I will contact you as you directed."

* * *

The short night had made it a long day for Craig. He'd taken a nap in the afternoon but had heard nothing from his sentries, from Harper ... or from Susan.

He had missed dinner. Now it was almost 10:30 p.m. and the natives were growing restless as they prepared to spend another night in the cave with no news telling them how long they might be there.

Craig's phone rang.

He glanced at the caller ID.

The Fighter Wing in Portland? Whatever the reason for the call it probably wasn't good.

"Craig here."

"Colonel Craig, this is Major Morgan, 142nd Fighter Wing command post. I just received notification from an Airman Gore at WADS headquarters. She reported two Apaches headed toward the Oregon border from near JBLM."

"Then this is the beginning of the attack."

"Yes, Colonel Craig, it's the beginning but, unfortunately, we won't be getting any further radar tracking reports from WADS."

"Why is that, Morgan?"

"Airman Gore's commanding officer had her arrested as she was talking to us. It sounds like he's a Walker sympathizer and doesn't want her interfering in anything the president is doing, constitutional or not."

"Was Airman Gore following standard operating procedures?"

"Sounds like it. She said she was trained to contact the Fighter Wing in Portland to intercept any suspicious or hostile aircraft, and the Apaches flying toward the Oregon border were definitely suspicious. Her commander told her everything's changed with the secession of Oregon. Airman Gore replied, 'then you'd better tell me what to do if that had been a Russian bomber or a Chinese warplane. Who should I call in that event, sir? It seems to me somebody's not doing their job and it's not me'. She was a spitfire. It's a shame we can't help her. She was arrested for assisting a fighter wing she normally works with as a team."

"It's a mess if you're in the military when a nation splits," Craig said. "Chain of command loses its continuity. That young woman wouldn't know who to trust. If there's any way we can help her, we need to try. Regardless, we won't be getting any further info about incoming air traffic."

The roar of an engine came through the phone.

"Back to the Apaches," Morgan said. "The Guard doesn't want the Apaches entering Oregon's air space, so we've scrambled three Eagles to stop them."

"I don't want them here either. They're coming to launch an attack against the militia here in Central Oregon."

"That's why I called. Do you want us to patch you in to our comms, Colonel Craig?"

"If you see no problem with that, yes, I have a vested interest in hearing what happens to the two Apaches coming to kill me and my people."

"Governor Harper has already given her blessing. Patching you in now. You'll only be in listening mode, but the command post can talk to you directly."

"I understand."

Static came through Craig's phone for a second or two.

"This is Eagle One. Initiating contact with Apaches. Calling their bluff. Do not know what to expect."

He paused for several seconds. "Pilots of the AH-64Es, you are over airspace of the Sovereign State of Oregon. Turn around and leave, now."

No reply.

"Hostile Apaches, the cavalry has arrived. If you do not respond immediately you will be shot down. Neither your countermeasures nor your missiles can save you."

"Apache niner niner four here. You are interfering with our training route."

"Training route my—consider this Apache niner niner four and your accomplice. If you do not turn and leave Oregon air space now, you both will have two AIM-120s flying up your exhaust mixers, welcoming you to Hades. I'm assuming you have a reservation for said destination, or you wouldn't be trying what you're currently trying."

"Apache niner niner four changing course to three-five-zero, headed home."

"Watch him Eagle two. He may be positioning to fire his Stinger."

"He's preparing to fire, major."

"At 'em boys. Give 'er the gun!" It was the major's voice in Eagle one. He was about to kick the Apaches out of the wild blue yonder.

Craig waited for at least ten silent seconds.

"Eagle one here. Both Apaches turned bandit on us. There are now two smoking holes at 45.51 north and 121.89 west. And two small wildfires burning along the nearby National Forest Road."

"Command post copies, Eagle one. Too bad they didn't listen. Command post is notifying ranger district about fires. Come on home, Eagles."

"Command post here. You still there, Craig?"

"Still here, Major Morgan. Got a question for you."

"Shoot, Craig."

"We just shot down two U.S. helicopters and killed four of our men. Who's going to investigate this incident and who will they report it to?"

"Uh ... good question. We need some new procedures for reporting combat against U.S. forces."

"Yes, we do. That's all I've got. Craig out." He ended the call.

# Chapter 25

*11:00 p.m., Skylight Cave*

Craig tucked his cell in its pocket on his cargo shorts and climbed down the ladder into the Skylight Cave. The fifteen-degree temperature drop raised goosebumps on his arms.

In the shadowy cavern, too many were milling around for anyone to be asleep yet, except Baker, who would stand the first watch.

"Listen up, everybody! Let's gather near the cave entrance. I've got some news you all need to hear."

Baker had been napping on his sleeping bag. He yawned and rose to his feet. "If you're in here, who's guarding the entrance?"

"We're safe for now. I'll explain once everybody gets down here."

The last to arrive were the unmarried women whose beds were in the back of the cave.

The entire group needed to know what was happening, but he shouldn't frighten them. After all, this was good news, so far.

"Walker's attack has begun."

Gasps came from the group standing in a semicircle around Craig.

"Don't be alarmed. So far, I have only good news to report. Walker sent two Apaches from JBLM. Obviously, he hoped they would take out all the militia leaders' houses that Walker had located. But a brave, young airman at the Western Air Defense Sector notified the Fighter Wing at

Portland, because she suspected the Apaches were up to no good. She was arrested for warning the Air Guard, but the F-15 Eagles scrambled and intercepted the Apaches shortly after they crossed the Columbia River. The Apaches tried to shoot air-to-air missiles and the Eagles shot down both Apaches. So Walker's first wave of the attack failed miserably."

"But it won't be the last wave," Steve said.

"Steve's right. We can expect another wave, probably ground troops that must come in either via motor vehicles or Chinooks. We can stop motor vehicles. But if any Chinooks got through after Airman Gore was arrested, their range is only three hundred miles. They will need to refuel after the drop off or just before."

"Then we can get advance warning," Drew said.

"Yes. So I'm sending ten men with RPGs to the Madras airport and ten to Richards Field in Redmond. If they try to refuel at either location, we can capture or destroy the Chinooks.

"That traps the ground troops here, within an area that we'll be watching. We will get them, eventually. But they will try to hit our houses first, since they know the Apaches didn't accomplish that. Therefore, I'll send half the men at each of our sentry locations to Crooked River Ranch to protect our houses."

Craig's cell rang. "This is one of our sentries reporting in. Excuse me while I take his call."

Craig walked to the ladder and sat on the second rung. "Craig here."

"Craig, sir, this is Simmons. I'm on the ridge above the Otter Creek Trail watching two Chinooks unload in the plateau below. You'll never guess what was in those two birds."

"Do I really want to hear this, Simmons?"

"Probably not, sir. But you need to. You know those armored vehicles slated to replace the Humvees?"

"Do you mean the JLTVs that the House refused to fund in the last continuing resolution—those armored vehicles that cost four hundred thousand dollars apiece?"

"Yes, sir. If this is Deke's team, there are twelve men total and two JLTVs. I put my binoculars on them and I can see a big chain gun and four rockets."

"Are those rockets or possibly missiles?"

"They're pretty big sir. I'd say missiles."

"Good grief. Those JLTVs have almost the same firepower as an attack helicopter. I thought we were out of hot water when the Fighter Wing took out the Apaches."

"These are like slow-moving Apaches with armor. But we can't tell what armor kit they used, so we don't know if our RPGs can damage them."

"Simmons, they will try to hit all of our families' houses on the ranch. We're all out, but I want to stop the JLTVs, and I'd like to know what that's going to take." He paused.

"Set up an ambush and hit them with the biggest RPGs you have, probably the thermobaric ones, and the most powerful machine gun you can get your hands on. But keep our men safe. Just hide, hit them, and run. Then report back to me. I'm praying we can stop them."

"Got your orders, sir. Will let the team here know. I'm also praying we can stop these machines. The Chinooks are taking off headed north. Yowser! One of the JLTVs just took off across the desert. It knocked the gate out at the trailhead and hit the pavement at fifty or sixty miles per hour. Gotta go, sir, or these guys will get to Brock's and KC's place before we can engage them. Will call you back ASAP."

The two Chinooks headed northward, would probably refuel at Madras.

Craig called the Madras sentry.

"Sanders here."

"This is Colonel Craig. Has the militia team arrived, Sanders? I sent ten men up to assist you."

"They just arrived, sir. What do you want us to do?"

"There are two birds headed your way from the south, Chinooks. They should be there in four or five minutes and they need fuel. I want you to get in close and arrest the pilots and guard the Chinooks. You can arrest them on my authority. They are guilty of assisting in the attempted murder of Oregon civilians. Call the Madras police and ask them to hold them on my authority and tell them that Colonel Craig is willing to take any heat for holding them in custody. The chief there knows who I am and should cooperate."

"Got it, sir."

"Sanders, get the men in place hidden near the fueling area. Don't complete the arrest if it puts any civilians or their property in danger. In that case, it's better to let the pilots go."

"Yes, sir. But what about the Chinooks after we arrest the pilots?"

"They're ours. Acquired gear. Leave someone to guard them."

He ended the call.

Before he could turn to address the people in the cave, his cell rang again.

"This is Simmons, sir."

"What have you got, Simmons?"

"Sir, we engaged a JLTV at the Daniels' house and the rest of our group engaged the other one at the Bancroft's place. We hit them with everything we had—RPGs, an M2. Nothing got through the armor. We couldn't even give them a flat tire. Nothing stopped them. Unless they run out of fuel, they're unstoppable."

"They have a lot of armor. The amount and configurability of the armor on an JLTV is classified. But we know the version they sold to the Brits had armor that could stop our biggest RPGs."

He wasn't going to dispute Simmons *unstoppable* assessment now, but there had to be a way to stop them. "Do they still have twelve men in two JLTVs?"

"Yes, sir."

"What did they do to the houses?"

"They looked inside, sir. Saw there was no one there and left."

"When did they leave?"

"Just now."

So they know the leaders of the militia and their families have left. But did they have any idea where the families were now?

"Where are they headed, Simmons?"

"Down Rim Road toward Chinook Drive. They turned onto it, headed south."

They could be headed toward the Sisters area, but what information might they have that could send them toward the Skylight Cave?

The answer to that question was moot if he couldn't find a way to cripple those two vehicles and catch the men in them. If the JLTVs reached the families, this could be worse than the nighttime ambush in Afghanistan, where Craig lost most of his men. He needed to focus or this *would* be worse. "Which way are they headed now, Simmons?"

"They turned west on Terrebonne-Lower Bridge Road."

"They're headed in the general direction of Sisters, but that's also the general direction of the Skylight Cave. I need to get our families out of here, just in case. Keep tailing them and bring as many men as you can. Tell them to prepare for an intense battle. If you can spot any vulnerabilities in the JLTVs let me know. We've got to find one. Talk to you in a few minutes."

Craig ended the call and placed another to the lead sentry guarding the perimeter around the cave.

He answered on the first ring. "Wilson here."

"Wilson, leave a couple of men watching the approach from Sisters and the rest of you double-time it here to the cave. We've got a situation developing and only a few minutes to resolve it. I need you to hear our plans."

"We're on our way, sir."

Craig ended the call to Wilson and turned toward the people in the cave, "Our location may be compromised. To be safe, we've got to leave."

# Chapter 26

*11:30 p.m., Skylight Cave*

Craig tried to maintain a sense of organization after his announcement that they needed to leave sent the residents of Skylight Cave into chaos. "Ladies, pack up everything you can in five minutes. I need to finalize our escape plan with my warfighters."

The women turned and ran for their sleeping bags and other camping equipment. Susan ran to the far end of the cave, where the single ladies had been sleeping, out of earshot of the men.

"Men, we're going to drive down National Forest Road 1028 to Highway 242," Craig said. "Go west on 242 toward the observatory." He paused.

"Steve, how far is it to the shortcut across the lava flow that takes you over to Highway 126?"

"About two and a half miles beyond the observatory. It's a small unnamed road on the right that cuts through the lava flow, between the Belknap Crater and the Twin Craters, then links up with a network of small dirt roads that will take you to Highway 126 a little south of Clear Lake."

"Clear Lake. That's where we will all rendezvous after we stop Walker's black ops team in the lava flow. We'll gather in the picnic area at Clear Lake. There are two large gullies in the flow with bridges across them. Are the bridges still usable?"

"Last I heard the bridges were fine, sir."

"Let's change that, Steve, if you've got enough C-4."

"If I understand where you're going with this, I've probably got enough C-4 but not any extra. Now how are we going to get them to follow us? We can't use our families as bait."

"I'll be the bait," Baker said. "I've got the fastest vehicle here, and I've heard those JLTVs can't go over seventy miles-per-hour."

Shauna, with a rolled-up sleeping bag under her arm, charged through the group to Baker's side. "You can't let a runt like him bait a detachment of special ops soldiers. If the runt stays behind, I need to be there with him to keep him safe."

Baker glanced her way and, for the first time Craig could ever remember, fear showed in Baker's eyes. "I'm not saying Munchkin isn't man bait, but we can't let these people get close enough to see us. I say she rides with Jeff and Allie."

They couldn't afford this relational stuff holding them up right now. "This is precisely why we didn't allow women on combat teams, at least not during my tenure." Craig blew out his frustration in a sharp blast. "Baker, RPGs detonate at 920 meters. If you stay a thousand meters ahead of them and keep moving, you'll be safe," Craig said. "Besides, if she's with you, I know you'll stay safe."

"Is that an order, *sir*?" Baker huffed out the last word.

"We don't have time to argue about it. It's an order, Baker."

Shauna bumped his shoulder with hers but didn't say anything.

Baker's eyes on the other hand ...

Craig turned back to face Steve. "Set charges on the first bridge. I'll detonate them after they cross."

Steve looked puzzled for a moment. "So Baker's leading them and you're following them? What if seeing headlights behind them makes them a bit nervous? They might turn around, and that would destroy our whole plan."

"They won't see any headlights. Mine will be off. I'll use my NVGs."

"Sir, I don't have any remote detonators. I've only got instantaneous electrical detonators."

"Can you rig it up with a trip wire?"

"Would you rather yank on a wire up close and personal, or shoot at a small target from forty or fifty yards away?"

"The farther away the better."

"Done. I suppose you want me to rig up a trip wire for Baker to blow up the second bridge after he crosses it to strand the JLTVs in the lava field."

"Can you think of any other way to stop those JLTVs? Our RPGs didn't faze them, even when we shot them in the front grill. Just make sure there's enough to take out that second bridge or this plan falls apart. Worst case, if the first bridge doesn't go, they'll have to backtrack to Highway 242 and drive around. That's an extra 30 miles. We'll have time to lose them. Should that happen, I'll call with an alternate plan. Worst case, I can lead them on a wild goose chase."

"I've seen those vehicles in action," Baker said. "Can't they make it across the lava if they take it slow and pick their way? Each wheel has its own computer-controlled suspension."

"They're going to be surrounded by hundreds of acres of lava boulders four to six feet high with grooves in the flows ten feet or more feet deep," Steve said. "I don't think those monster trucks with six-foot-high tires could make it across, let alone these JLTVs."

"Then that puts Walker's troops where we want them, on foot," Craig said. "Then we attack with all our forces. We take them out completely and only take prisoners if they voluntarily surrender. Got it?"

"Got it."

Susan, Shauna, Kate, Itzy, and Sam emerged from the far end of the cave carrying their sleeping bags.

"We will rendezvous at the Clear Lake picnic area," Craig said. "Let's load up now."

After everyone exited the cave, they loaded the kids into their vehicles first. With the children corralled, they loaded the equipment and supplies.

After Steve, Julia, and Itzy left in the lead vehicle, Susan approached Craig. "David, can I please ride with you? I'll stay out of the way. I promise."

Baker cleared his throat and waited for Craig's attention. "Sir, you already set a precedent. And it's not like she hasn't earned her stripes."

Craig shook his head.

"You owe me this much, Mr. Craig."

She wasn't going to back down, and he didn't want to have this argument in front of his men. "Throw your things in the Jeep and climb in. I'll be there in a minute."

Before he could change his mind, she headed for his Jeep SUV.

Craig turned to the militia members that had been guarding the cave. "Assemble on National Forest Road 1028 and head South to Highway 242. We will meet the enemy at the lava fields on a small road two and a half miles beyond the Dee Wright Observatory. There's help on the way. Half of the sentries we deployed for this mission are on their way here, but ahead of them are two JLTVs that we've been unable to stop with just our RPGs. But that's about to change, men."

# Chapter 27

Susan got out of Craig's Jeep and, in the dim moonlight, carefully made her way back toward the cave entrance.

What was taking David so long? And what was he doing by the cave entrance?

The militia men had climbed into their vehicles and were leaving in a hurry.

She glanced behind her.

The last militia vehicle pulled away from the cave.

Craig turned from the cave and strode her way.

"Hurry, David. The others have all left."

Movement to her right.

A dark form leaped from the trees and took Craig to the ground.

Craig rolled and shoved a man in camouflaged clothing away from Craig's body.

Metal flashed in the moonlight and a dark stain grew then ran down the outside of Craig's shoulder. He had been cut.

The assailant leaped toward Susan as Craig pulled out his handgun.

An iron arm wrapped around her waist and a sharp sting radiated from her neck up the side of her face.

She tried to move her neck away from the knife, but the man pushed it farther until the tip broke her skin.

"Don't even think about it, Craig." The man holding her growled out the words. "Shoot and you won't like whose blood is spilled, and I can make sure it *all* spills."

It was Deke. He had seen them together at the restaurant and with his knife at her throat, Deke knew he held the advantage over Craig.

Craig lowered his gun.

"Drop it on the ground and move away from it."

When Craig dropped it, three men came from the trees behind him and held their guns on him.

Deke's hold on her loosened.

She tried to pull away from him. "He's bleeding. Let me stop the bleeding."

"First, we see if you have any weapons."

She was only wearing shorts, a tank top and running shoes. Susan had no place to hide a weapon.

Deke studied her for a moment and must have drawn the same conclusion. "All right. You two cooperate with me, and I'll let you stop the bleeding from that scratch on his arm."

She tried to pull away from Deke and go to David.

Deke yanked her back. "Not yet, my red-haired beauty."

"What do you want, Deke?" Craig spat out the words.

"What I want ... perhaps I shouldn't say that in mixed company. But hear this, Colonel Craig—retired, has-been, Colonel Craig. If you don't tell me where the other militia leaders and their families have gone, Ms. O'Connell will suffer. We can make her suffer with pain or with shame or both. Maybe I should start with my beauty treatment, a face shift." Deke drew the point of the knife so it scraped a burning, stinging path across Susan's cheek.

"Stop! I'll tell you what you want to know," Craig's voice trailed off in resignation.

"No, David. You can't. The women and kids are with them."

Deke laughed a mocking, derisive noise that sounded more like a dog barking. "Women and children. This gets better all the time. Maybe they can be used to gain concessions from a certain governor."

Susan stifled the urge to spit in this man's vile face. "Governor's do not make compromises with terrorists," she said.

Deke repeated the mocking laugh. "Just like militia leaders don't compromise with, as you say, terrorists?"

"One way or another, Susan, from you or from me, he's going to find out."

"I won't tell him no matter what he does to me."

David shook his head. "There are things you know nothing about. I won't put you through them all for nothing."

"Nothing? You think those kids' lives are nothing?"

"The other leaders all took a shortcut about two miles beyond the observatory on Highway 242," Craig said. "It cuts through to Highway 126, and that will take you north to Clear Lake where they'll be waiting for me."

David had told them. It was unbelievable that this strong leader of the militia, a man who had won the Congressional Medal of Honor, could do something so dishonorable. And he had betrayed their friends and their entire families.

Craig had betrayed more lives than her fiancé, Jerry, had in betraying her. Not only that, but Craig had likely killed them.

It was best that she found this out about him now than to continue their fast-growing relationship. But did it really matter? In a short while, they would all be dead, thanks to their fearless leader, Colonel David Craig.

"Ms. O'Connell, I thought you wanted to bind up his life-threatening wound."

Susan stared at the rocky ground. "Let him bleed."

She shouldn't have said that. Only a few hours ago she was asking him to tell her if he was ready to make a commitment to her.

She blew out her pain and frustration, glanced at David's bleeding arm, and took a step in his direction.

Deke grabbed the neck of her tank top and yanked her back toward him.

It choked her, sending her into a coughing spasm.

"You're getting what you want. Cut it out."

"Look, Craig, you have your fun and I'll have mine."

His knife flashed in the starlight, coming within an inch of her stomach. In a few seconds, Deke had sliced the band from the bottom of Susan's tank top and cut it to make a long elastic strip of cloth.

"Here. Go tie off that dangerous wound."

Susan ripped the band from Deke's hand and walked slowly toward David.

He sat emotionless and silent while she tied the fabric tight enough to stop the bleeding. The wound looked like it could use several stitches, but like other issues, at this point that was moot.

* * *

Deke studied Susan O'Connell's shadowy but shapely form as she finished tying off the fabric covering the deep cut on the outer edge of Craig's shoulder. As the story was told to him, his brother had a fascination with another redhead, KC Banning, now KC Daniels.

For now, he would keep all the militia prisoners alive for information and for use as hostages, if needed. And he could think of several reasons for keeping Ms. O'Connell alive.

His cell rang, playing the *Colonel Bogey March.* Colonel Towry.

"Zip tie those two," Deke said, then he answered his phone.

"This is Colonel Towry. Major Deke, our Chinooks are loaded and we're waiting for a safe time to fly."

"Safe time? What's up Towry? We made it here just fine."

"Yes. But you took the eastern route. We're too heavily loaded to do that. We'd run out of fuel." He paused. "Didn't you hear? The two apaches were shot down by F-15s out of Portland."

Deke swore. "Why is it that attack helicopters never seem to be able to attack?"

"Somebody must have tipped off the Fighter Wing. But with this indefinite hold we're in, maybe you should abort the mission. We can always—"

"Abort the mission? What kind of fool talk is that, colonel?"

"I'll overlook the impertinence, Deke. But we won't be there to protect you if the Oregon Guard or more militia show up."

"Look, Towry, we're not aborting. I've captured the militia leader, Craig. Soon we'll have all the leaders. If worst comes to worst, we can use them as bargaining chips, but that won't be necessary. With the JLTVs we can run right through the militia and the Guard, blasting them to blazes as we make our run."

"What about air support. If they call in the Fighter Wings and the F-15s attack you, the JLTVs will be history, and your men inside will never know what hit them."

"That hasn't been proven, Towry. We're running the JLTVs with the B-kit armor. It's never been tested against a Hellfire Missile, but it has withstood a Javelin, and that's no small accomplishment. Besides, there are no signs of the Oregon Guard responding at this time."

"No comms?"

"We have heard some comms on our frequencies. They were between Steve Bancroft of the state militia and

Governor Harper's Guard troops. Bancroft let her know there was trouble. I'm continuing my job to behead this ragamuffin band. I may not have much time for phone calls for a while. If you talk to President Walker, tell him what I'm up to and what we've accomplished. This mission can still be a success."

"I'll tell him," Towry said. "Take care, Deke. Don't underestimate these people. You are intruding on their homes and threatening their families. Remember what the Russians did to Hitler when he intruded?"

"I'm not a rabid Nazi, Towry. I know enough to be wary if I corner a wolfhound. With Craig and his mistress in hand, and knowing where the others are hiding, I've got the rebels right where I want them." He ended the call.

Now what? Sending the JLTVs ahead while he stayed behind to question Craig had become an attractive option, because one cannot come away from a mission like this one with nothing, especially after losing two Apaches.

With such heavy losses, Deke may not get approval from JBLM for another mission. That would leave him on his own with only Walker for support. Money but no troops.

If Deke questioned Craig, he would be a treasure trove of information, provided Deke could get him to talk. The most important information was the location of one Julia Weiss. She had a debt that she needed to pay. The blood of Deke's older brother still demanded revenge.

There were other reasons, such as Ms. O'Connell. But he might not have time for her.

Craig could probably help with the purely military issues which included how the Air Guard knew about the two Apaches that were shot down. That had nearly caused the mission to implode. Craig probably knew who had alerted the Air Guard.

Then there was the issue of Governor Harper, an issue near and dear to President Walker's heart. Craig could likely tell Deke who protected Harper—how many men and their vulnerabilities. Even that bit of information would placate Walker and keep Deke on his payroll.

"Major Deke, what are we going to do now? We don't have much time before first light."

"Here's the plan. Ballinger and I will stay behind for a few minutes. We need some intel from our prisoners. Your JLTV will be loaded with ten men."

"But there's only room for—"

"I know. Four of them can ride up on top. You won't be engaging the militia until after I arrive. Got it, Hill?"

"Yes, sir. We'll leave immediately."

"Did you get the information about the shortcut to Clear Lake?"

"Got it, sir. A little over two miles beyond the observatory the road turns to the west and crosses a big lava field."

"Get your men and be on your way, Hill."

The men piled into and onto one JLTV. Soon they rolled away toward the Forest Service road that would take them to Highway 242.

Deke and Ballinger approached Craig and Susan.

What was the quickest way to get Craig to talk?

*The quickest way was using a certain rare woman—a beautiful redhead with blue eyes.*

# Chapter 28

Susan studied the two men who approached her and Craig. They resembled vultures circling a dying animal on the desert floor. But these two hadn't come to clean up a dead carcass. They had probably come to leave one ... or two.

Even in the darkness, the evil look of the two shadowy forms sent chills up the back of her neck.

She needed to do something to stall them, anything to prevent them from starting their torture of Craig. But as easily as they had gotten the location of the other militia leaders from Craig, they might try the same approach again. If so, Susan would be their next target.

She stood. "I need to use the latrine."

"Of course, you do, Ms. O'Connell," Deke said. "At this critical juncture you just happen to need to—"

"Deke." She raised her voice. "Did it occur to you that this critical juncture might actually cause a woman to have such a need? Do I get to go or ..."

"Take her to the latrine, Ballinger. And treat her like the officer and gentlemen you used to be."

"I need my hands in front of me," Susan said. "Can you move the ties, please?"

Ballinger grabbed her wrists, raised them, and sliced the ties with his knife. "Lead the way." He turned on a flashlight and used it to prod her forward in the opposite direction of the latrine.

Evidently, Ballinger hadn't had time to become familiar with the area around the cave. Maybe she could use that to her advantage.

Susan led the man along the spine of the Skylight Cave which paralleled their path. Thirty feet below them lay the floor of the lava tube, a rough bed of jagged lava rock.

The flashlight flickered, dimmed, and in a few more steps went out.

Ballinger grabbed the back of her tank top and pulled her to a stop. He cursed the light. "I don't have any batteries with me."

"I know the way to the latrine. I've certainly walked it enough."

"Then you lead, but don't try to run off, or you'll regret it."

"I ran into a rattlesnake near here last night. I'm not going to run off."

Where was the first skylight?

The ground was rough, punctuated every few feet by large, protruding lava rocks ... and one dark spot. The man behind her would not be able to see it with her body blocking the barely visible four-foot-wide skylight.

Susan skirted the hole on the right side of it then quickly stepped to the left as she passed it.

Ballinger hurried to catch up to her.

Susan swung her right arm around behind her, driving it into his right side.

Ballinger lost his balance and stepped to his left to recover. He started his slide down into the hole. His fingers raked her back as he went down. But they didn't catch the fabric of her tank top.

His brief cry was cut off when Ballinger's head struck the rough lava rocks forming the edges of the skylight.

The momentum of Susan's blow, which caused her to twist to her right, sent her right foot skidding down into the edge of the skylight.

Her feet churned like an ant trying to claw its way out of an ant lion's trap.

Ballinger's body crunched on the rocks thirty feet below.

She squelched the cry that rose in her throat and frantically sought traction to avoid Ballinger's fate.

Susan leaned forward and fell face down on the edge of the hole.

Her feet dangled in the skylight and her belly lay on the edge.

She slid back an inch. Then two more inches.

If she couldn't stop the sliding, she would soon join Ballinger on the rocks below.

Susan stuck out a hand into the darkness and grabbed for something, anything.

Her fingers curled over the top of a protruding lava rock.

The porous, igneous rock cut into her fingers, but she held on, trying desperately not to cry out and alert Deke.

She pulled hard, ignoring the stinging cuts on her fingers.

Slowly, almost imperceptibly, she inched her body forward, away from this deadly trap by night that created beautiful columns of light by day.

Susan pulled her knees under her and pushed up with her hands. She stood, stepped away from the hole, and tried to hear other sounds through her furious panting.

Her breathing eased, and she heard only the low murmur of Deke's occasional words breaking the silence of the night.

It seemed Deke was unaware of what had happened at the skylight.

No sounds came from inside the cave, so Ballinger either lay unconscious or dead.

She needed to hurry back and try to help Craig before Ballinger awoke and cried for help.

Even if Craig was a traitor, he had tried to save her life.

But he had betrayed their friends to save her. Did that mean he loved her in a sick way, so sick that he would let others die so he could have her?

There was another possibility. Maybe he knew something she didn't. No, that was giving the man too much credit. He'd have to earn that kind of trust, and that would not be easy to do with a woman who had been treated as badly by a man as Susan O'Connell had.

Susan carefully moved off the spine of the Skylight Cave and onto a trail that paralleled the cave. This trail should take her back to a spot between the JLTV and where Deke held David.

Soon the silhouette of the JLTV, created by Deke's light, loomed over her.

Sliding sounds came from the other side of the vehicle.

Deke had stood. "Ballinger, you need to get back here! We're running out of time."

Susan picked up a lava rock that weighed about five pounds. She quietly rounded the JLTV and approached Deke from behind.

Craig's gaze seemed to focus on her, but his body language gave no appearance that he saw her.

Deke yelled for Ballinger again.

The night was warm. He took off his helmet and wiped his forehead.

Susan raised the rock over her head and brought it down with all her strength on his bare head.

Without making a sound, Deke crumpled to the ground.

"He has a knife clipped onto his belt," Craig said. "Get it and cut my ties before he wakes up, if he wakes up."

"He's still breathing," Susan said.

She unclipped the knife and cut Craig's zip ties.

"Well, we've got ourselves a JLTV, but we've got to hurry. I'm supposed to blow up the first bridge before the other JLTV can turn around and backtrack. It may already be too late."

The picture came into focus. Craig was leading Deke's men into a trap. "You mean you were setting a trap for those men when I thought you were betraying us?"

"I thought you'd be more convincing if I didn't try to correct you."

"But I was ready to—"

"But you didn't. I knew you'd forgive me, Susan. That's the kind of person you are."

"I am a fool, David Craig. That's the kind of person I am."

"Only if you don't let us leave before he wakes up or before his partner returns." Craig scooped up his own rifle and Deke's too. "What happened to his partner?"

"I led him astray."

"You played the femme fatale? You wouldn't, would you?"

"No. I couldn't begin to do that. I led him to a skylight and knocked him in. It was quiet in the cave after he hit. I don't think he survived."

"Remind me never to go on a walk in the dark with you. Regardless, he's probably out of the battle. And Deke might need brain surgery after what you did to him. As for this JLTV, I'd disable it, but I haven't seen one up close and personal before, and I don't have time to reverse engineer it here in the dark. Let's head for my Jeep and pray we can still trap the other JLTV in the lava flow."

"David," She gave him a quick hug. "I am so sorry."

"Come on, Susan. We have ten guys in a JLTV that need to be made sorry ... sorry they ever set foot in Oregon."

# Chapter 29

*Clear Lake parking area*

At 1:15 a.m., Steve Bancroft put his cell back in his pocket after his third try to reach Craig failed.

Baker's Jeep Trackhawk slid to a stop in the parking area.

Steve strode toward the big Jeep.

Baker and Shauna climbed out and met Steve at the edge of the tree-lined parking lot.

Baker approached Steve. "We blew bridge number two."

"Nobody will be crossing that bridge," Shauna said.

"How far ahead of them were you when you detonated the charges," Steve asked.

"The JLTV was slowing to turn from the highway. They were about six or seven hundred yards behind us. Unless they were looking right at the bridge, they wouldn't have seen it blow. You did a good job with the C-4. I don't know what the acoustics are like in a JLTV, so it's possible they could have heard it."

"Did they keep following you?"

"They did," Shauna said. "But we couldn't see any signs of Craig. Then we headed down into the forest and lost sight of the lava field."

"So we know they didn't cross the lava field, but don't know if they were able to turn around and go back?"

"That's about the size of it," Baker said.

"I haven't been able to reach Craig. Something must have gone wrong," Steve said. "I'm going to call Governor Harper and let her know what's happened so far."

Governor Harper answered on the first ring.

"Governor, this is Steve Bancroft, David Craig's second in command."

"Hello, Steve. I hope nothing has happened to Colonel Craig."

"So do we, governor. Here's our situation. Craig hasn't answered my calls for the last hour or so. During that time, we've tried to trap a black ops team sent by President Walker. We believe there are twelve members and they have two JLTVs."

"JLTVs? Could you please translate that, Steve?"

"These are armored vehicles with a lot of firepower. Like a small tank. They were intended to replace the Humvees currently in use. We tried to trap them in a lava field, because we could think of no other way to stop them. But we don't know how that turned out because we can't contact Craig."

"I'm afraid I have more threatening news for you. The Portland Air Guard just contacted me and said more troops might be coming from JBLM. If so, it means Walker must be preparing for a battle."

"You don't have any clues as to how many troops might be coming, do you?"

"No. I don't. But one would think they would bring at least a company. Isn't that about two hundred men?"

"Yes. Two hundred or more. Can you help us, governor?"

"Where are you now?"

"The leaders of the militia were targeted. Their families too. So we left our homes and have gathered at the Clear Lake picnic area off from Highway 126. It's a few miles east of Santiam Pass. I'll text you our location as soon as we end this call."

"I have about one hundred fifty Guard troops who can be ready to go in about an hour. Will that be enough?"

"We'll make it be enough. We have about fifty militia, so we should be able to handle a company of two hundred. But I'd feel a lot better if Craig were here to help plan our attack."

"Hopefully, Craig will contact you before I get there. See you in about two hours."

Steve opened a message and hit the location icon. A map image appeared, marking his location. It included the GPS coordinates. He sent the message and glanced at the time on the cell phone.

*1:30 a.m.*

He tried Craig again. Still no answer. He left a message, but as he did, something had happened on the other end of the parking lot. All eyes seemed focused on one spot in the trees.

Steve sent the message and walked slowly toward the group. They stood, huddled in the dark except for two wandering beams of flashlights.

"Do not move! Put down your weapons now, or we will open fire with RPGs." The loud, raspy voice came from the trees to Steve's left.

He needed to take charge of the situation or people could be killed. "Lights out everybody. Don't move. Let me talk to them."

The flashlight beams disappeared.

"We have you surrounded! Turning out the lights? That was a stupid move, on your part! Haven't you heard of NVGs, make-believe militiaman? Tell your people to freeze, or you'll all burn together. And put all weapons on the ground."

* * *

A light from the trees came on, a strong beam shining on Steve.

Shauna nudged Kate who stood beside her.

"Now who's stupid?" Shauna whispered to Kate. "He just lost his night vision goggles advantage."

"How do you know that?"

"Some runt told me all about NVGs. Now give me the gun?"

"Are you crazy, Shauna?"

"Come on, girl. We both shot the gun at the range several times. My skin's dark. I'm wearing dark clothes. I can sneak out of here and give them fits with Siggy while we wait for Craig and the other men."

Steve and the leader of the men surrounding them argued in loud, angry voices as Steve negotiated their terms of surrender.

"Quit stalling! This is your last warning. Guns down and hands on your heads ... everybody, or we open fire."

Shauna flinched when the cool metal of the Sig Sauer P226 touched her hand.

She took Siggy and scurried toward the trees opposite the source of the loud voice, using the group to shield the man's view of her and praying the guy was lying about surrounding them.

"All right, everybody. Guns on the ground. Hands on your heads." Steve's voice.

Shauna needed to circle the parking area and move closer to the raspy voice. If she needed to shoot from where she stood, she would be shooting through the families. It wasn't worth the risk of hitting one of them.

She crept to her left toward the lake trail she'd spotted while they waited for Craig.

Still no gunmen. The man must have lied to them.

Shauna needed to finalize her plan. She was in the trees, within shooting range of the loudmouth. But, even if he exposed himself, she dare not shoot him if he had other men who might use the RPGs on the women and kids.

She continued her stealthy movement to her left until an opening appeared revealing the form of a person.

It was a man partially hidden by the trees lining the parking area.

Shauna raised her gun, felt the bulge of the laser button with her middle finger, waited for an opportunity ... and prayed.

# Chapter 30

Craig was so far behind their planned schedule that running without headlights wouldn't help. It would only slow him down.

He raced down Highway 242 and then slowed after passing the observatory. .

He spotted the cut-off and took it.

Soon, his Jeep rolled along a road that bisected a lava field.

The headlights hit a bridge ahead.

Craig stopped and cut the lights. Ahead they saw no lights. He cut the engine, grabbed his M4, and climbed out.

"Be careful, David."

"And you stay in the jeep. The blast could send some shrapnel our way."

There were no sounds of engines up ahead. If the JLTVs were there, they weren't running.

This was not going according to plan, but it would be wise to carry out his role.

Craig reached through the driver's window, hit the Jeep's light switch, and spotted the target Steve had left for him.

He raised his M4, aimed at the target, and pulled the trigger.

The bridge disappeared in a flash of light and a sharp crack.

Dust and debris fell in the lighted area ahead.

"So much for the bridge," Susan said. "Did we trap them?"

"I doubt it. I'm not sure where they are, but I'm guessing they turned back and circled the mountain on 242 to get to Highway 126, just like we're going to do."

They would lose a half hour in driving time plus the fifteen minutes it had taken them to escape from Deke.

Steve would be concerned.

"Susan, here's my phone. See if I've gotten any messages from Steve."

"I can see that you got five calls from him. What's your voice mail pin?"

"If I tell you, I'll have to kill you."

"Do you want to hear your messages now or not?"

"It's ... 1234."

She giggled. "How clever. I would have never guessed."

"Yeah. Yeah. I know. Just play Steve's messages."

Susan fiddled with the cell for a moment, then Steve's tension-edged voice came from the phone. "Craig, where are you? Harper says federal troops are on the way. She's sending some help, a hundred and fifty troops in about two hours. Gotta go now. Something's happening here."

"You need to call him, David. At least let him know we're coming."

"Normally, I would agree. But that last bit of the message, 'something is happening here', worries me. I've listened to that voice for twelve years. Something's wrong. My call could put him in danger or even get people killed."

"So what are we going to do?"

"We're going to hurry." He shoved the accelerator to the floor. "And when we go in, we go in quietly."

Several minutes later, the headlights lit the intersection with Highway 126.

Craig slowed and took the right turn lane.

"Check that sign for me, Susan."

"It said Clear Lake seventeen miles."

"The problem is, if my hunch is right, we don't have seventeen minutes. If there's trouble, Steve will try to stall. Ten minutes max would be the best he could do."

"Sixty times seventeen divided by ten," Susan said.

"What's that?"

"It's how fast you'll have to drive to make it there in ten minutes."

"Well, Einstein, what's the speed needed?"

"A hundred and two."

"That's doable."

"You've got to be kidding."

"This is a good road, Susan, with only a few sharp curves."

"One sharp curve is all it takes."

"Hush. Let me concentrate on the road."

Craig stomped on the gas pedal and put the lights on high beam. "You might want to tighten your seatbelt, and you can be thankful we're not in Baker's Trackhawk."

"Thankful? Why? Are you a better driver than him?"

"I doubt it. But the Trackhawk has 700 horsepower."

"I'm just going to close my eyes and pray."

He had no choice but to hurry. If somehow Deke's men or federal troops had captured the families, Craig would have failed again. Failure would become the bookends on a career that somehow had a Medal of Honor in the middle. He didn't deserve any medal, not if Lori, Peter, beautiful Sam, Itzy, those brilliant cousins, or their parents were hurt in any way or, heaven forbid, killed.

He pushed harder on the gas pedal keeping it mashed to the floor.

Nine minutes later, Craig slowed and turned in at the Clear Lake entrance.

"Can I look now?"

"Yes. Can you pray with your eyes open?"

"Of course. If I need to."

"Right now, I'd say you need to."

Before the road narrowed to a single lane, he pulled off onto a wide spot on the shoulder and stopped.

"David, we need to get closer to see what's happening." She laid her hand on his arm. "Are you okay?"

David Craig wasn't okay, but he didn't have the time or the inclination to talk about it.

"See the treetops lit up ahead. The whole parking area is as light as day. It's not a good sign. We need to sneak in not drive in." He pulled his M4 out of the back seat and got out.

Susan climbed out and followed him. "It's lit up all right. At least we'll be able to see what's going on."

After they had walked ahead about three hundred yards, the road straightened and headed toward the parking area which lay two hundred yards ahead.

He pulled Susan with him behind a bushy fir tree on the right side of the road and peered around it at the scene ahead.

"They're surrounded by armed men. It must be the rest of Deke's men. It took us too long to get to the lava flow, so they probably backtracked and took the same route we did to get here."

"It's not your fault, David. Let's figure out a way to—what do you call it—extract them?"

"I'm the one who failed them, so I'm the one who should get them out."

"This isn't like you. You're no failure. I only *thought* you had sold us out. I really didn't know what to think. But you just used my uncertainty to trick them."

"Some trick that was. I've led them into a death trap. I'm incompetent, Susan. Others don't see it. They see what they want to see. But no matter how I try to cover it, in the end, that's what I am."

"Stop it right now. That's not the truth and you know it."

"It's the truth, Susan. But Walker's men don't know the truth about me, so maybe I'm a big enough prize in their eyes to trade for the others."

Susan blocked his way. "No, I won't let you."

"I failed and now the women and the kids are in danger. They don't deserve that. No one deserves to die but me. They will probably want to keep me alive to parade me around as Walker's prize example of why people shouldn't oppose him. Then they'll lock me up for life, so I won't become a martyr."

He stood to walk toward the dirt parking lot where Deke's men held his friends. "I'm sorry for all my unkept promises to you, for all your expectations I couldn't live up to. Goodbye, Susan."

She didn't reply, but in the glow of light from the parking area, her cheeks glistened with tears.

He needed his wits about him if he was going to free the women and kids. In his twenty-five years as a warfighter, he'd never had problems concentrating on the battle ahead, regardless of the circumstances. But this was different. His adopted family might be killed, and he'd already killed the love he'd never found before he met Susan.

*You've got nothing to lose, dude, so you might as well go lose it.*

Craig worked his way down the right side of the narrow road keeping himself hidden by the dense forest.

He stopped about ten yards from the clearing containing the parking lot.

One gunman had his weapon pointed at Peter's head.

The biggest brute backhanded Steve, sending him sprawling on his back on the dirt. "Next time, just answer the question."

With these creeps it always started with threats and intimidation. Craig needed to stop this before the torture and killing began. He took a deep breath to announce his presence. "This is David Craig!"

Every head in the parking lot turned his way.

"That's pretty good," the brute said. "But, you see, Deke has Craig and is probably in the process of mangling his fingers to get information. I don't know who you are, but you've got five seconds to show yourself or little Peter is going to have a long nap. Then you'll have five more seconds until Lori joins him."

"Look, I *am* David Craig and I will trade myself for the women and children."

Brutus pointed his gun in Craig's direction, but obviously could not see him in the darkness while the man's eyes were adjusted to the light. "Sure, Colonel Craig, you walk right in and surrender and we'll let the women and kids go."

"No. You let everyone go, then I surrender." Craig moved to where he could peer between trees and clearly see the leader's face.

"Even if by some unfortunate circumstance, you *were* David Craig, you don't have that much leverage. We can take out everybody here in a few seconds then come after you, and there's nothing you can do to stop us."

"I don't think so. That may have been the case a minute ago, but it's not anymore."

Shauna's voice? It came from a few yards to Craig's right.

"Don't move or I will take your head off, Big Mouth!"

The man's face turned toward her voice. "Now we have two bluffers in the woods about to meet their makers."

A red laser flashed across the man's eyes and settled on a spot right between them.

He froze.

"I could have just gone bang, bang you're dead. But I'm giving you one more chance to put down your guns. You've got three seconds until you get a one-way trip to Hades. First, you get it, Mr. Mouth, then your Team Daddy, and then as many of the others as I can shoot before you scatter like fleas on a dog that's getting dipped."

She paused, probably waiting for a response.

Silence.

"Okay. Rest in peace."

"Okay, okay." The team leader paused. "Men put down your weapons."

"But, sir—"

"Do it, sergeant," Brutus said.

"Keep in mind," Craig said. "I am David Craig and my M4 is trained on your Team Daddy, so Shauna can take the runt and then I'll take Mr. Butterball. We can alternate through the other goons until we've got all ten."

"But if you make even one move toward the others, we'll pick you off in the order that you move that direction," Shauna said. "You will all die in the dirt of the Clear Lake parking lot. Is that clear?"

The women and children had been slowly backing away from Deke's team creating more separation and a greater likelihood that Shauna's prediction would come true.

After the guns dropped to the ground, Craig burst in to help take charge.

Shauna followed him into the open area.

"Steve, collect their guns."

"Hold it! Everybody freeze!"

Deke's voice.

How had he gotten here so quickly? He would have tried to take the short cut because he hadn't heard about the bridge being blown up. The other JLTV had already backtracked and gone the long way around.

But had Deke's JLTV actually navigated the deep lava gulley, bypassing the blown-up bridges, or running over their remains to get back on the road? Maybe Craig had underestimated the JLTVs capabilities ... either that or he underestimated Deke's desperation to get here.

"Your turn to put down your guns, Craig," Deke said. "Or I will shoot one person each minute until you do."

He snatched the closest child to him. "What's your name, little girl?" He pulled Lori to his side.

"It's Lori. Are you going to shoot me?"

"Well, Lori, if your illustrious leader will surrender his weapons to my men, nobody needs to be shot. So why don't you tell Craig to drop his guns."

"That would be a bad thing for Mr. Craig to do. I can't tell him to do bad things."

"Craig, my first hostage isn't cooperating. I'm afraid she has to be put down now. You've got ten seconds to comply or a hollow point bullet is going to—"

"That's enough, Deke." Craig couldn't see Deke after he'd stepped back in the darkness of the trees.

There was nothing Craig could try without risking an innocent person's life. And he couldn't let it be one of the children.

"As contemptible and cowardly as it was, you've made your point."

Deke stepped into the edge of the clearing. "When my men give me the all-clear, I will point my weapon at something other than insolent little Lori's head. Maybe at— what's your name, son?" He pointed at Drew and Beth's son.

"Peter."

"No!" Beth's voice. "You do anything to him, and I swear I'll rip your eyes out of your skull and nothing you can do will stop me."

Deke moved back into the shadows.

Beth took a step toward Deke's hiding spot in the trees.

"Beth, don't!" Drew's voice.

A scream pierced the soft night sounds of the forest. A man's scream. A low moan followed.

Deke's men raised their guns and pointed them in the general direction of the moaning.

"Tell Deke's men to stand down. Deke's my prisoner now." Drew's voice.

"I told you," Shauna raised the gun she still hadn't surrendered. "Drew's just like Chuck Norris."

Baker snatched an M4 from the dirt where it lay beside the man Shauna had called Mr. Mouth.

The man swung a foot at Baker's head.

Baker dodged the kick, shoved the leg further upward along its line of motion, sending the man flat on his back in the dirt.

Baker pointed the gun at Mr. Mouth's midsection and glanced at Shauna. "Like Chuck Norris? And I suppose runts get no respect," Baker said.

"I didn't say that." Shauna's voice had softened.

For the third or fourth time today, Craig debated the wisdom of letting serious relationships develop among what was rapidly becoming a co-ed combat team. Sooner or later something was going to happen, and they would all suffer when it did.

For now, it appeared to be a romantic suspense story with a happy ending. But with the challenges that still lie ahead, this was only book one of a series.

Craig prayed the final book would be named, America Restored.

Susan moved beside him at the edge of the open area. "David, do you understand now? It's God who makes heroes. He makes them out of anyone He chooses. No matter their struggles or failures, they're still heroes who we can look up to. Just like He's done with you."

Craig wrapped an arm around her as his vision blurred with unshed tears. Next time, he would remember Josh's recitation from First Samuel, "for the battle is the Lord's, and He will give you into our hands."

The enemy had ended up in David Craig's hands, but it had involved more than David Craig's efforts. And now that Deke and company had been captured, they needed to be secured before part two of this battle began.

# Chapter 31

*2:15 a.m. PDT, 5:15 a.m. EDT*

Walker's fingers drummed his desk at a frantic pace. Why was it that the people he needed to count on the most, actors where the stakes were highest, always turned out to be the most unreliable?

Deke would get an earful when he called—if he called. It was possible that he'd been killed by F-15s or shot by the militia. Possible, but not likely.

During normal times, Walker would have been fulfilling his presidential duties by preparing to host a lunch with an ambassador of some small country seeking favors, or meeting with the representative of some organization that had a complaint they thought he could help them with.

Lately, the only normal thing on his agenda was the daily intelligence briefing with the National Security Council. Only a small fraction of the usual attendees had remained in Washington DC and actually attended. And the role of the NSC, to advise and assist the president on national security and foreign policies, had dwindled to mostly internal security issues related to the *de facto* secession of several states.

Congressional members had all gone home to look after family. The president and his advisors *were* the U.S. government.

Walker did not feel at ease discussing the most sensitive security issues in the NSC meetings. Those issues he kept to himself and his Secretary of Defense, Will Richards.

Walker jumped when his cell rang the alert for an incoming call.

"This had better be Deke." He answered the call without checking the caller ID and prepared to dress Deke down.

"Deke, you had better—"

"Mr. President?"

It wasn't Deke's voice. "Excuse me, President Walker here."

"This is Colonel Towry. I take it Major Deke hasn't called you yet."

"So all the Chinooks got through, even after the problems Deke had? How did you manage that?"

"Western Air Defense Sector replaced Airman Gore, the leaker. They replaced her with a young man who understood that he should not alert the Air Guard at Portland for U.S. military aircraft operations. He should not call for interceptors unless the Russians, the Chinese, or some other hostile nation or group were attacking. Our Chinooks circled far to the east and came back in over Eastern Oregon. We don't think anyone knew about us flying to Oregon."

"Where's Deke? I haven't heard his status in several hours."

"I'm not sure of his status. He was headed for a place called Clear Lake, where some of the militia were thought to be congregating. But I haven't heard anything for a while either, and he doesn't answer when I try to call him."

"So what is your plan now?"

"We just landed in a large open area six miles west of Redmond. This location gives the troops easy access to Highway 126. We think it's inside the perimeter of the militia's sentries so we'll be approaching from behind them and can take them out as we proceed. The Chinooks need to refuel soon. We could refuel them seven miles away at Richards Field, but that's the regional airport, and it would bring more scrutiny than going to a smaller airport, like Madras."

"What do you intend to do about the possibility of encountering Harper's troops?"

* * *

Colonel Towry heard the question but chose not to reply. Instead, he would give an indirect answer and hope it would suffice. Who knew what Harper would do? But it was likely she would stay on her side of the mountains.

"Mr. President, we've studied maps of the Clear Lake area. It's an hour's drive from here, maybe two if we approach cautiously. We can move in from the north and trap any troops there against the lake. If they are there, as we expect, we can eradicate the militia's leaders. But if their families are in the way, there may be collateral damage."

"I don't care. They should know better than to take their families with them when they're in a war zone."

"Uh … Mr. President, we made it a war zone, while their families were simply living in their homes. What do you plan to tell—"

"I plan to tell the world that they're all in violation of the Constitution. They're all guilty of treason. Even their women and kids have fought for them and killed our men."

Was the president losing it? "Seriously … are you going to admit to the nation that their kids killed our seasoned warfighters and took down an attack helicopter?"

"I wouldn't couch it in those terms. But we can't let the women and children go free to spread their propaganda and lies."

"Well, don't expect me to gun them down. But if we don't do something, they will try to kill my men."

"Perhaps you should watch them until they try to attack, then kill them in self-defense."

"Sir, regardless of my orders, no commander in my situation could expect that all of his men would open fire on women and children under any circumstances."

"Then find the ones who will and have them handle the families of the militia. We don't need adolescents becoming young men and then coming after us for revenge after we kill their parents."

"We need to move out now, Mr. President."

"Very well. You have my orders, Colonel Towry."

"Yes, sir."

The president ended the call.

*Orders? I have your strong suggestions, which you carefully worded so as not to be orders. Very clever, Mr. President. But I will not fall into your trap, nor will I become your fall guy when one of my men violates the United Nations additions to the Geneva Conventions, especially Article 13, Paragraph 2. "The civilian population shall not be the object of attack."*

"Men, make sure you're ready."

"Colonel Towry, have we heard what happened to the meat eaters that beat us down here?"

"Meat eaters? Oh, you mean the special forces team Deke is leading. No, sergeant. Major Deke hasn't reported in several hours. Regardless of Deke's circumstances, and of the fact that I'd like give him a swift kick on the fourth point of contact, we meet the enemy in less than two hours. Let's move out!"

# Chapter 32

Craig's cell buzzed his leg. He pulled it out of his pocket.

What person not already in his contact list would call him at 2:30 a.m.? Maybe he should use caution when answering.

"Hello."

"Craig, this is Peterson standing watch at the Follette Butte lookout. You're not going to believe what I'm seeing."

"Peterson, weren't you supposed to be at home healing up and guarding your family?"

"If my family is going to be endangered, I will see it first from up here and can move them if needed. Don't you want to know what I saw?"

"How can you see anything at two thirty?"

"Drew gave me his NVGs. We leave them up here for whoever is on duty. You need to know what I'm seeing right now."

"Okay, shoot."

"Ten Chinook helicopters landed in a field about three miles east of here, just off Highway 126. They unloaded eight big Humvees and probably a hundred men."

"Walker's troops?"

"I'd say so. But, Craig, they're leaving now. Looks like they're heading west on 126."

"Sounds about right. They're looking for us. If Deke called in earlier, they know where we are. Good job, Peterson. Now you get home and watch out for your family. This whole area could become a battlefield. Did you see any other birds?"

"No, just the ten Chinooks."

"Let me know if you see anything else on your way home."

Craig ended the call and waved the beam of his flashlight over the cluster of men nearest him. "Listen up, everyone. We've got a minimum of about sixty minutes until Walker's troops, a hundred of them in Humvees, come driving up. Gather your gear and get ready to move out."

He turned to Steve. "You, Drew, and Baker know this area best. We need a plan to defeat a force of equal size. We've got to keep the women and kids safe and decide what to do with our prisoners."

Susan stepped into the beam of the light Craig held. "But I know the area even better than Steve. I grew up not far from here in McKenzie River."

For a moment, he studied that face now permanently etched into his memory. "So what is my Intel Specialist suggesting?"

"Hide the women and kids at Sahalie Falls. There's a loop that runs through a parking area. It's lined by trees and will hide us."

Craig's phone buzzed his leg and he pulled it out of his pocket. "It's Harper. Let me see where her troops are."

"This is Craig."

"Craig, our convoy is on Santiam Highway approaching the intersection with Highway 126."

"After you turn south on 126, you should reach the Clear Lake turn off in about fifteen minutes."

"What a night. I'll see you in a few minutes."

"Governor, the night is just beginning."

He ended the call.

"So the Guard troops will be here in fifteen minutes?" Susan looked up at him, studying his face. "You know, when you shine the flashlight up like that, your face looks rather ghoulish."

Nothing could make Susan's look anything other than beautiful, but that was an entirely inappropriate thought for a commander forming a battle plan. "Ghoulish. I've been called worse. But what were you about to tell me? Does it factor in about one hundred and fifty Guard troops?"

"It can," Susan said. "I'd put the women and kids at Sahalie Falls and leave some militia to guard the bridge just south of the lake, using one of the JLTVs."

"The JLTVs have thirty-millimeter chain guns," Steve said. "But I say we use the explosives we found in the JLTVs to rig the bridge so that, if things go badly, we can blow it to keep the women and kids safe."

Susan continued. "The lake and eventually the river encroach on the highway near the south end of the lake. Line the highway at the south end with Harper's troops all the way down to the bridge. But put them on the side opposite the lake. Then you can either chase Walker's troops or lure them down toward the bridge. You could trap them on the narrow sliver of land between the road and the lake. If Walker's troops have their backs to the water, you'd have a turkey shoot at that point."

"I agree," Steve said. "If you station the Guard along the highway on the west side, then put a strong militia force to guard the bridge—blow it up if necessary—then bring one of the JLTVs out of the Clear Lake resort entrance, we would have Walker's troops trapped on three sides, with the lake on the other side. Like Susan said, it's a turkey shoot."

Intelligence analyst, war strategist—his admiration for this woman grew with every danger they faced and every contribution she made. But this was not a time to be counting the qualities that placed Susan far above any woman Craig had ever known.

"We've only got about ten minutes to finalize our plan. What about the prisoners, Steve?"

"I'd hog-tie them, put them a safe distance south of the bridge, and leave Baker and Shauna to guard them," Steve said.

"Baker and Shauna?"

"Sir, she earned her stripes tonight. Give her some responsibility."

"Yes, she did. Okay, Steve, split our men between the two JLTVs. One JLTV, with you in it, will lure them to the bridge. I want you near the bridge in case we need to blow it. Drew, Blaine, and Rodriquez will go with me in my JLTV up to the resort turn in. That's where we'll meet the Guard and give them our plan."

"So I take my group down and get them positioned but with Baker, Shauna and the prisoners far enough on the other side of the bridge so I can blow it if necessary. Then I bring my JLTV back up 126 about a quarter mile below the turn in to the resort?"

"You got it," Craig said. "After you start luring them toward the bridge, I will use my JLTV to chase Walker's convoy toward the bridge. They probably will not want to take on a JLTV with only Humvees." He paused. "Since she knows this area, Susan can lead the wives and kids, along with our VIPs Brock and KC, Lex and Gemma, Zach and Kate, to Sahalie Falls."

"Brock and I brought our M4s along, just in case."

"So you still have those from nine years ago?" Craig grinned at KC.

"We take them out a couple of times a year—out into the desert to, you know," Brock said.

"Yeah. I know that military-issue, fully automatics are not legal. But I'm glad you have them tonight."

"Craig?" Steve waited for his attention. "Are you sure the federal troops will realize it's us in the JLTVs?"

"We have Deke's phone," Craig said. "It's rang a half-dozen times over the last hour, according to Drew. They'll know it's us and they'll chase you to the bridge. If they don't seem to be taking the bait, I'll chase them and start firing. And when you turn on them, that's the signal for the turkey shoot to begin. I'll explain it all to the Guard troops. We don't want anybody jumping the gun and alerting Walker's troops too soon."

Someone poked his shoulder. He looked down into the wide eyes of Shauna. "Craig, do you want Baker and me to march these guys down to the bridge?"

"No. Not by yourselves. After they're hog-tied, you and Baker will have them for the duration of the battle."

Craig summoned up his battlefield commander's voice. "Listen up. I need ten militia volunteers to help escort our prisoners down to where we'll hold them."

Fifteen men scurried through the throng around Craig. "Taylor, it looks like we have more than enough volunteers. I'm guessing munchkin might have something to do with that. Pick out nine other guys from the volunteers and start the prisoners down the road. Steve will show you where to put them, and I want them on their bellies, hog-tied with no possibility of escape. Their comfort is not my concern. But our security is. Gag them too. We can't take the chance that Walker's troops might hear them. Use duct tape if you need to."

Kate laid a hand on Shauna's shoulder. "You don't know how to handle a military rifle, do you?"

"If I have to I can."

"Here." Kate pulled her Sig Sauer from behind her back. "This served you well earlier. You'll need this more than I will."

"Are you comfortable with that weapon, Shauna?" Craig asked.

"Kate and I shoot it at the range at least once a month." She glared at Deke who sat on the pavement with the other prisoners. "I put the laser on his forehead while my finger was on the trigger. Is that good enough?"

Baker stepped beside Shauna. "Munchkin could have pulled the trigger if she needed to." He looked down at Deke. "Don't think this is your chance, Deke. She can use that gun. You're lucky she didn't."

Kate grinned at Shauna. "See if I give you my gun anymore. Look at all the trouble you've stirred up. Want my advice? If they wiggle, shoot them."

"You took the words out of my mouth," Baker said. "Let's go. Our escort is rounding up the prisoners for a little march."

Deke glared at Kate, then he sneered at Shauna.

Craig could envision smoke coming out of the man's ears. Deke was angry and dangerous. "Keep your eye on Deke, Baker. That man's trouble. Kate gave you two some good advice about wiggling."

"You all have your assignments. I'll call Steve, Baker, and Susan if our plans change. Now, let's move out."

Susan gripped his arm. "But, David, I thought—"

"Susan here's an M4 and Deke's Glock we confiscated. Give Kate the Glock, you take the M4. KC can show you how to use it. Once you get to the falls, you're in charge. Don't let any strangers into the Sahalie Falls turn off and keep everybody there hidden in the trees. Keep them apprised of any developments and remind them to stay out of sight. We don't want any antics, especially from the three cousins."

KC pointed at Josh, Caleb, and Benjamin. "Lex, Gemma, and I will make sure those three mind."

Beth, with Peter clinging to one hand, came alongside KC. "I'm glad Peter isn't about four or five years older."

"Three is enough," Gemma said. "I don't think Central Oregon could survive four of them."

Sam left AJ's side and stopped beside Gemma. "The boys aren't that bad. I think they're cute ... and really smart."

"It's clear what you're thinking, Sam," AJ said. "You're wishing they were about four years older."

"Mom, there aren't any boys my age in our whole group."

"Well, I think that's a good thing."

"You wouldn't if you were thirteen," Sam said.

"Let's speed it up," Susan said. "It's three o'clock, and we need to be hidden in the trees at Sahalie Falls by three thirty."

# Chapter 33

Thirty minutes later, Craig sat on top of the JLTV at the exit from Clear Lake Resort.

Vehicle lights lit the trees at the curve about a half mile up the road to the north.

It was either the Guard or Walker's army.

His cell rang.

"Craig here."

"This is Sandra Harper. Steve Bancroft said your people were in the picnic area. What's your exact location, Craig?"

"Shouldn't I be talking to your troop commander, governor?"

"Sandra will do just fine. And no, the troops gave a no-confidence vote to every commander I proposed. It seems the Oregon deep state is deeper than we thought. The men wanted someone they trusted, and I won the job."

So Sandra Harper was leading the Guard. That raised hundreds of red flags—no combat experience, no military experience for that matter. But lack of trust on her men's part—Sandra was right. For now, the commander had to be her. She had the guts for it, and her assignment tonight required little else.

"Are you still there, Craig?"

"Yes, uh ... Sandra. We're waiting in the Clear Lake Resort exit. It's about a half mile down the road from your position. Double-time it down here and we'll brief you on our plan."

"Why the hurry?"

"We might have visitors in another twenty or thirty minutes."

Craig ended the call and speed dialed Steve.

"Steve, Harper and her troops are arriving now. I'll brief them and then—"

"Hold it, sir. Don't you mean Harper's troops are arriving?"

"No. That's why I'm calling, to let you know she's commanding the Guard."

Silence.

"Think about it, Steve. The guardsmen we can trust are the same ones who now trust the governor. Who else can they trust in Western Oregon?"

"I see your point. It probably doesn't matter much anyway. After you tell them the plan and give them their assignment, they won't need much advice."

"My thoughts exactly. But let your men know so she gets the respect a commander deserves. That'll be a good bonding experience between the militia and the Guard. The Guard has probably had a tough time since the state flipped. Loss of trust. Loss of friends. Worry about their future."

"I'll let our men know, sir."

"Gotta go, Steve. Guards are here."

He slid off the JLTV and stood in front of the vehicle. "Hit the lights, Blaine."

The first Humvee braked quickly to a stop. The figure of a woman stepped out. It would have been a slender figure were it not for the police body armor she wore.

Sandra Harper pulled a combat helmet from her head and pushed the hair back that had fallen in her face. "How in heavens name did you wear something like this in Afghanistan in one hundred-ten-degree heat?" She wiped her forehead and rubbed the sweat on the pant legs of her fatigues. "So what's the plan?"

Craig unlocked the military grade F110 tablet computer and zoomed in on the map of the area. "Governor ..."

She raised her hand. "Just Sandra, please."

He nodded. "Sandra, here's where we are. In about thirty minutes or maybe a little less, they will be coming down 126, the way you just came. Our sentry said they have about a hundred men in large Humvees."

"How do we take them on? I brought one hundred fifty men. And you have about fifty?"

"Yes. And since we outnumber them, here's what we plan to do to exterminate them."

Sandra's eyes widened. "Exterminate? That's a harsh word for harsh action."

"Sandra, these are federal troops President Walker sent to wipe out the entire leadership of our militia ... while we slept ... including our wives and our children. Men capable of carrying out those kinds of unconstitutional commands deserve a harsh response."

Governor Harper blew out a sigh that sounded more like a small explosion. "Then I will tell my men about them and that we shoot to kill."

"In a firefight, that's the only way to shoot. Now let me show you our battle plan."

Craig laid out the plan that had come from Susan's sharp mind.

After the briefing, Harper strode back to her Humvee and started the Guard procession down the highway.

As Craig watched them roll down the road, something niggled just beyond the boundary of his conscious thought.

*Have I forgotten something?*

# Chapter 34

At 4:00 a.m., Craig stood on top of the JLTV. He had one hand on the M230 chain gun and the other on the battery containing four Javelin anti-tank missiles. He peered eastward through the tops of the tall, slender fir trees. The eastern horizon had brightened over the past twenty minutes, and the silence was now broken occasionally by the soft cooing of mourning doves.

Now that all of their vehicles were stopped, an eerie calm settled over the dimly lit roadway that ran along Clear Lake. What made it seem even eerier was the certainty that the calm would soon turn to chaos.

Below Craig, in the bowels of the JLTV, Drew, Blaine, and Rodriguez sat in silence. All of them had fought battles of various sorts. And, like Craig, they were probably filled with adrenaline and trying to contain the hormone's attempt to drive them into action.

In the distance, the rumble of an engine sounded.

"I hear them. Start the engine, Blaine," Craig said. "And back up about twenty feet. Make sure no lights are on except for the control panel. We don't want them to spot us when they pass by."

"Yes, sir. I'll keep us behind the trees lining the highway."

Craig waited as the familiar galloping of his heart announced the beginning of another battle.

In a couple of minutes, the first Humvee passed on the highway, traveling about forty-five miles-per-hour.

Craig counted each Humvee. Nine passed, but only unbroken darkness cloaked the road to his right.

Where was the tenth Humvee? The militia and Guard had only seconds left before they would have to spring their trap. The first Humvee should be approaching the bridge by now.

He could wait no longer, but Craig would have to keep an eye out for a Humvee behind them.

Craig crawled inside the JLTV and backed into the swing seat under the turret of the M230 chain gun. "Let's go, Blaine. Drew, if anything should happen to me, you take the weapon controls. Get ready, men. We engage them in ten to fifteen seconds."

The engine revved and they tore out onto the highway four hundred yards behind the last Humvee. Blaine drove without headlights, using the taillights of the last Humvee to navigate.

Could the troops in that last vehicle hear Craig's JLTV? Would they think it was the tenth Humvee? Probably not if they could hear the engine roaring.

"Blaine, stop at 300 meters. I'll take the last Humvee out with a Javelin and work up the line until we've shot all four. I'll save the chain gun for number five, if Steve doesn't get it before us."

"Preparing to stop at 300 meters, sir."

The deceleration swung Craig forward in the seat that resembled an old-fashioned playground swing. He caught himself with one hand against the side of the turret narrowly missing the weapons-control monitor that he would soon use to acquire his target.

He scanned the screen and the controls. Craig had studied them, but this would be his first time to shoot either the anti-tank missile or the thirty-millimeter cannon. The cannon's one-hundred-dollar bullets measured nearly a foot long, and they could penetrate nearly an inch of steel.

With that kind of firepower, he couldn't afford to let the target acquisition system select the wrong target. Steve and his team would be only a thousand yards ahead ... directly ahead. Beyond Steve and the bridge, Shauna and Baker held the prisoners. They were more vulnerable than Steve in the JLTV.

Missiles hit their targets and exploded there. But the big chain gun bullets would keep traveling until something stopped them. Craig would avoid using the chain gun unless Blaine could give him an angle that wouldn't send ricocheting bullets beyond the bridge toward Baker and Shauna.

Steve's headlights appeared in the distance. He had turned around.

The line of Humvees stopped. They sensed the danger.

Craig marked the nearest Humvee and fired the first of his four Javelin missiles.

A brilliant blast obliterated the Humvee before Craig heard the explosion.

He waited for the smoke to clear, then he marked and fired on the second Humvee. It disappeared in flames and smoke.

The other Humvee drivers evidently realized their peril. The third and fourth Humvees turned, one to the right, the other to the left, trying to find cover in the trees along the road.

The one that turned right ran directly into Harper's troops' gunfire. They would make short work of the vehicle and any men who tried to jump out and run away.

The Humvee that turned left hit a steep bank at the roadside. Before it could negotiate the bank, Craig's third missile gave the would-be murderers in it a foreshadowing of Hades.

The fifth Humvee was Craig's. Its driver tried a bold maneuver. It turned and accelerated directly at Craig's JLTV. The attempt may have been bold, but it was stupid.

Craig fired his last Javelin and, in a white flash, the Humvee disassembled in a few microseconds.

The battle, if one can call a one-sided affair a battle, had lasted a little more than a minute.

The only thing moving on the battlefield was Steve's JLTV. It seemed to be crawling toward them.

"Approach the Humvees with caution, Blaine. Watch for any survivors, men. I doubt that we will find any. But if you see anyone on foot, be cautious. They will be desperate."

"You got it, sir," Blaine said. "Approaching cautiously."

Craig switched to the M230. He pointed the powerful gun off to the left side of Steve's vehicle and away from Harper's Guard in the trees on the right.

Now that the cacophony of rifles, rockets and explosions had ended, an eerie silence pervaded, despite the destruction covering the road ahead. Even the few remaining flames licked silently at the flammable materials on the Humvees.

As the JLTV reached the remains of the first Humvee, the odor of death brought back unwelcome memories and emotions from Northern Afghanistan, the place where young Lieutenant Craig had failed his team and sent most of them to their graves.

It had not been that way today, but the day wasn't over until the tenth Humvee and its men had been accounted for.

Blaine zigzagged through Humvee carnage until they met Steve's JLTV coming from the opposite direction, taking a similar inventory.

When an antitank missile hit an unarmored Humvee, the devastation was complete. And as Craig suspected, there were no survivors.

But thoughts about the missing Humvee niggled.

Before anybody began celebrating their victory, Craig needed to check with Baker near the bridge and Susan two miles down the road.

He called Baker first.

"Baker here."

"Baker, are you and Shauna okay?"

"We're fine. Shauna is a bit shaken up, but—"

"What happened?"

"Sometime during Steve's onslaught with the JLTV, an RPG shot came from one of the Humvees. It was a bit high and landed in the ditch on the other side of the road."

"First time in a combat situation, with explosions around you, can shake a person up," Craig said.

"That's not it, sir. When the smoke cleared and our ears stopped ringing, we noticed Deke had disappeared."

"Disappeared? But he was hog tied."

"Yes, he was, sir. We don't have a clue how he got loose. But one thing's for sure, he had to go south, either down the road, or down the river. Either way, he—"

"He'll be headed toward Susan and the kids. How long ago was that?"

"A couple of minutes."

"In another ten minutes Deke could be at the falls. Watch the others, Baker. I'll be coming through shortly headed toward Sahalie Falls."

*And we still don't know where the tenth Humvee went.*

# Chapter 35

*8:30 a.m., Washington, DC*

Walker's gut twisted with the strong premonition that something had gone wrong. He had placed four calls to Deke and had heard nothing from him.

In late July, it would already be daylight on the West Coast. Something must have gone wrong.

His secure cell vibrated and danced where he'd set it on his desktop.

Victory dance or writhing in agony?

The caller ID said it was Towry calling. Walker would soon find out.

"President Walker."

"Mr. President, I wanted to let you know about a modification of our plans."

"Have you heard from Major Deke?"

"No, sir. That is a concern, but Deke tends to be a lone wolf. I wanted to tell you that my troops should be engaging the militia about now. I took a few men and a Humvee and circled the mountain in the opposite direction in case the militia tried to escape or evacuate their families using this route."

"Where are you now Colonel Towry and have you seen any militia?"

"My Humvee has reached Highway 126 and we are approaching Clear Lake from the south. It's about five miles ahead. We've heard no sounds of conflict yet, but I assume we'll find my men and the militia near Clear Lake. I need to end this call and prepare for a skirmish."

"Very well. But when you find Deke, make sure he finished his job."

"Yes, Mr. President."

*The job you wouldn't do, Gutless Wonder.*

\* \* \*

Colonel Towry snorted in derision then tucked his phone into his pocket.

Make sure Deke finished his job? President Walker probably meant slaughtering the militia leadership's families.

A president who violates the Geneva Conventions when fighting a civil war in his own country—who would punish him for it? Nobody, unless Walker were impeached. And if that happened, Towry was inclined to testify against the president.

The Humvee slowed to a stop and the headlights went off.

"Sir, we saw some flashes of light ahead on the left. We're close enough to Clear Lake that it's a concern."

"We'd better investigate, Ramsey. We can't afford to be caught in an ambush. You take our men with you and work your way up the river to that open area where the flashes of light came from. Take as much time as you need to make sure no one sees you. Text me what you find. In the meantime, I'll wait here to watch our vehicle and answer any incoming calls."

"Rogers, Cummings, let's move out." Ramsey and the other two slid out of the Humvee and disappeared into the trees on the left.

Towry sat alone in the front seat of the Humvee. "Now I wait and hope this solves the mystery of disappearing Deke."

\* \* \*

211

Susan stood near the entrance to the Sahalie Falls parking area. It was rather small for such a well-visited tourist attraction. And the parking lot consisted of two adjacent loops with parking on the outside of each loop.

She had just checked the loop closest to the falls and intended to check the loop nearest the highway on her way back to her post, where she guarded the entrance.

Trees and bushes lined the sides of the loops. There were so many that someone could—

Arms circled her from behind, capturing her arms with a ferocious bear hug.

Susan gasped then reacted. She pushed her gun away from her body.

The arms loosened but then resumed their powerful squeezing in an even stronger bear hug.

She whipped her body in a violent twist to her left.

That maneuver exposed one side of the person behind her.

She jammed the butt of the M4 into the person's groin.

The voice of a man moaned, and he lost his grip on her.

She yelled a warning, "Brock, KC, attack!"

The attacker was all over her now. Sticky hands that smelled like dirt clamped over her mouth.

An arm wrapped around her neck and squeezed the sides of her neck by bending the elbow.

No choking sensation. That surprised her. So did the early morning gray fading to black.

When she awakened, she had obviously been out for only few seconds.

The man holding her had one arm wrapped around her and a handgun pointed at her head.

That didn't matter. She needed to warn the others. "Brock, KC, don't negotiate with these terrorists!"

"Shut up, Carrot Top, before I scatter your brains and red hair all over this parking lot."

Another man stepped into the open dragging Peter and seven-year-old Lori.

A tall man emerged pushing Itzy and Sam with his weapon and eyeing the two beautiful girls in a way that revealed the evil running through his mind.

The man holding Susan told her again to shut up. "Listen, if you people want to keep your sons and daughters safe, all you have to do is come out into the parking lot and put down your weapons."

"We've got no choice." KC's voice.

"Yes, we do, Kace." Brock's voice. "Regardless of what happens here, these men are dead. They just don't know it yet."

"Good try, Hulk." The man glared at Brock. "Don't even bother trying to explain. I'm not listening to any of your bull. Just get everyone who's hiding back in those trees out here, now, or we start shooting the kids. One every minute until—"

"You wouldn't dare!" Susan wrenched free from his grasp and whirled to face him.

He shoved his handgun against her forehead.

"Don't provoke him, Susan," Brock said.

"That's good advice, Carrot Top. Better listen to Hulk over there."

"You don't know who he is, do you?" Susan met the man's gaze as he ground the barrel into the skin on her forehead.

"Don't know and don't care."

"He's Brock Daniels," Jeff said as he and Allie moved into the open. "Normally, I would warn you about harming such an American icon. You'd have two-thirds of this nation after your head. But, like Brock, said, you won't live that long."

"All right," the man said. "Mr. Not-an-icon, how am I and my three buddies destined to die?"

213

"He's an American icon too." Allie's voice. "Jeff Jacobs is an Olympic Gold Medalist who holds a world record."

"In what, synchronized swimming? Ice Dance?"

"The decathlon," Allie said. "If you macho men, who talk big and hold guns on little kids, tried to take on Brock and Jeff in a fair fight, you three would get the ever-lovin' crud beat out of—"

"Enough, Allie," Jeff said. "No matter what you say, there won't be a fair fight. Regardless, these men won't live much longer. The shooting and the rockets ended a while ago. Their people are probably all dead."

The man's arm squeezed tighter on Susan and each powerful breath blew her hair. "You mean *yours* are dead, because we killed them with our JLTVs."

"No." Susan said. "Our men, led by Colonel Craig, captured Walker's black ops team and took their JLTVs. They used them to destroy the rest of your troops that came in Humvees. And they will come here looking for us, if we don't answer when they call, and they will kill you."

"She's lying, Ramsey," one of the other men said.

"I agree, Rogers." He gripped her shoulder and spun her around. "That's a tall tale, isn't it, Carrot Top."

She opened her mouth to flame him with words worthy of an angry, stereotypical, Irish redhead.

"Susan," Brock said. "Don't."

Brock was right. They needed to keep the kids safe. They needed to comply with these men's demands for now and wait for a chance to turn the tables. It would come whenever Craig came. But first there would probably be a phone call from him. She needed to be prepared with the right words, provided these scoundrels would let her answer the call.

"Everybody else, out of the woods before we start shooting the kids."

Beth, Lex and Gemma, Hunter and AJ, Kate and Zach emerged from the shadowy darkness of the trees into the early morning twilight.

One of the men took their guns.

But where were the three boys? They didn't come out and their parents, Lex, Gemma, KC, and Brock, didn't mention their boys.

# Chapter 36

*6:00 a.m.*

Josh scampered through the forest. He headed southward, away from the falls. It was the direction the three men must have come from. He turned to look behind him. "Cabe, Benj, hurry up. We've got to find their Humvee and make sure they can't get away."

Benjamin pulled alongside Josh. "Why do we want to keep those men here?"

Josh huffed a sigh. Surely Benj could figure that part out, but they didn't have time for twenty-one questions. "Because all our families are hostages, even Sam and Itzy."

Caleb poked him in the back. "The girls? Josh, why'd you mention the girls. We're too young for girls. Besides, they're too old for us."

"That's not the point." Josh slowed to a walk and gave the other two the stop sign. "As long as those men need hostages, all our people will be safe. We've got to keep them alive until Craig comes to rescue them. If we mess up their Humvee so it can't be fixed, they'll need hostages, because they can't get away without the Humvees."

Josh turned and angled through the trees toward the highway.

A Humvee came into view.

He planted both feet in the forest floor and stopped.

Someone had parked it on the side of the road.

Josh started to point toward the abandoned vehicle, but nearly choked when he sucked in a breath.

The driver's door had swung open.

A man in uniform climbed out.

"There's a soldier in it," Benjamin said. "What do we do now?"

"He's not wearing a helmet and he's not carrying a gun," Caleb said.

"It's probably in the seat beside him." Josh paused.

They needed a powerful weapon. "Benj, do you still have your slingshot in your pocket?"

"Yeah. It's the one Dad and I made out of surgical rubber tubing."

"What's the best ammo you got? Rocks?"

"No. I've got some four-ounce lead fishing weights. Dad gave them to me in case I ever needed something like a gun. He said I didn't need a carry permit for a slingshot even though it was probably more powerful than some handguns."

"If you shoot as hard as you can, how powerful are those lead weights?" Josh said.

"I shot one clear through the half-inch plywood that we mounted our target on. Dad said it might crack a man's skull or go clear through it into his brain. Either way, it could kill a person. And if I hit somebody in the chest, it could break ribs. It might even stop their heart."

"Okay. It'll have to do," Josh said. "But we've got to surprise him."

"And since it's my slingshot, I suppose that I have to shoot him," Benjamin said.

"Yeah." Josh stretched the rubber of an imaginary slingshot. "You get to do the honors. But you've got to sneak up behind him. Get so close you can't miss. And, Benj ... shoot him in the head."

Benjamin grimaced.

"You have to do it, Benj, because you're a year older than Cabe and me. You can shoot it harder."

Benjamin nodded. "Suppose I knock him out. What then? Do we have to decapitate him?"

"I think you mean incapacitate," Josh said.

Caleb gave the slit throat gesture. "I think that lead weight could almost do what you said, Benj."

"After we knock him out, we have to get rid of the Humvee," Josh said.

"We could take the keys," Benjamin said.

"No. They might hotwire it," Caleb said. "We have to figure out how to drive it and wreck it so they can't use it."

"We can't work the pedals and see out at the same time. If one of us drives it, we'd wreck it for sure," Benjamin said.

"But look at that steep bank up ahead. It goes all the way down to the river."

"Now you're thinking, Josh," Benjamin said. "And I heard that all the military vehicles have granny gears."

Caleb's forehead wrinkled. "What's a granny gear?"

"Makes it go really slow and have a lot of power. It just keeps on going even if you don't press on the gas."

"Then we'll figure out how to do that and give it a trip to the river."

"We'd better pray the river's deep enough to drown the engine or—"

"See that bank?" Josh said. "Even if it doesn't die, they would have to escape by pulling it out using one of the JLTVs, but we have them all."

Benjamin had a funny look on his face, half grinning and half scared.

"What are you thinking, Benj?" Josh studied that look and shivered. Whatever Benj had in mind, it was going to be dangerous. But it would also be fun.

Josh pointed ahead. "Go up to the road about fifty yards, Benj, and sneak across while he's not watching."

"Look," Caleb said. "He's staring toward the falls."

"And now he's getting a phone call," Josh said. "I'll distract him when you come around the Humvee behind him. But you gotta get so close that you can't miss."

"Josh, you and I should walk out and let him see us while Benj makes his shot," Caleb said.

"Okay. That's our plan. Go, Benj."

A minute later, Benjamin was sneaking through the bushes and trees on the far side of the road, moving steadily toward the Humvee, keeping it between him and the man.

Josh tugged on Caleb's hand and they scurried to a position about ten yards in front of the Humvee.

When he and Caleb stepped onto the road, Josh hadn't a clue what the man's reaction would be.

"Come on, Cabe. Time to distract him." He pulled on Caleb's arm.

Caleb didn't move. "Josh, do you think he might shoot us?"

"No. Who's gonna shoot two harmless nine-year-olds?"

"He would if anybody told him we took down an Apache."

"Can't change our plans now. Let's go." Josh tugged again and Caleb followed.

They stepped out onto the roadway and walked side-by-side toward the soldier.

He jerked around to face them and raised his gun.

"We're lost," Josh said.

Benjamin crept around the Humvee and slowly stretched the powerful rubber tubing on his slingshot.

Josh tried to watch Benjamin but keep his eyes on the man with the eagles sewn on his uniform. He must be a colonel.

"Stop, you two." The man held his rifle like he was ready to use it, but he had pointed it down toward the pavement.

Benjamin let his lead weight fly.

It parted the man's hair as it flew over his head.

"What the—" He turned toward Benjamin and the rifle swung upward.

"I can't look." Cabe covered his eyes.

Benjamin had another lead weight loaded and the rubber stretched all the way.

But who was going to win the shootout?

The man's mouth dropped open and he hesitated when he saw Benjamin. Then he raised the gun all the way.

Benjamin let go and a thud sounded.

The sound made Josh's stomach roil.

Blood splattered from the man's forehead and he crumpled in slow motion to the ground.

The man hadn't shot and he wasn't moving.

"Come on, Cabe." Josh ran to the man and picked up his rifle. "Here, hold it, Cabe."

Benjamin scurried to Josh's side.

Josh placed two fingers on the man's neck. A steady pulse. "He's alive."

"Yeah," Benjamin said. "He's still breathing. So we'd better hurry."

"Hold the gun on him, Cabe. If he tries to get up, pull the trigger."

"Maybe the safety is on. I don't know how—"

"He was about to shoot Benjamin. The safety won't be on."

Josh and Benjamin climbed into the Humvee. There were too many gauges and switches to figure them all out.

Josh looked for keys and the gear shift. "Look. Above the key. It shows how to start, run it, and stop it."

"But, Josh, it has two shifters."

"We want to go as slow as we can. I think we need to start it in N and shift this other one to L, and this one to 1."

"What then?" Benjamin asked.

"We should start rolling down the road. Then we open our doors and get ready to jump. I'll turn off the road between those trees."

He looked out at Caleb holding the gun on the man. "Is he still out, Cabe?"

"Yeah. But he moaned and moved a little."

"If his eyes open, tell him you'll shoot if he even wiggles. And if he does, you gotta do it, Cabe."

"You guys hurry so I don't have to do it."

"I put the gear shift on the N, Josh."

Josh turned the key to start. "It won't start. Maybe it has to be in P to start. Like our dad's cars."

Benjamin pushed the lever to P.

Josh hit start.

The engine turned, sputtered a few times, and started.

He scooted forward on the seat until his toe reached the gas pedal. He pushed the pedal and the engine revved.

"Okay, Benj. Push the gear shifter to 1 and then the other to L."

"Here goes."

The truck lurched, then crept ahead on the roadway traveling at less than walking speed.

Josh turned the wheel until he was following the centerline of the highway. "Push your door open all the way, Benj. When we go over the edge, we jump out and roll away from the Humvee so it can't run over us."

Josh cranked the wheel hard right. The big vehicle slowly angled to the right and headed toward the steep bank along the river. He steered for the opening between the trees.

"Jump, Benj."

Josh landed on the edge of the drop-off. His feet clawed for traction on the steep bank. His hands had found a small bush. He grabbed it and pulled.

Crashing noises below grew louder.

The engine sped up, followed by a big splash.

Then noises came from the river. They sounded like a monstrous snake hissing and Josh's dad gargling with mouthwash both at the same time.

Josh pulled himself onto the shoulder of the road and looked down.

Only the top of the cab was visible.

The engine noises stopped.

The Humvee had drowned.

Benjamin hurried to Josh's side. "We did it, Josh. But we better go back and help Caleb."

Caleb stood in a firing position with the gun barrel pointing at the man's stomach. "Don't even think about it. This is an automatic. I can cut you in half."

"Don't do anything crazy like that, kid."

"Kids do crazy things all the time. You read about them on the front page of the paper."

Josh and Benjamin ran to Caleb's side.

"Josh, I don't think he believes I'll shoot him. That almost got him killed."

Benjamin pulled his slingshot from his backpack. "I have another lead weight. I can shoot him in the head again."

The man swore. "Don't do that, kid. Just tell me what you want me to do."

"We need something to tie him with," Josh said.

"But he'll grab us if we get that close," Caleb said.

"Not if I stand with my slingshot aimed at his head while you hold the rifle on him."

"Mister," Josh said. "Is there tape in the Humvee?"

"Yes. In the first aid kit under the driver's seat."

"But it's underwater, Josh." Benjamin said.

"What did you do to my Humvee, kid?" He looked right at Josh.

"It repented of doing all that bad stuff, so we baptized it," Benjamin said.

Caleb laughed.

The colonel mumbled something that didn't sound very nice.

"I can get the tape. I can stay underwater longer than you guys," Josh said. "Be right back. Both of you shoot him if he moves."

Josh ran down the road to where the Humvee went over the edge.

He slid down the bank and stopped at the edge of the river. He peeled off his shoes, shirt, and socks, then waded into the icy water.

It was torture to stay underwater while his head turned to an ice cube and froze his brain. But a few moments later, he had the first aid kit in hand, and he waded out of the river.

Josh pulled the tape from the box. It looked and felt like Duct Tape. It wasn't gray, but it would do.

He put on his clothes, scrambled up the bank, and ran back to Caleb and Benjamin. "Here's the tape." He turned to the man lying on the pavement. "Listen, mister, because I won't repeat my instructions. It would be a lot easier to shoot you than to tie you up."

"Get on with it, kid. But you do know about my men who went after the people—probably your parents."

"We know, and that's why I'm thinking we should just shoot you to even the odds."

The man moaned again. "Just use the tape, since you went through all the trouble of fishing it out of the river."

"How did you know the Humvee was in the river?"

"I heard the splash," the man said.

"Crawl on your stomach to the edge of the road and hang your head and shoulders into the ditch but keep your hands behind you all the time."

"That's pretty smart, Josh," Caleb said. "He can't try anything without ending up in the ditch."

"He's crawling too slow," Benjamin said. "I think he's stalling. Probably hoping his men will get here."

Benjamin picked up a marble-sized rock, placed it in the slingshot's pouch, and sent it zinging into the man's somewhat over-sized rear end.

The man said some words Josh wasn't allowed to use, then he groaned. "Cut it out, kid." But he did crawl faster.

"What do we do if his men show up?" Caleb said.

Benjamin shrugged. "We either shoot him and run or use him for a hostage."

The crawler had reached the ditch and his head hung out over the four-foot-deep trench.

"Put your feet together." Josh kicked one foot.

The man slid his black boots together.

Josh ripped off his chukka boots and taped his ankles together. He held up the boots. "We'll throw these into the river."

"Kid, don't do that. I'll need shoes whenever I walk out of here."

Josh ignored him. "Get ready to shoot while I tape his wrists. At least he can't kick us now."

Josh wrapped five layers of strong tape around the man's wrists.

"Better do his mouth too," Caleb said.

"Yeah. So he can't holler for help," Benjamin said.

Josh slid down into the ditch, then he turned to face the man.

The man craned his neck up.

Josh stared into the man's glaring eyes.

He moaned again.

"What's your name, mister?"

"I can't tell you."

"That's a lie. In the movies, it says you're allowed to give your name, rank, and social security number."

"Serial number, kid. But my name is Towry. Colonel Towry."

Benjamin stepped beside the man and drew his slingshot. "We knew you were a colonel."

"Yeah, because you had the birdbrain insignificant on your collar," Caleb said.

"Insignia," the colonel said. "And the bird is an eagle."

"But birdbrain is right," Caleb said. "What colonel would let three boys shoot him with a slingshot, capture him, and take his Humvee and wreck it."

Standing in the ditch looking at the colonel, Josh almost felt sorry for him. But that was quickly replaced by anger when he thought of those men capturing his mom and dad and all the others.

Josh slapped the tape across the man's mouth and wrapped it twice around his head.

There, it was done. He wouldn't be going anywhere or saying anything until someone came to free him.

"Come on, guys," Josh said. "We need to see what they've done with our parents."

"There were *three* men. We could surprise them and get two at once with the rifle and my slingshot," Benjamin said.

"That would still leave one to shoot us. And what if you missed?" Josh said. "If they're holding everybody captive, we need to sneak by the falls, on the other side of the road, and go back to where Shauna and Baker are. They can call Craig to help us."

"If Craig's still alive," Benjamin said.

"Benj, you heard Craig's plan," Caleb said. "And you heard the shooting stop. So who do you think got killed?"

"You're right," Benjamin said. "Craig probably blew them all up with his missiles."

"Let's go call him," Josh said. "But be really quiet when we pass the Sahalie Falls turnoff. If one of those men spotted us, we'd be toast. And, Cabe, if anything happens and you think you need to shoot that rifle, be sure you know who you're shooting at."

"Yeah, be careful," Benjamin said. "My mom says the barrel keeps trying to go up if you shoot in automatic mode. And you never want to shoot a bullet straight up."

"I know," Caleb said. "We tried that out in the field with a bow and arrow. Did you know an arrow from a homemade longbow can go clear through the roof of a big Dodge pickup?"

# Chapter 37

"Blaine, it's 6:30 a.m.. We need to check on Shauna and Baker and the prisoners," Craig said.

"Crossing the bridge now, sir. We'll be there in just a moment."

"They had the prisoners spread across the roadway. Although it's tempting, Blaine, try not to run over those would-be murderers."

Susan hadn't answered her phone on his last two attempts and they still had one Humvee unaccounted for. Those two puzzling occurrences may not be a coincidence. "If Baker and Shauna aren't having any problems, we need to continue on ASAP to Sahalie Falls."

"I see Shauna, Baker, and their captives," Drew said.

Craig studied Shauna's face. She looked worried.

After Blaine stopped the JLTV, Craig and Drew hopped out.

He scanned the hog-tied prisoners as he walked by them.

Shauna met his gaze then hung her head. "Yeah. We're short one. During the shooting, somehow, Deke escaped."

"Escaped after the way we hog tied them?"

"The last time I saw him he was flying down the bank, and then he dove into the river. I watched for about five minutes but never saw him."

"That's not all the bad news," Craig said. "Susan's not answering her cell. That missing Humvee might have something to do with that. I think we could use some help from the Oregon Guard."

He called Harper.

"Well, did we get all of them, Craig?"

"We did, governor. But I could use about half of your men to help me with a situation."

Craig explained his concern about Susan and the others at Sahalie Falls and about the Humvee still unaccounted for.

"I'll send fifty of my guardsmen in Humvees now."

"Tell them to stop near my JLTV and we can formulate a plan. Maybe I'll know more by the time they arrive."

They ended the call.

When Craig looked up after slipping his cell in his pocket, Shauna walked his way with a hand on Benjamin's shoulder and the twins followed behind them.

What were they doing here and where were their parents? Regardless, maybe now he would get some answers about events at the falls.

The expression on the twins' faces twisted his gut in a knot. Something had happened and it wasn't anything good.

"Well, here they are, sir," Shauna said. "I'll let them tell you their story. These guys aren't in the habit of lying, are they?"

"No. But I suppose there's always a first time. Benjamin, Josh, Caleb, what happened at Sahalie Falls?"

Josh stepped in front of Benjamin.

Shauna backed away and stood, listening.

"Craig, sir, some soldiers sneaked in around us. One of them captured Susan then used her to get the rest of us."

"Then how did you three get here?"

"It's a long story."

"I need the short version, especially if the others are in danger. Let's hear it. Now, Josh."

"We snuck back into the woods and got away, but we discovered the Humvee the men came in. But there was a man there, Colonel Towry, the commander."

"You obviously got away from him. What happened?"

"We snuck up on the colonel and knocked him out. We knew the men couldn't leave if they didn't have a Humvee. Then they would have to keep everybody alive to use as hostages, so we taped up Colonel Towry, destroyed their Humvee, and came back here to tell you."

"Josh, I need the truth. Your mom's and dad's lives depend on it."

"I told you the truth."

"Can this Colonel Towry get away?"

"Not after what we did to him," Caleb said.

"All right. Into the JLTV, guys. I'm belting you in and you will stay in that seat until I say you can get out. Got it?"

"We got it, sir," Josh said.

Drew chuckled, then his face turned serious again. Beth was one of the hostages as was their four-year-old son, Peter.

"Blaine, take us to Sahalie Falls, but ease in quietly and stop about four hundred yards this side of the turn in."

"You got it, Colonel Craig."

The JLTV circled the hog-tied bodies on the road and headed south on the highway.

"Now tell me how you destroyed a Humvee."

"We drowned it," Caleb said.

"Save that story for later unless you think there's some way they might be able to make it run again."

"They would have to pull it out of the river and fix a lot of stuff," Benjamin said.

"How did you knock out Colonel Towry?"

"Benjamin did it with his slingshot."

"And you weren't playing David and Goliath and imagined this whole thing?"

"No," Josh said. "We don't lie. I just hope Colonel Towry doesn't have allergies."

"Allergies?" Craig studied Josh's face. "What did you do to him?"

"I told you. We taped him up really good. And we gagged him with tape. I'm afraid he might die if his nose gets plugged up."

"Yeah. He couldn't breathe," Caleb said.

"I don't think you have to worry about that. Adrenaline is a pretty effective antihistamine," Craig said. "He'll be able to breathe."

"Probably breathing fire after what the boys did to him," Blaine said. "Stopping just ahead, sir."

"And you're sure that there were three gunmen?" Craig asked.

"Yeah," Caleb said. "They had guns that looked just like yours."

"Thanks for your help. Now you three stay here or you could be endangering your parents."

"We'll stay," Josh said.

"Harper's men approaching from behind, sir."

"Blaine, you stay here and guard this vehicle with your life. If you can handle it, man the chain gun from the turret. Just be careful what target you acquire, because that gun can make Swiss Cheese out of a metal vehicle."

"I can handle the M230, sir."

Craig climbed out of the JLTV and soon Harper's troops formed a tight semi-circle around him.

"Men …" Craig kept his voice low, "… we have a hostage situation in the parking area at the falls. We will surround the Sahalie Falls parking area, then slowly move in."

He scanned the men around him. "If any of you have not had stealth training, step forward."

Three men and a young woman stepped forward.

"You four will remain on the highway until we make our move," Craig said. "You will guard the entrance to the falls. Don't let anyone in military garb escape through the entrance. They do not have any motor vehicles, so they'll be on foot. Just make sure you pick a spot for cover in case shooting starts. If we do our job right, there will be no shooting."

Craig paused. "The rest of us will surround the double-loop parking area using stealth techniques to move through the surrounding forest. But I want everybody in position, completely surrounding the parking area."

"I need three snipers who will acquire targets closest to the captives. We have intelligence that told us there are three men in military garb."

Six men stepped forward.

"You six pick your best three snipers. Remember, the militia men have wives, kids, and fiancées among the hostages. Don't volunteer unless you can handle this assignment."

Two men stepped back. After a short conversation, another man moved back.

"You three who stepped back, we need you to be spotters for the three who will do the shooting. Pick your partner now, and when we move out, stick with them.

"After we're in position, I'll announce our presence and do the negotiation. Snipers, if you see that a hostage will be killed, shoot if at all possible. But once a shot is fired, the other two snipers must take out their targets. You six will remain in proximity while in the woods, so coordinate to make sure you've got the targets covered between the three shooters."

"We'll split the group right here." He made a chopping motion with his hand. "I'll lead the right half as we circle to the right around the area. Drew, you lead the left half."

"Are there any questions?"

No one spoke.

"Let's move out."

He prayed God would guide him through the hostage rescue. This time he was confident God would answer and would direct his steps. But what frightened Craig was what God might allow to happen.

# Chapter 38

Craig had moved with stealth and in eight minutes deployed his half of the men in a semicircle in the trees surrounding the parking area.

In another minute, Drew approached from the other direction and flashed the okay signal.

Good. They had made it in less than ten minutes. After that amount of time, things might be overheating in the parking area.

Craig gave the signal to slowly close in, tightening the circle as much as possible without being detected.

He peered between branches of a thick bush. What he saw jolted him.

One of the men was trying to force the barrel of his gun inside Lori's mouth. Allie was crying and Jeff looked like he was about to jump the guy, but the gun in Lori's face restrained him.

*Time to put an end to this.*

He took a deep breath and prepared to announce his presence. "Colonel Craig, Oregon militia! The militia and Oregon Guard have you surrounded. Put down your weapons.

The apparent leader jerked away from Lori and scanned the trees in Craig's vicinity.

"Guns to their heads, guys." Two put guns to KC's and Brock's heads, while the leader held his gun against Susan's head. "Back off or your civilians are dead."

"That's a good one," Craig said. "All your people *are* dead. Looks like there are only three left and there are snipers with guns on each one of you. It's finished. Put down your guns."

"And why should we believe you?"

"Because we took Deke and his men and commandeered their JLTVs. The road is guarded by those vehicles, with their M230s and four missiles apiece."

"Like I said, why should we believe you?"

"Men, by my command, close on the parking area."

A line of troops appeared surrounding the area with rifles in a ready position. "Maybe you believe me now."

The man looked around. "Tell your men to open up and let us pass through or we'll kill these three."

"If I give the signal, or they feel it's justified, bullets traveling at Mach 3 will drop you before you can even squeeze the trigger."

"Are you willing to bet her life on that?" The man beside Susan pushed the gun into the center of her back. "Rumor has it that she's your girl, Colonel Craig."

"Don't listen to him, David."

"Shut up you..." The vile description he gave of Susan pushed Craig to the limits of his patience.

They had to stop this now.

Susan dropped to the ground. Two shots rang out. KC and Brock had also dropped.

Four more shots.

It was over.

Three stubborn, vile men had gotten themselves killed. Perhaps they deserved it. Craig would leave that up to God. But right now, he felt no remorse.

Susan ran into his arms.

"I'm sorry, David I didn't hear them sneaking up from the south." She pressed her forehead into his chest.

"It's not your fault, Susan. If it's anyone's fault it's mine."

When she looked up into his eyes, he tried to maintain some measure of dignity as he stroked Susan's cheek, then released her.

He scanned the group of people around them. "Is everybody okay?"

"We think so," KC said. "But Benjamin and the twins disappeared."

"We have them safe and belted into my JLTV. And according to them, they shot the Colonel, the commander of Walker's troops, disabled his Humvee by sending it into the river, left the colonel with a likely concussion and tied up with Duct Tape along the side of the road a quarter of a mile from here."

"That sounds like a story they would tell," Brock said.

"No," Gemma replied. "It sounds like something they would *do*."

"A concussion?" Lex said. "I'll bet Benjamin shot the guy in the head with his slingshot."

"Using the four-ounce lead weight I gave him," Brock said. "The guy's lucky he didn't get his skull cracked open."

"We'll pick up the colonel on the way back to the bridge, where we'll meet with Harper to debrief. But despite losing track of one Humvee that circled the mountains to the south of us and surprised us, we won an overwhelming victory."

"All of Deke's men left alive are in custody, except for Deke. He escaped during the firefight. All of Walker's troops are dead, except their commander, the colonel, who has probably had every bit of his dignity stolen by Benjamin and the twins."

"We've confiscated all the federal troops' weapons and ammo." He paused. "And I had a call from our sentry at Follette Butte, John Peterson. He spotted the Chinooks when they arrived with Walker's troops in them and he warned us. Now, we have added ten Chinooks to our army.

"I'm hoping that we can get some pilots from the Pendleton Guard to fly them for us. If so, I think we just formed the Central Oregon Air Cavalry. With those birds, we can deploy three hundred troops from Redmond to any place in the state in one hour. That should make Walker think twice about attacking us or any target in Western Oregon. Good job, everybody. Let's go palaver with Harper, then go home."

"Drew, take everyone to the road. They can ride back to the bridge in the Guard's Humvees. We'll be there in a few minutes after we take the JLTV to pick up Colonel Towry. Men ... and women, let's go."

When Craig turned to walk back to the JLTV, Susan blocked his path. "With a dozen extra people, those Humvees will be overloaded. May I—"

"Yes, you may. If you don't mind three boys exaggerating their exploits each time they tell you about them."

With Susan safe by his side while they walked back to the JLTV, Craig relaxed for the first time in two days.

As they approached, Blaine waved to them from his perch on top of the vehicle.

"Craig, looks like a successful extraction."

He opened the JLTV back door for Susan. "Unfortunately for the bad guys, their sort seldom shows common sense. We shot them all."

"What do you mean by 'their sort'," Susan climbed in behind the shotgun seat.

"These guys were not the cream of the crop, the 'proud to be an American' type. Susan, they were willing to torture civilians, even little kids, even murder them to obey unconstitutional orders from a compromised president."

Susan's gaze dropped to the floorboard. "There were other types of threats, but we don't need to get into that."

"Are we gonna' pick up Colonel Towry?" Josh hollered from the far rear corner seat.

"If he's alive, we'll pick him up."

Blaine climbed into the driver's seat and fired up the engine.

"We didn't mean to kill him," Josh said. "But I've never gagged anybody before."

"If anything might kill him, it was the concussion I gave him with the lead weight," Benjamin said.

Blaine accelerated up to about forty-five miles-per-hour. "How far up the road, guys?"

"Don't worry. You'll see him," Josh said.

"Yeah." Caleb said. "When you see something on the other side that looks like roadkill, that's Colonel Towry. His head's hanging down into the ditch."

"I can see a half mile down the road and there's no roadkill," Blaine said.

"Do you think he got away?" Benjamin craned his neck, but the window was too high and too small for any of the boys too see the road through it.

"Mr. Blaine, you'd better stop or we'll go too far. I can show you where we put him."

Blaine braked to a stop.

Craig pointed ahead to their left. "What's that in the ditch on the left?"

Josh had already unbuckled the seatbelt that held him and Caleb in one seat. He pressed his nose to the small window. "Oh man. We warned him not to wiggle. He fell in the ditch."

"But there wasn't enough water to drown," Caleb said. "Mostly mud."

Craig and Blaine bailed out and both opened the rear doors.

The cousins jumped down to the pavement and ran toward the body in the ditch.

"Whoa, young men." Craig collared the twins and Blaine grabbed Benjamin's collar. "Never approach a body until you know it's safe."

"He's all taped up," Josh said. "He can't hurt us."

"Never take that chance, Josh," Craig said. "If he had gotten loose, made it look like he was still taped up, then jumped you when you got too close, what would you have done." Craig scanned the twins and then Benjamin. "Well ..."

Benjamin lowered his head. "We'd probably pee our pants."

"And good soldiers never have to do that in their pants." As Craig said the words, he thought of a half-dozen times good soldiers had performed that embarrassing action when things went awry on the battlefield. "Come on. Let's pull Colonel Towry out of the ditch."

A low moan came from the ditch where Towry lay face down in a muddy trench that had an occasional puddle of water in it.

He raised his head, revealing a scraped-up face.

He had obviously scraped the side of his face until he loosened part of the tape over his mouth.

"Is that you, Rogers?" Towry tried to roll over.

"Rogers is dead," Craig said. "I'm Craig, the militia commander. Are you injured, colonel?"

"My head is and now my back. I fell headfirst into the ditch. Twisted my neck and back. Now I can't move."

"Didn't the boys tell you not to move?"

"They did, but they're only boys. I thought—"

"Well, you thought wrongly, colonel. Those boys have IQs off the scale. It only took them five minutes to figure out how to take down an Apache coming to attack them."

"Somebody should have warned me," Towry muttered. "What about my men?"

"All one hundred of your men are dead. The last three violated the Geneva convention and received swift justice."

Craig and Blaine hopped into the ditch.

Blaine followed them.

Susan had gotten out and she stood watching the operation in the ditch.

"Blaine, we need to turn him over." Craig looked up at Susan. "Susan, catch." He tossed her his cell. "Call Harper for a Humvee and a stretcher. He'll never be able to climb into the JLTV with a bad back."

"You'd better twist at the same time," Josh said. "Or you might really mess up his spine. You might even paralyze him for life."

"Or kill him," Caleb said.

Towry moaned again. "Just do it. I'm not sure I want to live anymore."

On the count of three, Craig turned Towry's shoulders while Blaine turned his hips.

With a minimum of moaning, they had turned him over. Towry now lay on his back with his taped hands underneath.

"Dude, what happened to your face?" Blaine said.

"Blaine, he *is* a colonel. Show some respect," Craig said.

"Colonel, what are those red welts all over your face ... and neck ... and your arms too? Is it catching? Craig, we may have to get vaccinated."

"It was mosquitoes. Those blasted kids left me here to involuntarily donate my blood to the Clear Lake blood bank."

"Can you breathe okay, colonel?" Craig asked.

"I think so."

Susan was still on the phone.

"Susan, tell them to include a first-aid kit with an EpiPen. I think the colonel's having an allergic reaction to all the bites."

Moments later a Humvee rolled up and stopped. A medic and another man hopped out.

The medic carried a small pack. He made eye contact with Craig. "You can head back to the bridge, we've got this."

"He twisted his back and was shot in the head with a four-ounce lead weight, and he's having a reaction to being eaten alive by mosquitoes," Craig said.

"We got all that from Ms. O'Connell. He won't need an EpiPen. We'll just give him a dose of diphenhydramine."

"So you've got him?"

"Yes, we do, Colonel Craig. You've got some anxious parents back at the bridge."

"Load up," Craig said.

Towry raised his head and made eye contact with Craig. "In about eight or nine years, the CIA would be glad to take those three off your hands."

"I'm sure the boys appreciate your vote of confidence, colonel, but first we've got to make sure that we have a United States of America in eight or nine years."

Five minutes later, they consummated a happy reunion of parents and rascals. Each rascal got a warm hug from Sam.

Then it was time to divide the spoils and decide the charges.

Craig gave Governor Harper a short debriefing.

"Colonel Craig, I suggest that the militia take Walker's ten Chinooks. After all it was your troops that confiscated them."

"We also confiscated nine of their pilots. We need pilots, but we could never trust anyone loyal enough to Walker to carry out his raids," Craig said. "And that raises another question. What do we do about prisoners of war?"

Harper rested against a Humvee parked alongside the road by the bridge. "For the prisoners, here's what I recommend. Any that we suspect of crimes—treason, murder—we put them in the state penitentiary and try them."

"Can you legally try them for treason in Oregon?"

Governor Harper nodded. "It's been a crime since Oregon entered the union."

"Hey, I like your thinking—part governor, part battlefield commander."

His remark drew a smile from Sandra Harper. "Craig, I believe that's the first compliment you've ever given me."

What a difference that smile made. For the first time, Craig saw a resemblance between Harper and Kate. He laughed.

"So now you're mocking me?" Harper's smile faded.

"No, Madam Governor. For the first time I'm seeing how much you and Kate look alike."

"Colonel Craig, that's the second compliment."

"Enjoy them as long as you can, governor," Steve said. "They are a rare item from Craig."

"Back to the business at hand," Harper said. "I would also recommend that anyone we don't intend to charge with a crime in Oregon, should be sent home. We don't want to run POW camps."

"And I agree. That would include the Chinook pilots that my men captured today. Some of the other troops might have been caught up in this operation without knowing the whole story behind it. They aren't a threat to us and, if we treat them well, we may win them over to our side."

Sandra Harper sighed. "Then there is the matter of the Chinooks. To protect Western Oregon, we can use the Chinooks and pilots from Pendleton. I can station several on the west side so we can rapidly deploy the Guard when needed. But I was thinking. There are probably more pilots than helicopters at Pendleton. Perhaps we can get eight or nine loaned to the militia."

"We would need some mechanics to keep them airworthy. We already have one pilot in our group, Baker, whom you have flown with once or twice."

"There is one other matter, Craig. We barely had room in our Humvees for the men we brought. Now we have nine prisoners to take home too."

"Sir?" Baker said. "If you'll drop me off where those Chinooks landed, I can take the prisoners, and some troops to guard them, back to Salem."

"I guarded those prisoners too," Shauna said. "I earned the right to see them locked up where they belong."

"That she did, sir," Baker said. "Munch—uh...Shauna did a great—"

"I'll bet she did. All right. Take her to Salem, Baker. Do I need to send a chaperone along for the return trip? How about Sam? She'd love to go along."

"Sam is coming home with me and AJ," Hunter said. "She's had enough excitement for one day."

"I guess that wraps it up for today, governor. Call us and let us know when you need depositions, testimony and such."

"Don't worry. We'll be in touch as soon as I figure out which of my lawyers I can trust."

"Trustworthy lawyers? Isn't that an oxymoron?" Steve said.

"That's enough lawyer jokes," Craig said. "Militia and families, let's all head back to the picnic area at the lake. Between the JLTVs and the vehicles we came here in, everybody should have a ride home. With a little luck, we'll all be home before nine o'clock."

As the group started walking up the highway toward the picnic area, Craig headed toward the JLTV where Blaine, Rodriguez, and Drew were climbing in.

Susan came alongside. "David, is there any chance I could hitch a ride back in a JLTV? I left my car at Julia's house and there was hardly room for me in their SUV."

"Do you mean a ride in a JLTV to complete a continuing education course in military vehicles? You know, for your intelligence analysis certificate?"

"Of course. What other reason would there be?" She gave him a warm smile that defeated every objection that came to mind.

"Drew."

"Yes, sir."

"Would you like to ride home with your wife and your son?"

"Would love to, Colonel Craig."

"Better hurry and catch up. I saw them leading the group headed back to the cars."

"Rodriguez, would you like Blaine to give you some OJT on driving a JLTV on the trip home?"

"You mean I get to drive this incredible piece of engineering?"

"That was the general idea."

"You bet, sir."

Blaine looked from Craig to Susan. "I guess that means you two will be sitting in the back."

"Yes. That's where I will be debriefing my intelligence officer."

"Debriefing? If that's what you call it, sir."

# Chapter 39

*10:25 a.m. EDT, Washington, DC*

President Walker scanned the outstretched arms as a cacophony of voices cried out.

"Mr. President."

"Mr. President."

He would allow one last question then this press conference was over.

Walker motioned toward a cute blonde reporter in the second row. "Yes, you."

"Mr. President, with two thirds of the land mass of the U.S. declared as red territory, and a dozen militias already formed or being organized to defend red territory, how do you plan to defeat the militias and unify the nation, and are you willing to turn our military's guns on U.S. citizens?"

He had already turned weapons on U.S. citizens, but now was neither the time for that admission nor the place to defend his decision, especially since the outcome could only be described as a failure.

"We are finalizing our plans for defeating the various militias and restoring the union. It wouldn't be prudent to disclose that information at this time in this setting. Thank you all for coming. That is all for today."

"Mr. President."

"Mr. President."

He turned and strode out of the press briefing room.

Didn't attractive young women have better things to do with their time than becoming annoying reporters? Didn't she realize, that if she played her cards right, she might become the first lady?

"After all, I am the most eligible bachelor in the nation."

"Pardon, Mr. President, but did you say that you're—"

"I was just mumbling Ms. Bailey. Just mumbling."

His Press Secretary turned but didn't annoy him by pursuing an answer.

"Please let the staff know I will be in my private study handling some sensitive calls and do not wish to be disturbed unless there is a nuclear attack." Why had he said that? It was true, but far more hyperbole than needed to convey his message.

"Yes, Mr. President. We will direct all but nuclear emergencies to Will Richards."

He studied Erica Bailey for any evidence of defiance or smugness, but Ms. Bailey turned and headed down the hallway in the opposite direction.

Back to the subject at hand, the attack on the Oregon militia. It must not have gone according to plan or Deke would have reported the outcome hours ago.

At 11:00 a.m., Walker sat in his study drumming his fingers on the desk. Concern had morphed to anger. How could his most trusted operative have failed to report? Surely he wasn't dead. If Deke could report, Towry also should have.

His secure personal phone rang. "President Walker."

"Mr. President., it's Major Deke."

"Your report is rather late, and I haven't heard a peep out of Towry."

"You won't, sir."

"Surely Colonel Towry didn't disobey orders and abandon the mission."

"No, sir. Colonel Towry was taken prisoner by the militia. Before I fled the area, I heard talk about three boys, geniuses, taking him out with a slingshot."

"I'm in no mood for David and Goliath stories, Deke. Just tell me what happened."

"Sir, all of Towry's men were killed by the militia which was reinforced by the Oregon Guard led by Governor Harper."

"Harper? Sandra Harper commanding the Guard? You've got to be joking. And how did Towry lose all his men?"

"That's a long story, Mr. President."

"Just give me the short version. And it had better not involve three boys and a drone."

"The militia took our JLTVs and used the Javelin missiles to blow up Towry's men in their Humvees."

Walker swore until he had exhausted his vocabulary of such words. First, he swore at Towry and Deke for being incompetent. Then he moved on to Craig and his ancestry.

Craig was the real danger here. Almost single handedly he had recruited, trained, and now commanded a militia that seemed unstoppable.

"Back to you, Deke. What happened to your men and the JLTVs? Those two vehicles were worth almost a million dollars."

"They lured us and our JLTVs into a lava bed and almost stranded us there. I trailed militia leaders and their families to a lake and captured them. Using them, I forced Craig to surrender."

"Something tells me there's a big but coming."

"A scrawny girl, with what looked like a Sig Sauer, got the drop on us and we lost control."

"You let another kid take you prisoner?"

"She wasn't a kid. Just a short person who knew what she was doing. Then Craig helped her. I had to surrender or lose my men. While the militia and the Guard took out Towry's troops, I escaped."

"That's the only positive thing that happened last night? You escaped? What about the Chinooks Towry flew down on?"

"The rebels have them, sir. I saw one of those birds fly away toward Western Oregon early this morning."

Walker swore again. "So we lost all of our troops. The rebels stole our JLTVs and a half a billion dollars' worth of helicopters. They can even fly them. Now they have an airborne attack capability and JLTVs that are the equivalent of a light tank. Tell me, Deke, what should I do with you?"

"I have a good reason to want Craig dead. Let me go in alone after him."

"And what about defeating the militia and Harper's Guard?"

"Don't play strategy games with them. Just go in with such an overwhelming force that you can simply wipe them out. But, Mr. President—"

An anapestic knock sounded on the study door. "Just a minute, Deke. Will Richards is here. I need his input on this disaster."

Walker let Will in and briefly described the situation Deke had related. "So, Will, what do we do to defeat the Oregon rebels and show all the red areas what happens if they rebel against me?"

"Don't you mean rebel against the United States of America?"

Walker didn't reply.

"You only have one option, Mr. President. You assemble a huge army, an overwhelming force, and wipe out the resistance."

"And that's what I will do."

"There's one problem," Deke said. "You have to find a large army of say ten thousand men who will obey you as commander-in-chief. Maybe you can, Mr. President. But the odds are shrinking every day as resistance forces strengthen."

"He's right," Will said. "You need to make your move soon, or it may be too late."

Walker's head was splitting. He needed a pain pill and then he needed time to think.

"Deke, you may go after Craig alone. Call me tomorrow and I'll arrange supplies and finances for you. Will, we'll talk tomorrow about which troops to use, the logistics, and the timing."

He ended the meeting and ended the phone call.

Will left and Walker locked the study door.

Wipe them out with an overwhelming force—to do anything less would only encourage other states and regions to emulate Oregon. That would allow the resistance movement across America to strengthen.

If that process continued, they would reach a tipping point where America would lose the legitimate government. The rebels would take over.

What would they do to him if he survived such an event?

They wouldn't hang a president, would they? Surely, for the sake of the nation, the new administration would pardon him as they had Nixon.

But that was an eventuality Walker would do anything to prevent. And *anything* demanded sending an army so overwhelming it would run roughshod over the militia and storm Salem, taking control of the entire state.

*That will show other red states what happens when you try to rebel against Wendell Walker.*

He looked down at a paper Will had dropped on his desk. What was this?

He scanned it. Maybe he should read it, though it appeared to be more treason from the poison tongue of Zach Tanner.

*President Walker, you cannot order or force us to unity,*

*especially unity with you as a dictator over us. If you want compliance from us, you've got to convince us, not just command us. And you cannot convince us with your lies and your lying media, but only with common sense, clear logic, verifiable facts, and clear compliance with the U.S. Constitution. If you don't do this, you're done, because we're done with you. We will ignore you, defend ourselves, and then vote you out of office. Do not attempt military force. We are one hundred million strong, with an average of five weapons per person, and we're the largest army in human history, twenty times over. We are the citizens of the United States of America.*

*You cannot defeat us and that is by design, the design of our founders. Let this nation return to being the United States of America. Let its people return to being Americans, or we will force you to do that, and we will be a lot more effective at forcing you than you have been at trying to force us to do things we do not wish to do.*

*Mr. President, civil servant whom we have elected, what's it going to be? Serve us or get served with a pink slip ... or perhaps a death certificate if you choose to fight us?*

*I believe you need a reminder of Thomas Jefferson's words on this subject. "The tree of Liberty must be refreshed from time to time with the blood of patriots and tyrants." Maybe it is time for the latter.*

*And to you, my fellow Americans, our republic is showing signs of failing and turning to the tyranny our founders feared. It's late in the ball game. It's time to decide how much you're willing to give to win it. Do you want to be one nation, under God, or one Marxist mob, under Satan?*

*As Bob Dylan wrote, You Gotta Serve Somebody. It's time to choose this day whom you will serve. I know you good people will make the right choice. And after you do, then step up to the plate. Don't just stand there and go down looking. Swing the bat for goodness sake! Swing for the fence! Swing at the ball before the ump says, "Game over!"*

Walker's heart pounded out a presto tempo. He had been briefly drawn in, perhaps even inspired by Tanner's words. How could he let this babbling, rebel idiot affect him like that?

Walker swore until his thumping heart brought a pounding headache that drove him to find his bottle of pain pills.

# Chapter 40

*8:30 a.m., Terrebonne, Oregon*

Susan woke and sat up in bed.

What time was it?

She wasn't in the cave. This was *her* bed.

She looked at the clock.

*4:30 p.m.*

She had gotten home at 9:30 a.m. then had fallen into bed, exhausted. Seven hours of sleep at the wrong time of day left her dopey headed and still a bit disoriented.

The meeting at Steve's and Julia's house was set for six o'clock. Maybe she should get ready and stop by Crooked River Espresso to pick up coffee and maple bars and take them to David's place at the RV park on the ranch.

The coffee shop—they had left the new girl, Gloria, alone to run it while the whole group, including the Crooked River Espresso team, ran away to hide from the president. Hopefully, Gloria had managed yesterday and today without any help. Susan would soon find out.

At 5:15 p.m. Susan rode the brakes on her SUV as it rolled down the hill onto the ranch plateau. She turned in between the 11th and 12th fairways on the golf course and navigated the short, paved road to the ranch RV park.

What if David wasn't home?

Maybe surprising him wasn't as good an idea as it had first seemed.

After she circled the grassy campsite, she rolled slowly through the upper loop of the RV park and spotted David's large motorhome with his Jeep in the driveway.

The light in the kitchen area provided further evidence that he was there and probably up, preparing for the important planning meeting at six.

She parked beside his Jeep. While balancing two coffee drinks in one hand and carrying the bag of maple bars with the other, Susan had walked as far as the picnic table when the front door opened.

David stood in the doorway dressed in what he called his civvies—Docker shorts, a polo shirt, and cross trainers.

Only one word came to mind to describe him, *magnificent.*

His eyes seemed to be alternating their focus between her and the coffee she held.

So she had made the right choice. But she was competing with coffee for his attention. Providing she eventually won, it was all good.

He walked down the steps and met her by the picnic table. "The table's in the shade and iced lattes beat air conditioning anytime." He motioned toward the table. "Shall we, Ms. O'Connell? Oh, and thanks for the coffee. Since it's in Crooked River Espresso cups, I assume the young lady Kate hired kept things running while we ran off exploring caves and lakes."

Exploring caves and lakes. Downplaying the danger. That was something David and the other warfighters did continually. It probably helped to keep them sane while they lived a life often filled with danger, death, and uncertainty.

"She did very well, and here's some proof, the iced version of your favorite, a vanilla bean latte and ..." she opened the bag, set it on its side, and slid the pastries to the front, "... maple bars."

He devoured his maple bar and started sipping coffee. "I missed breakfast and lunch. Thanks, Susan. Caffeine and sugar ... just what I needed to wake up from a six-hour nap."

When she downed the last of her maple bar, he took her hand, stood, and pulled her to her feet. "We've still got a half-hour and nice breeze is blowing up the canyon. Would you like to walk the trail to the lookout by the gorge?"

"I'd love that." Carrying their coffee cups, they walked hand-in-hand down the dusty trail through the Juniper trees and scrubby desert bushes to the wooden platform that hung out over the Crooked River Gorge.

He pulled her up the steps and onto the platform. David set his cup on the wide railing that topped the fence surrounding the lookout.

She set her half-full cup beside his.

As it always did, Susan's first look down into the four-hundred-foot-deep gorge caused an ache in the pit of her stomach as she imagined herself falling. But studying the blue ribbon lined with green that wound through the canyon took away her anxiety.

David turned and looked a quarter of a mile across a patch of desert to the white church that gleamed in the late afternoon summer sun.

It was a beautiful church, but a modern-day civil war had limited its use for activities such as weddings.

"If there's ever a lull in this war with Walker, Kate and Zach get first shot at the Ranch Chapel for their wedding. That's if Baker and Shauna don't beat them to it."

Craig chuckled. "Munchkin and the runt. Those two don't even realize what's happening between them yet."

"Kate has told me otherwise, David."

Who'd have thought it. I'm going to be commanding a militia of old married men."

"What do you mean by old?"

"Well, I'm forty-five and—"

"They say sixty-five is the new forty. We have lots of time."

"Time for what?"

"I ought to punch you in that shoulder."

"Please don't. We didn't put any stitches in that cut, only a butterfly bandage. And I don't heal as quickly as I did when I was twenty-five ... but you didn't tell me why you were punching me. Time for what?"

"You know, time for what everybody else around here is doing."

"Training for the militia?"

"Don't play dumb, Colonel Craig. Raising a family. Somebody's got to carry on the traditions we've started. We can't let Crooked River Ranch go crooked or be populated by wusses who let the government tell them what to do while trampling on their constitutional rights. The people here are models of the stuff that keeps America strong and free. Like Zach said, 'Freedom only lives in the hearts of people, and if it dies there, the legal system, the justice system, the Constitution—nothing can bring it back to life'. So we've got to keep it alive."

"Zach's right. I'm not sure freedom can be reborn in people's hearts after they die to it. And the measure of freedom Americans have had, backed by a government that supports it, has only occurred once in six thousand years of human history. If we let someone take it from us, we may never see that kind of freedom again in this age."

"You have a way with words, David. Maybe you should trade places with Zach."

"Trade places? No. Kate's a nice girl ... for Zach. But I think David Craig has finally found the place where he belongs. It's beside the woman he began looking for years ago but never found until he met you."

For the first time, he had opened his heart to tell her what he had been holding inside.

She looked up into his eyes and what she saw there stole her breath.

He kissed her, for the first time of his own free will ... without any provocation.

Well, maybe she had looked up at just the right moment and had given him the perfect opportunity.

After that tender moment, Susan pressed her cheek into his chest and held the man who had proven to her that Susan O'Connell was enough for him and that David Craig, a man of honor, would never betray her or abandon her.

She looked up into his eyes. "And together we have a job to do."

"Yes. And so far, we've resisted a power that wanted to destroy our freedom and our nation."

"But, David, now it's time to restore this nation to what our founders envisioned, so we can experience *our* pursuit of happiness."

"If there are enough liberty-loving hearts that want a godly nation, a constitutional republic, He will help us restore it."

"Yes, He will."

God was faithful even when people were not. And God had brought this man into her life when her world seemed to be crumbling into dust. Certainly, the nation was crumbling. But with people of faith and commitment banded together, resisting an evil president—people with incredible abilities and fortitude—Zach, Kate, KC and Brock, Drew and Beth, Julia and Steve, Lex, Gemma and even those three genius cousins, God could restore America and create a place for her and David to raise a family.

"It's almost six o'clock, Susan. We'd better head up the hill to that strategy meeting. We need to prepare, thoroughly. We humiliated Walker today. He will come with a big army seeking vengeance after his defeat. We wiped out his entire force and confiscated three hundred million dollars' worth of equipment. We've got to be ready this time for an even bigger response from him."

She studied his piercing eyes that turned warm when they returned her gaze.

With God's help, David would prepare the people here in Central Oregon, and he would take care of them. Now he was resisting an evil head of state. But soon he would help them restore the nation she loved, the United States of America.

And, over the past few weeks, God had painted a picture now clearly seen by the eyes of Susan O'Connell's heart. The picture spoke a message to her.

*David Craig was born for such a time as this.*

It was God's message, so it had to be true.

To Be Continued

Book 3, *Restoration*, is coming soon. If you enjoyed *Resisting*, please consider leaving a rating and a brief review on Amazon. Reviews are difficult to get and greatly appreciated by authors and readers. You can find *Resisting* and all my other novels on H. L. Wegley's Amazon Author Page.

# Author's Notes

### The Characters

Parts of seven of my books have been set in Central Oregon. Of course, I knew the heroes and heroines of those books very well. I thought it was a great idea in the *Riven Republic* series to use them all as the supporting cast while introducing some new characters in the leading roles.

While this seemed like a good idea in theory, it proved difficult in practice. First, I had to recall a lot of details to make the characters consistent with the previous stories. Second, these characters were, in many instances, larger-than-life people. How do you keep them from stealing the show? Third, I had to age them all nine years and, in many cases, give the couples some children.

I've given it my best shot, and I hope those of you who have read my other series, *Against All Enemies* and *Witness Protection*, enjoy spending time again with these folks. Together, they do make a formidable army when allied against you. Even the twins, Josh and Caleb, geniuses who are now nine years old, get in on the action.

### Military Equipment – Chinooks, F-15s, and JLTVs

The hero of *Resisting*, retired Colonel David Craig, becomes the leader of the Central Oregon Militia. His experience and new responsibilities bring a lot of military jargon, equipment, and tactics into the story. I've tried to keep this realistic without bogging things down with Tom Clancy-like details.

The Chinook helicopters and F-15 fighters have both been around for decades. The F-15 was accepted by the USAF in early 1973 making it nearly 50 years old. But a lot of technology has been applied as upgrades over the years to make this aircraft a formidable weapon capable of speeds approaching 2,000 miles-per-hour.

Chinook helicopters have been around since the fall of 1961 and were used extensively in Vietnam. This aircraft has also seen its share of upgrades, even some electronic warfare and infrared countermeasures have been added.

The new kid on the block is the JLTV. It's a shame our warfighters in Afghanistan didn't have a vehicle that could be configured with armor like the JLTVs. The improvised explosive devices (IEDs) that took so many of our soldiers' legs and arms wouldn't have been effective against JLTVs. But these vehicles are more expensive than Humvees and so their future use remains a question mark beside a dollar sign.

### Political Ideologies

The *Riven Republic* series illustrates the breakup of the USA, fragmenting along ideological lines. When I was young, and up until the late '60s, our politicians were mostly liberal or conservative. They wanted either a larger government with more spending or just the opposite. They argued in the halls of Congress, went to dinner as friends, and hammered out compromises. The wheels of the federal government turned, though sometimes slowly.

Once Marxism took hold in academia and professors began proselytizing students, the opposing political ideologies morphed to two which are completely incompatible, Constitutionalists and Radical Leftists (neo-Marxists). Today, their beliefs are disjoint sets of ideas. There is no room for compromise, and that is what I presupposed in this book series.

If you wish to read more on Marxism and about the man who codified the political/economic philosophy, here are a couple of articles providing an overview of Karl Marx:

https://www.intellectualtakeout.org/blog/karl-marx-was-pretty-bad-person/

https://stream.org/why-karl-marx-hated-god-and-marxists-hate-christians/

Karl Marx was a racist (proficient in his use of the "N" word) and a sexist who refused to work. He also refused to bathe or groom, and so he suffered from boils all over his body, and I do mean all over. That rat's nest he wore as a beard is a direct result of his slovenly attitude toward cleanliness and grooming.

As a young man, he was a lazy student, and the money his father sent him for tuition was spent at coffee houses and taverns where he got drunk and argued about Hegelian philosophy.

He married but, bigot that he was, he hated his daughters as he did all women. He was unfaithful to his wife and fostered out his illegitimate son. Because he refused to provide for his children, four died before reaching adulthood. In fact, Marx said, "Blessed is he who has no family."

Okay, maybe you don't need to read those two articles. *Grin.* As you can see, I hold Marx in very low esteem but for many good reasons, and I'm in good company on this.

### The Central Oregon Setting

Central Oregon is a beautiful place with great diversity in geography, flora, and fauna. *Resisting* takes the reader from the desert up into the Cascade Mountains to lakes and rivers. I tried to depict this area as it is with no embellishment.

Sahalie Falls is beautiful and it's only a couple of miles from there to Clear Lake. If you visit the lake on a day with calm winds, you'll understand how it got its name.

I made a couple of distortions of reality in *Resisting*. First, I added a road through the lava fields near Dee Wright Observatory. The road doesn't exist, but I needed it for my story. Second, I exaggerated the depth of the Crooked River Gorge a little bit. From Crooked River Ranch to the bottom of the gorge is about 400 feet—I said 600 feet once or twice—and it's nearly 800 feet from the promontory on other side of the river to the bottom of the gorge.

Crooked River Espresso, along Highway 97 in Terrebonne, is called Crooked River Coffee in real life. Sometimes it's called The Wagon, because it sits inside a huge Conestoga Wagon façade, much like in the story. If you're ever in Terrebonne, The Wagon has great coffee.

Book 3 in this series, *Restored*, should release by Christmas 2020. Christmas will take us beyond the 2020 election, an historic event that could produce a lot of fodder for more political thrillers. But I hope it brings peace to our nation.

May God bless America as we navigate these treacherous waters that we find ourselves in.

H. L. Wegley

# Discussion Questions

1. David Craig made what we might call an "honest mistake" as a young lieutenant. It resulted in most of his men getting killed, and it left him with a complex about being a failure. Have you ever made such a mistake, one that wasn't a sin, just a mistake from lack of knowledge or experience? What should we do to get beyond the guilt and sense of failure produced by such events in our lives?

2. Susan had a problem with self-esteem, i.e. how she viewed her personal value. Her problem stemmed from an absent father, lack of love from her mother, and finally a fiancé who abandoned her for a vile lifestyle. Where does our value as human beings actually come from? What are the drawbacks of seeking value in the adoration received from people?

3. This quotation precedes the prologue of this book: "Liberty lies in the hearts of men and women; when it dies there, no constitution, no law, no court can save it; no constitution, no law, no court can even do much to help it." Judge Learned Hand
   If this is true, why does liberty abide in our hearts? Who put it there? Can you cite a reference(s) supporting your answer?

4. How would you define true freedom, the kind that resides as a longing in our hearts?

5. God gives us a lot of information about conducting war. War is a frequent subject and activity in the plot of *Resisting*. What principles of war do you see given in Deuteronomy 20? Which is more important to God, the size of the army or the heart of the army?

6. What characteristics of a wise leader does David Craig exhibit? What things does he still need to learn?

7. In both *Riven*, and *Resisting*, Marxist theory is spoken of disparagingly. What do you know about Karl Marx the man? How have his ideas played out in the 20th, and 21st Centuries? If you wish to know more, here are links to two brief overviews of Mr. Marx, a man whose ideas have killed upwards of 100 million people in the 20th Century alone:

https://www.intellectualtakeout.org/blog/karl-marx-was-pretty-bad-person/

https://stream.org/why-karl-marx-hated-god-and-marxists-hate-christians/

8. If the United States of America actually does divide along geopolitical boundaries, what hope do we have for reunifying this nation? Do you think God can provide a Great Awakening in our time? Will you pray that He will do so?

Don't miss H. L.Wegley's award-winning, political-thriller series, with romance, *Against All Enemies*:

Book 1: <u>Voice in the Wilderness</u>

Book 2: <u>Voice of Freedom</u>

Book 3: <u>Chasing Freedom (The Prequel)</u>

Read all three books in the *Witness Protection Series*—action and romance with thriller-level stakes—clean reads that are never graphic, gratuitous, or gross.

This series can be read in any order.

## No Turning Back

When a young man much like her father offers her protection, will trusting him bring another massacre, one that takes her life too?

*Witness Protection Series*

Book 1: No Safe Place

Book 2: No True Justice

Book 3: No Turning Back

**2020 Finalist in the Cascade Writing Contest**

When her father is murdered, he left her with a warning, an assassin on her trail, and his secret history contained in a set of journals. As Allie tries to elude the assassin and read the journals, she learns that the loving father who raised her was not the man he appeared to be, and the man she must now trust with her life is someone Allie must never trust with her heart.

At strong safety, Grady Jamison could defend against opponents in the red zone, but he couldn't stop the drunk driver who hit his car and killed his sister. Does Allie Petrenko's call for help mean Grady has been given a second chance, a chance to do things right?

*The Janus Journals*, an epic, dual timeline story of story of love, courage, forgiveness and faith.

**Romantic suspense with thriller-level stakes**

Vince van Gordon inherits control of break-through, virtual-reality technology that could make him one of the wealthiest and most powerful people on the planet. But, if commercialized, the technology would likely shred the fabric of American society beyond mending. Keeping it a secret only delays the inevitable. And, once the secret is leaked, there are people who will kill for the wealth and power. Stopping it may literally require an Act of Congress, and Vince will need the help of brilliant Jess Jamison, his childhood soulmate, the girl who shattered his heart seven years ago.

Virtuality

Made in the USA
Coppell, TX
14 August 2021

60483939R00162